THE TRIANGLE MURDERS

By

Lynne Kennedy

Also by Lynne Kennedy:

TIME EXPOSURE
PROVENANCE
PURE LIES

ISBN-13: 978-1535572859
IABN-10: 153557285X

Author's Note: This is a work of fiction, however, much of the historical detail and many of the historical characters woven around the Triangle Shirtwaist Factory fire of 1911 is accurate to the best of my knowledge.

Acknowledgments: Thanks to my critique group, Ken, Dave, Barbara and Maynard, for sticking with me through myriad versions of this novel and others. You're the best.

To John, thank you for your patience and faith in me.
All my love.

Prologue

New York City

March 25, 1911

At twenty minutes to quitting time, Fiona stopped typing and let her hands fall still. Something was wrong.

She smelled it first, a familiar odor, like she'd left the iron on a shirt too long. Then she saw it. Wispy ribbons of smoke coiling up into the room from a gap at the bottom of the door. Fiona could almost taste it now, foul and acrid, an insidious miasma curling around her feet, her legs.

She leaped up, rushed to the exit and threw the door wide. In the corridor, a screen of smoke shimmered like a gathering of ghosts in the hallway but no flames were visible. The floor felt warm. Hot. She tread on the balls of her feet toward the elevator. That's when she heard it. The sound of glass breaking. Not a tinkling like a whisper, but a painful splintering. Then a rumble shook the building. Fiona's heart thrashed crazily and for a moment that was all she could hear. She had to get out, down, all the way down to the street. Ten floors.

The next sounds she heard threatened to close off her lungs. Screams. Workers, her friends, mostly women, coming from the production floor below. Fiona raced to the exit door and down the stairs. At the ninth floor, she garnered enough courage to push open the door. A blast of heat and a horde of half-mad women assaulted her. Before she could turn and head further down, the door slammed behind her. And locked.

Belligerent flames rolled across the huge expanse of the factory floor, devouring the wood planks, thrusting deadly tentacles toward the ceiling. She couldn't fathom how quickly the blaze had spread. Yet before her radiated a living hell.

Through the conflagration she could see the windows on the Washington Place side. The glass in the frames seemed to ripple and undulate. One by one, they exploded into fragments.

Fiona spied her friend, Becca, sprinting to a second stairway door. She followed on her heels. This exit, too, was locked. Becca wrenched at it, shrieking. Fiona tried to drag her away, but her friend, like the door, wouldn't budge. Sparks from the blaze caught Fiona's dress and the wool began to smolder. She slapped at the hot embers and darted through the firestorm. Her scalp prickled in pain and she heard a crackling sound. She reached up. Her hair was on fire.

Suddenly Fiona found herself drenched. Someone had thrown a pail of water over her. She couldn't see who to thank so she thanked God. Somehow, she managed to reach the Greene Street door. Dozens of women had already beaten her to it, their faces fiery red, their dresses blackened and scorched.

"It's locked, locked."

Fiona shivered despite the heat and backed away. Workers not paralyzed with fear became a struggling stampede and charged toward the elevators. Out of the corner of her eye she could see the freight elevator door closing, a crush of women pinned inside and several leaping onto the elevator roof. Too late for her. Fiona's eyes blurred with tears.

A bin of cotton fabrics inches from her whooshed into flames and she mewled like a maimed kitten. Then the line of hanging blouse patterns began to burn. It erupted into an orange and red blaze. Unearthly utterances emanated through her lips and she understood the plaintive sound of terror.

The fire escape. I must reach the fire escape.

The crowd of panic-stricken women seemed to catch her thought at once and rushed as one wriggling, squirming mass to the fire escape window. Someone threw a chair through the glass. A dozen panicky women crawled out. Voices shouted.

"Not too many, it's dangerous, it won't hold."

"It don't go down ter the street."

Fiona found herself suspended in fear and disbelief. Her lungs were about to implode from the thick, poisonous smoke. She dropped to the floor to catch a breath and snaked her way toward the fire escape ladder.

When she reached the wall, she rose, held a cloth over her mouth and nose and leaned out over the broken window. At that moment, Fiona heard a terrible groaning of metal on metal, the screeching of bolts coming undone. Before she could shout out, the fire escape, a mere flimsy ladder, was shearing away from the building. Plummeting nine stories to the basement skylight along with twenty or more workers clinging for their lives. She watched, aghast, as it bounced twice against the building, crushing limbs before it landed, dumping its cargo into the dark pit of the cellar or onto a spiked iron fence at the bottom of the shaft.

Fiona pulled back, deafened by the shrieks. She found herself pushed and prodded toward a large open window on the Greene Street side of the building. It looked out upon the New York sky. A beautiful sapphire sky, turning to charcoal as fingers of greasy, sooty smoke drifted out from behind her.

Hollers from the street below: "The ladders don't reach. The nets don't hold," passed through her consciousness without taking hold. Her mind couldn't accept the wretched plight before her. Women were hurtling themselves out the windows into the air, one by one, with a grim acceptance that death by falling nine stories was somehow better than death by fire. Fiona's throat and eyes burned gritty from smoke and ash. Her mind numbed to the bedlam.

I am trapped.

At that instant, a violent, piercing pain punched her in the back. She fell to her knees. Her hand came away bloodied from the wound.

I. . . don't. . . understand.

She turned from the window to face the devil himself. In the wavering air, Fiona could see the gun in his hand. The raw, crimson scar on his cheek stood out in relief on his pasty white skin. The scar she herself had wrought. At that moment it became clear. She had misjudged badly. She should have trusted Cormac, her love, her life. She should have revealed the letter to him sooner. Now it was too late.

Blood pooled beneath her and her legs wobbled.

The devil grinned as he approached. Without a word, he lifted her to her feet and maneuvered her to the window. The pain radiated to her arms and legs. Fiona's brain grew dull. She couldn't match his strength as he propelled her forward until she, like the others, faced the dimming azure sky.

He forced her feet upon the windowsill, his insistent, unforgiving hands guiding her. Her will faded. She was so terribly tired. In the distance Fiona spied a hawk sweeping in endless circles. She reached out to touch it, to sprout wings and take to the air. She dearly regretted that she would never see her tiny son soar like that bird.

Time had run out and she had only herself to blame.

Fiona leaned out of the window to grasp the hawk's red tail, the clouds, the sky, higher, farther, finally tearing the last earthly strings that bound her

One Hundred Years Later

Chapter 1

March 21, 2011

3:30 p.m.

The body was still recognizable despite falling nine stories to the pavement. Female, early to mid-twenties, honey-colored hair, blue eyes glazed to eerie pale ice chips. Her arms and legs bent at astonishing angles. Blood leaked from her mouth and ears, but nowhere near the volume behind her head, the dark syrupy liquid painting the sidewalk with grisly tentacles.

Francis Aloysius Mead squatted as close to the dead girl as possible without disturbing the scene. The smell was always what got him first. Fresh death. Different from those in the morgue. Fresh death did not assault the senses in a numbing way like decay and putrefaction, but invaded the body viscerally, sharp and painful like inhaling salt water up your nose. He breathed through his mouth and studied the dead girl.

Worse than dealing with a corpse was the realization that a young life had been obliterated. He hated waste.

Frank rubbed his head, somewhere between buzz and bald, and looked up at the girl's killer—the ten-story Brown Building in the heart of Greenwich Village.

Helluva way to start his new assignment.

"Lieutenant?" A heavyset, pasty-faced patrol officer approached.

Frank stood, knees complaining, and looked up again at the building. A ninth story window was the only one open wide enough to fit a human being.

"Lieutenant?"

"I hear you." Frank turned to the beat cop.

"Looks like she went out the ninth story window, from what witnesses--"

"Yeah, no shit. Where are these witnesses?"

"Uh, in the lobby, of the building, that is."

Frank looked at the officer's name badge. Ivan Wynkosky.

"All right, Ivan, thanks."

Wynkosky twisted his lips into a sneer, clearly unhappy with the dismissive treatment. He turned and marched off.

Great way to make friends. Frank shook his head, pissed at himself.

He cricked his stiff neck and strode through the main doors, leaving the medical examiner and crime team techs to their job. Inside, four uniforms and a dozen bystanders stood around, pacing, squirming on lobby benches, standing, fidgeting, sitting again.

A tall, knobby man loped toward Frank. Frank had met the sergeant for barely ten minutes the day before, but knew he'd be a hard nut to crack in the welcome department.

"Jefferies?"

"Lieutenant. Apparently the vic's name was Stephanie Brandt. Twenty-three, reporter for the *Post*."

"Reporter? What was she doing here?"

"Good question," the sergeant said without hypothesizing.

Frank might like this guy after all.

"This building is part of the University, right?"

"Yup," Will Jefferies said.

"What else do we know?"

"Brandt was waiting for a history class on the ninth floor to get over with so she could talk to the professor. When the class ended, everyone left, or so they thought. Coupla' students down at the end of the hall heard a scream, ran back into the room, and noticed the window was open."

"Wasn't open during class?" Frank said.

"Uh uh. Too chilly. Nobody was in the room so they went to the window and looked out." He shrugged. "Room has two other doors. In fact, the professor left through one of them."

"Why would he leave if he was meeting with the reporter?"

"Says he just went to the men's room before their appointment."

"The witnesses definitely heard a scream?"

Jefferies nodded. "Don't think suicides scream before they leap, do you?" The sergeant fixed Mead with a direct eye.

"No, Sergeant. In my experience, most jumpers scream because they've been pushed."

"And you've had a lot of experience," Jefferies said, that challenge between them surfacing like a shark fin in dark waters.

Frank pulled Jefferies aside and spoke quietly. "Look, Sergeant, I know you and the rest of the squad are not happy with this situation. I wouldn't be either, matter of fact. An outsider moves into your territory and takes charge. After all, what the fuck does a D.C. cop know about New York? The fact remains, I am the new Lieutenant and you *will* take orders from me whether you like it or not. Get over it." He rested his hand on his hips and stared up at Jefferies. "I hope we don't have to have this conversation again. Now, we've got a murder on our hands. Which one's the professor?"

"Hyman Schueller, there." Jefferies nodded to a gray-haired, gray-bearded man wearing a shabby corduroy jacket and jeans.

Frank turned away and walked over to the man in question.

"Mr. Schueller." Frank held up his I-D and shield.

"Dr."

Pause. "Dr. Schueller. What can you tell me about Miss Brandt?"

"Nothing. I didn't even know her." He licked his lips, pushed rimless glasses up the bridge of his nose. "She left me a message at my office that she wanted to interview me, me and other people who worked at the Brown Building. So I said sure. She came early, sat in on the end of the class, and then we were going to talk in my office down the hall."

"You left for a few minutes and--?"

"And when I got back, well, the window, several students were looking down. Just terrible. Why would she do such a thing?"

"You mean take her own life?"

"Of course. Why? It doesn't make sense." Schueller shook his head and lowered himself to the bench."

"It may not be suicide, doctor."

The professor looked up, mouth dropped open. "Not, not suicide. Then what, someone pushed her? Oh my God."

"Dr. Schueller, why did Miss Brandt want to interview you and others here? Something special about the Brown Building?"

"Well, she said she was working on a piece to commemorate the tragic events that took place here a hundred years ago. When it was the Asch Building."

Frank scanned the lobby with its newly installed slate floor tiles, brass handrails framing the simulated marble staircase. He'd grown up in a neighborhood like this and knew a little about the architecture.

This building was early 1900's, neo-Renaissance-style. Original lobby probably of all wood--floor, stairs, and banisters. Not particularly attractive but then it was just an industrial building, a place used by garment workers, he recalled. That struck a chord. He knew about these events somehow. It was a fire. Catastrophic fire. How did he know this?

"Horrific disaster," Schueller went on. "Fire broke out on the top three floors, doors locked, people trapped. *Oy vey*, it gives me goose bumps still. Over a hundred people died of smoke asphyxiation and fire. Oh my God. So many young girls, garment workers, they . . . jumped." He wiped sweat off his brow. "They jumped to their deaths from the ninth story."

And then Frank knew. It was the worst disaster in New York history before the World Trade Center. In an era of Tammany Hall politicians, union progressives and suffragettes. This area of the city was the garment industry and the Asch Building was once home to the infamous Triangle Shirtwaist Factory.

Chapter 2

March 21, 2011

5:30 p.m.

"So you're the new Lieutenant?" A diminutive African American woman with close cropped hair and bright brown eyes held out her hand. "I'm the M-E, Serena Oliver."

"Frank Mead. Good to meet you." When she said no more, he smiled. "Anything you can tell me?"

She tugged her jacket closed and buttoned it all the way to her neck. "Gets chilly when the sun's gone."

He waited.

"Hard way to die, falling on the pavement like that. I'm sure there's lots of internal damage. I'll get back to you with the report." She gave a hint of a smile and walked off.

"How soon?" he called after her.

"When it's done." She disappeared around the corner.

Frank turned back to the scene where techs zipped up the body bag and lifted it to a gurney. That familiar melancholy hit him in the chest like it always did at this point. Even after twenty years, he could actually remember every single one of his dead victims. The once living relegated to body bags. How many were there now? A hundred, hundred and twenty? Lives squandered. For what? Greed, lust, hatred, jealousy. And what about Stephanie Brandt? Why was her life thrown away?

He popped a few Tums as his cell vibrated. He didn't bother checking the caller, just answered.

"Mead."

"Frank," his younger sister, Irene said. "It's Mom."

"What?"

"She fell. She's in the hospital."

"Shit. She okay? What happened?"

"Broke a few bones, not a hip, thank goodness."

"How did it happen?" he asked.

"I'm not altogether sure. On the stairs in the old building. Going up, going down, who knows."

"What did she say?"

"You know Mom. 'It's nothing, nothing. Phooey,' she says. Meanwhile, she's in the hospital."

"Her mantra is 'Phooey.'" Frank circled several times, phone to ear. "Irene, I don't know--"

"Listen, Frank, I understand if you can't come. It's your first week on the job."

"No, no, of course I'll come. It just may be a little while. How long will you be there?"

"Not to worry. I'll be here a long while, at least 'til I talk to the doctors."

Irene gave him the hospital information and clicked off. He stood there wishing he could handle this better, hating the helpless feeling that threatened to overwhelm him. He shoved the phone into the holder on his waist.

He looked around him, caught Jefferies hovering a few yards away. Frank used to frequent the Village when he lived in New York, the Lower East Side, where his Mom still lived. An old tenement she'd inherited from her husband, his dad, Frank Timothy Mead. It had been in the family dating back to Frank's great grandfather.

Why the hell didn't she get rid of the old relic? Nothing but headaches. Constantly needed fixing, plumbing, electricity, heating

for shit. Tenants always causing trouble, moving in, out, in, out.
Christ. Maybe Thomas was right.

He inhaled, turned and nearly bumped into the sergeant.

"What?"

"Problem, Lieutenant?"

"What makes you think there's a problem?" Frank said.

"Ya got that look on your face."

"Yeah, what look?"

"Never mind." Jefferies turned and started walking away.

"Sergeant," Frank said, stopping him. "Can you handle things
here? I've got to, I've gotta--"

"If ya gotta go, ya gotta go."

Frank smiled. Jefferies didn't.

"Go on," Jefferies said. "I'll get all the witnesses interviewed and
have notes ready for you later today."

Frank nodded, watched the sergeant meander back into the
building, its entrance now festooned in yellow crime scene tape.

Why now? When he was just starting out on a case. Back on his
old turf. Why did this have to happen now? And why the hell was
he so angry at Lizzie? She was dying and he was angry at her. How
dare she die on him? If only it was just a fall and not related to the
chemo treatments. Son-of-a-bitch.

The anger welled inside and he marched to the corner of
Washington Place and Greene Street then back, trying to calm
himself. In his pacing he faced the cornerstone of the building and
noticed a brass plaque. His eyes began to focus on the words.

Triangle Fire

*On this site, 146 workers lost their lives in the Triangle Shirtwaist
Company fire on March 25, 1911. Out of their martyrdom came new
concepts of social responsibility and labor legislation that have
helped make American working conditions the finest in the world.*

International Ladies' Garment Workers' Union

March 25, 1911. The hundred year anniversary was only three days away. The murdered girl was writing a story about the fire a hundred years later. So? Coincidence? Coincidence that she'd been pushed out of the ninth story window, where so many girls had jumped from that deadly fire?

Coincidences gave Frank the creeps. He didn't like them. He decided to follow his gut. As if he had a choice in the matter.

6:45 p.m.

Manhattan Memorial teemed with humanity, a microcosm of the rest of the City. Frank hurried past the emergency entrance where ambulances, their lights and sirens blaring, unloaded their cargo. He followed them into the puke green hallways and finally made his way upstairs to the intensive care ward floor. He collided with nurses, technicians, doctors, interns, wearing scrubs in green or blue, white jackets, stethoscopes dangling around their necks. Thick rubber-soled shoes squeaked past him and the smells of antiseptics, bleach and vomit filled him with dread.

Visitors of myriad shapes, sizes, ages and colors walked the halls or sat on orange-colored plastic chairs. Several turbaned men spoke in whispers, a gaggle of Spanish speaking girls clustered outside a room and a language that could have been Hungarian assaulted him from another doorway. English seemed to be an anomaly.

After an endless route of missteps Frank finally landed at his mother's bedside. Breathless, he shrugged off his jacket and pulled up one of the 70's chairs close to her. Irene must have gone for Starbuck's or something and would no doubt be back soon.

His mother looked God-awful. Ten years older than her seventy-two years. A hundred tubes hooked her fragile body to an array of electronics. Frank felt his stomach clench.

Why are all these machines needed? It was just a fall, right?

Lizzie's skin was a sickly gray; her hair had fallen out from previous chemo treatments and had grown back in soft fuzzy wisps. Her lips, once full and always smiling, had collapsed in on themselves.

Where are you, Mom? What did you do with my mother?

His head pounded.

Suddenly, she opened her eyes, like a cadaver looking at him. Then she smiled and it was okay again.

"Frankie." Barely a whisper.

"Yeah, Mom, I'm here. How ya' doin'?" He took her hand.

"I'm doing great. Just great."

Their eyes met. He swallowed hard and looked down. He didn't want her to see the tears in his eyes.

"Some water, there, please," Lizzie said.

Frank reached over for a glass with a straw and helped her sit up a bit to sip.

"Better. There, now I can talk. What would I be without my voice blabbing away, right?"

He grinned. "So what do the doctors say?"

"Phooey. I have a few broken bones here and there. Just a fall. Clumsy me. Par for the course. I'll be fine. I must look affright." She took a breath.

"You look fine. What bones are broken? What happened?"

"I wasn't paying attention, silly me. I tripped going up the steps. Natural instinct to throw your arms out to break the fall, so I fractured a coupla' those little bones in my wrist. That's it. Oh, and a rib."

"Oh, and a rib?" Frank mocked, shook his head. "Mom--"

"If you are even going to hint at me moving, the answer is no."

"Mom, maybe Thomas is right."

"Thomas is an asshole."

Frank couldn't help but smile. "Yes, well, but maybe he's right on this one. Maybe it's time to sell the old building."

"Frankie, listen to me. That old building is a classic, it's--"

"Exactly. And we could get a lot of money for it."

"I could up the rent from my tenants too, but I'm not going to. Money, money, money. Is that all there is?"

"You can't up the rent. The apartments are rent-controlled."

"Phooey," Lizzie said. "I'm not going anywhere. I'm fine. Just need to look where the hell I'm going."

He moved his chair closer and took the hand that wasn't bandaged, studied her face.

"Frankie?"

"Yeah?"

"You know that tenement has been in the family for three generations. It's special. Not many Irish in the neighborhood now, so it's doubly important we keep it."

"Okay. We'll drop the subject for now."

"Yeah. You tell Thomas."

He grinned, although that thought made him wince.

"Never mind me," Lizzie said. "Tell me about your new job. How are you getting along with the other cops? They giving you a hard time, being an outsider and all?" She paused. "Then again you're a New Yorker, not an outsider, really."

"Don't know yet how they'll respond to me. Haven't been in the office much. I expect they'll resent me for a while then get used to it. Get used to *me*."

"I think you're pretty easy to get used to."

"Yeah, you're my mother." He touched her cheek. "Besides, I'm not really an outsider as you put it. I've just been gone awhile."

"Awhile. Like eleven years."

"Eleven is my lucky number," he said.

"Frankie, tell me." Lizzie wriggled in bed and cried out.

"Mom, you okay?"

She waved a hand. "Fine. It only hurts when I move." She looked at Frank. "I'm just kidding. I'm fine."

Frank blew a breath out through tightly clamped lips.

"Are you on the case of that reporter girl? I saw it on the news." She tsked a few times.

"Yep, that's me."

"God in heaven. What happened?"

"We don't know yet."

"Did she jump?"

He shook his head.

"She was pushed, wasn't she? I knew it."

"What do you mean, you knew it? How could you know it?"

"Oh God, Amanda was helping her with research."

"Research on what?" Frank said, that familiar ache in his gut resurfacing.

"The Triangle."

"The fire?" he said.

She looked at him and frowned. "You don't know, do you?"

"What?"

"That building. You know, the Triangle Building."

"Yeah. I read about the tragedy. Saw the plaque on the cornerstone."

"No, I mean. . . that was your great grandfather's case."

"Cormac? Worked the Triangle fire?"

"Yes, that too." She stopped, looked at him funny. "You really don't know, do you? Your father never told you?"

"Told me what?"

"About your great grandmother."

"Fiona? What about her?"

Lizzie clucked and shook her head.

"She died in the fire," Frank said. "That's all I know."

"I can't believe he didn't tell you."

"Okay, Mom, I'm listening. What?"

Lizzie asked for more water before she could go on.

"She didn't just die in the fire. She was murdered. The fire covered it up."

She had Frank's complete attention.

"Are you sure you're not reading too many mysteries?"

"I still have all my faculties, thank you, despite what some people think." She sighed. "I have very good sources."

"What sources? Tell me. How do you know Fiona was murdered?"

At that moment, a nurse appeared behind Frank's shoulder.

"She needs some rest now, sir."

"Right, yes. Just a minute." To Lizzie, "Come on, Mom, what do you know?"

"Ask Amanda," she said, voice failing.

"Mom," he started. "Amanda and I don't talk much."

"You've got to change that, Frankie, it's not good. You're her father. She needs you. You need her."

Frank wasn't so sure his daughter needed him at all. He was pretty much absent for the last half of her life. But he said, "I know, I know, Mom. That's one of the reasons I'm back in New York."

"Have you seen her yet?"

He didn't respond.

"Frank."

"I will, I promise. I'm working on it. I've got to gather the courage, you know? She's not, er, too crazy about me." He smiled.

"She loves you."

Frank tilted his head. "We'll see."

Lizzie winked.

"Mom, tell me about Fiona."

"Sir, please," the nurse said.

He stood.

"Your great grandfather left his notes behind," Lizzie said. "From his days on the NYPD."

"Notes? On a murder investigation?"

"Cormac kept a whatcha' call it."

"What? What did he keep?"

Her eyelids fluttered. "He. . . kept. . . a murder book.

Chapter 3
Ellis Island, New York

April 18, 1909

Feet pounded the deck. Voices roared and cheered in joyous cacophony. Fiona forced her eyes open, wrenching herself out of a sickly torpor. If she moved, she might vomit. Mercifully, the sea had calmed and with it, her stomach. The steamship barely rocked.

Despite the scrambling around her, Fiona Kathleen O'Hara lay quiet. She gazed up at the brilliant, clear sky, felt the warm air. Fellow passengers hooted, cried, sniffled and sobbed around her. She shifted on the hard surface, her body aching and bruised.

Suddenly all went quiet. She could hear the whisper of a breeze, a seagull wheeling overhead.

She sat up, blinked, and rose to her knees. What had happened? Then she saw it. The green lady, her torch raised to the heavens in welcome. Tears came to her eyes and her heart felt as if it would burst from her chest. The journey was over. Everything would be all right.

She gathered her bags, steadied her wobbly sea legs, and made her way toward the ramp leading down from the steamship, *Nevada*. The air was warm and wet with the foretelling of summer; the sky shimmered a cobalt blue that seemed to mirror the ocean. From her vantage point, she could make out narrow patches of deep green grass and fat oaks abundant with leaves on the tiny island. A bit like Ireland and that gave her some measure of comfort.

Directly in front of her, loomed a giant fortress. A red brick citadel complete with copper-domed turrets, delicate limestone trim and huge arched windows. Fiona couldn't stop to take in the wonder, for disembarking passengers prodded her from all sides in their eagerness to reach the *island of hope.*

She felt her stamina and enthusiasm returning as she made her way inch by inch toward the incline. Behind her now--the many humiliations she'd endured for fourteen endless days and nights--the stench, the lack of solitude for even the most private bodily ministrations, the bug-infested food, toxic-smelling water, and the sea-sickness.

Fiona couldn't stem the tears of happiness.

"Don't cry, Dearie." An old woman nudged up beside her. "T'was a nasty business, weren't it?"

Fiona nodded and wiped her eyes.

"Aye, a misery of a passage, ye know, comin' cross that huge stretch of ocean, sick-like 'n all. I were sick the 'ole time."

Fiona looked at the woman, whose nose was crusted with mucus and wondered if she looked that horrid.

"But 'ere we are, Dearie, in a new country. What's yer gonna do 'ere then? Do ye 'ave relatives?"

Before she could answer, Fiona felt a tug on her shoulder strap. All at once she was shoved to her knees and her bag was wrenched from her arm. She leaped up in time to see a lad in a torn shirt, trousers held up by suspenders, and long hair tied back in a tail, vanishing into the crowd. He carried her satchel with him.

Fiona screamed, "No, no, Thief, stop. Come back. He's got my bag. Stop him." She hollered and pointed, jumped up and down.

The crowd around her was so thick she could barely move.

Tears scalded her eyes and rushed down her cheeks. "Please." No one seemed to hear her. Was everyone deaf?

Fiona had saved every penny of her sewing money to purchase a steerage ticket. Now the money was gone. Her body felt like dead weight. She couldn't move, despite the shoving from behind.

"Let's move, Lady. Come on," a voice shouted.

"Yeah, you're holdin' up the line," came several replies, echoed in other languages.

She picked up her bags, which seemed to weigh a thousand pounds and tried to push forward. She was blocked in every direction.

"Let me through, please." She shouted the words. "I must get off, I must--"

"We're all getting off, Lady. Wait your turn," came the responses.

Fiona tried to peer over the sea of humanity in front of her. Was the thief still there? She squeaked her body through several rows but was stymied near the ramp. Now, tears of frustration fell. Finally, she hopped off the ramp and onto solid ground.

As she struggled to get ahead, penned in on every side by the hordes, she caught a glimpse of the purse snatcher, his ponytail swaying. She whirled around with her two bags and elbowed through to one side where she spied a uniformed guard.

"Sir, can you help me? A boy stole my bag," she tried to explain. "Please. All my--"

"Over there, over there." The guard pointed, busy with the streams of passengers.

Fiona was sorely tempted to slap the man's face to get his attention, but that would only slow things down. She didn't have much time to save her purse.

She threw her bags behind the guard, hoping they weren't snatched too. Still, if she didn't get her money back, what difference would it make? She'd be deported.

Fired by adrenaline, Fiona took off in the direction of the boy. She fought her way through the lines until she spied him again. He was standing near a copse of trees and benches, searching through her bag.

Fiona took a deep breath and shot out toward him. The lad spotted her and took off but he was at the end of the dock and his only escape was the New York Harbor.

"Stop," she screamed.

The boy ran toward her, no doubt thinking a woman would hardly be a match for him.

Fiona raced right for him. She was unaware that a tall man was also dashing into the fray and the three collided in a tangle of legs and arms. Breathless from the tumble, she found herself nose to nose with the handsomest man she'd ever seen. He cracked a giddy grin at her.

At that moment, the thief squirmed beneath her and she had no time to think about anything else. She immediately began pummeling the boy.

"Give me my bag, you miserable thief."

Before she could tear her bag out of his hands, a crowd had formed around them. The tall man held down the boy as Fiona scrapped for her purse.

A voice shouted, "Tony, Tony, what are you doing?" A short, stocky man in a uniform leaned down into the fracas and grabbed hold of the boy's arm. With surprising strength he pulled him out from under Fiona.

The tall, handsome man helped Fiona to her feet.

The uniformed man turned to her.

"Did this young scamp steal your purse, Miss?"

"Yes. Yes, he did." She gasped for breath.

"Ahh, so he did. Here it is. Please check to see all your belongings are inside."

Fiona blew a wisp of hair out of her eyes and searched through her bag. The equivalent of twenty-five dollars was there. All the money she had in the world.

"Thank God, it's here. Thank you. . . thank you, sir."

The short man turned to another guard. "Take this rapscallion away."

Fiona turned to the tall man who had tussled with the boy as well. "And thank you, sir."

"My dear lady, don't thank me. You rescued your bag yerself, ye did. Astounding." He brushed himself off. "I'm only grateful ye didn't give me a black eye by mistake."

Fiona opened her mouth to respond and saw the glint in the man's eye. She half-smiled. Then she did her best to straighten her dress and hair.

Dozens of people gawked at her. She turned her back to them.

"Madam, please let me congratulate you as well," the short man said. "I am an Interpreter here on the Island. Fiorello LaGuardia at your service. Italian, Spanish. . . and some English." He grinned. "Please accept my sincere apology for this, er, incident. I hope you don't think all New Yorkers are thieves and rascals."

He took her by the elbow. "If you will allow me to assist you now, I believe I can make your process here a bit easier, make up for this bad first impression of our country. Of our city."

She nodded.

"Please follow me," LaGuardia said. "Do you have other bags?"

"Well, yes. I threw them behind another guard while I, er, while I--"

"While you did the police work and caught the thief."

"He's over there." She pointed.

"Let's go retrieve them."

Fiona stopped. "Wait, that gentleman who helped me."

LaGuardia spoke to him. "Sir, please accompany us. I will

assist you as well. It's the least we can do here for our new citizens."

The tall gentleman followed Fiona and LaGuardia into the great hall of Ellis Island. Fiona stole a longer peek at him. He was over six feet and broad-shouldered with thick reddish hair. His full mustache curled up with his mouth when he smiled. His eyes, a gentle robin's egg blue, crinkled as well.

LaGuardia stopped. "Now, whom do I have the pleasure of assisting?"

Fiona smiled. "I am Fiona Kathleen O'Hara, sir."

"And I am Cormac Fergus Mead."

"Ahh, both from the Emerald Isle?"

Fiona and Cormac nodded.

Fiona felt Cormac's eyes on her.

"This way." LaGuardia waved a hand. "Welcome to Ellis Island's great entry hall."

Fiona's mouth dropped open at the immensity of the space, its height and breadth dizzying.

"It's so huge, much as I imagine a museum to be," she whispered.

"I could stand ten ladders one atop the other and still not reach the ceiling," Cormac observed.

Fiona's eyes took in the huge arched, cathedral-like windows, which let in the light of day at the very pinnacle. Below, a balcony, hundreds of feet in length, ran along three walls.

"Look. Look there," a young woman behind them said.

They lifted their heads.

Hanging from the center balustrade hung the largest flag Fiona had ever seen. Red and white stripes and a blue box with stars in the upper left corner.

"The American flag," LaGuardia said, and held a hand over his heart.

"Our new country," Cormac said softly.

Fiona felt a shiver run through her and tears threatened again. All she did was cry since she'd arrived.

"This way."

Fiona stayed close to LaGuardia, Cormac right behind. At every step, she took in a new mélange of smells--was that baby vomit?--a medley of sounds--the balalaika?--and an array of costumes, both colorful and drab, from scores of foreign cultures. She glanced down at her own attire and winced at her old faded cotton dress. At least her wool coat remained serviceable. Still, she felt plain and gray like her wardrobe.

LaGuardia directed them into a small room off the great hall. "Here's where you will begin. This should cut about half the time off your process."

"Sir, how can I thank you?"

The little man did a quick bow. "It is I who must thank you, Miss O'Hara. For, um, tackling that little purse snatcher."

Cormac chuckled at her side. "It was, indeed, a feat to behold."

Fiona reddened. "We'll be fine, now, Mr. LaGuardia. Again, thank you."

"Welcome to America." The little man tipped his hat and hurried off.

Fiona and Cormac went through the first stage of entry, where they presented identification and answered numerous questions. Half an hour later they passed through the Registry.

Next came the physical exam. This caused Fiona some concern, for after two weeks of bare subsistence and sleeplessness, she felt light-headed and exhausted. And she'd heard so much about the eye exam. What was it, trachoma, a disease of the eye that would get one deported?

Screams of terror emanated from a tiny room to the left and all at once an old woman rushed out, chased by a young man.

"Madam, please, come back."

But the woman kept going.

Fiona looked at Cormac, who frowned.

"My God, *vas is dis?*" a girl behind them spoke. "I tink she's frightened of da hook in the eye. Ugh, me so too."

"Hook in the eye?" Fiona asked.

"Da. Dey use the button hook, you know to fix da buttons? Dey use on the eyes."

Fiona shook her head. "I'm just glad to be here, although I must say, it hasn't been a very auspicious start."

Cormac smiled. "Ah, at least there was a happy ending." He studied her.

She dropped her eyes, suddenly shy.

He picked up her bags and escorted her along the line.

"Oh no, please. I can carry those."

"Now you don't think I'm going to steal these, do ye?"

"What? Oh no, no, I--"

"Ach, Miss O'Hara. I'm jest teasing you. Besides, who am I to go against the likes of you and get meself beaten to a pulp."

This time Fiona grinned at the twinkle in his eyes.

"I am a gentleman, so I will be pleased to carry yer bags."

As they walked along, he talked. "Allow me to introduce myself formally, then. You know my name is Cormac Mead. I'm from Carrick-on-Shannon in County Leitrim. That is a ways between Dublin and Sligo, in case you're not familiar. And where do you hail from, Miss Fiona O'Hara?"

"Dublin, sir."

"And what did you do in that fair city?"

"Oh, I was, that is, I am, a seamstress. A very fine one, if I might say."

"You might, indeed. I understand this great city has a scarcity of seamstresses and would welcome you with open arms."

"I suppose we shall see."

"Is anyone meeting you here?" Cormac asked. "Many young ladies have men that sponsor them."

"Well, not a man, you see. My cousin, Patricia, lives here. I'm supposed to find my way to her apartment. Somewhere in Manhattan."

"Good. I mean, well, then, if I may take charge, would you allow me to help? It seems a lovely lass like yerself would be at a disadvantage in such a huge place as New York."

"Why would you do that for me?" She ducked her head, embarrassed at how much she wanted his help.

Cormac scratched his chin as they moved up the line.

"I could say because you look lonely and scared, although the way ye tackled that lad surely gives lie to that." He paused, smiled. "Then I could say because you're from my native country."

"You could, but you won't?"

"The real reason is that you're the loveliest lady, and dare I say, bravest, I've seen nigh on many a day. I'd be a fool to let you slip through me fingers."

Fiona's mind churned over his words. Who was this man? One to take advantage of her and depart? Would he use her then throw her away? It had happened to her before and it was many moons before she'd recovered from that devastation.

She looked directly into his eyes. They were kind, tender, honest. More than that, there was that one word he said that made up her mind. He'd called her a lady.

Chapter 4

Cormac Fergus Mead was accustomed to taking charge. He was good at it, in fact. It was no easy task, even for him, however, getting through the mounds of immigration paperwork.

"Ach, if I have to fill out another page, I shall go stark raving mad," he said, scratching his head with a pencil.

"Can I help?" Fiona asked.

"No. I'm just too impatient. Don't like filling out forms and such." He stopped, looked at her. "I must say, Miss O'Hara, you continue to impress me."

"Oh?"

"First at your, er, pugilistic skills. Now at your literary abilities."

"You mean that I can read and write?"

"Aye." He smiled.

"I might say the same about yours." She tapped her pencil on the paper in front of her.

"And where did ye learn these skills?" he said.

"Are you referring to my street fighting abilities?" She smiled, held up a hand. "I know what you mean, sir. My father was a very lear-ned man. Poor but clever. Read all the classics. He encouraged me to learn as well." She pursed her lips in recollection. "What about you, Mr. Mead? How did you acquire such skills?"

"Runs in me family. All literate from the great, great grandparents to the wee ones. Poets, writers, musicians--in the Irish tradition."

"How lovely," Fiona said, looking up. "Do you write poetry, then?"

"Ach, no, I'm sorry to say. I've taken a different path."

"Oh? Which path is that?"

"The path of law and justice."

Fiona furrowed her brow, but he had turned back to his forms.

"I wonder, then," Cormac said, "if this new country is as bureaucratic as it seems."

"I suppose they want to make sure they don't just allow anyone in. That's a good thing, no?" Fiona said.

He smiled at her optimism.

Once he and Fiona finally had their papers in order, they were sent to the final checkpoint. Their passports and papers were stamped three times.

"What now?" Cormac asked the processing agent.

"Welcome to America. The ferry to New York is at the landing just outside. Good luck to you both."

Fiona said, "Well, the ferry is all well and good, but I have no idea where I'm going when I get to the other side."

"Do you have an address?"

She fumbled through her pocket and retrieved a slip of paper.

"57 Essex Street. That's where Patricia lives. My cousin."

"I just happen to have a street map here. Let's see. Essex, Essex. Well, this is a bit of luck."

"Yes?"

"A relative arranged a flat for me as well. On Orchard Street. Two blocks away."

"How wonderful," she said. "We can travel together. That is, if you don't mind."

In answer, Cormac picked up her bags and escorted her to the dock. As luck would have it, the ferry had already departed.

"Oh dear," she said.

"Well, I guess we wait. Here," he said. He piled two suitcases one atop the other. "Please, sit. Your very own bench, Miss O'Hara."

She smiled and accepted. Their non-stop conversation ceased half an hour later when another ferry chugged into the dock.

"Here we go, then." He ushered her aboard, juggling all the bags.

There were no seats available so both of them leaned on the rail. They spoke little, merely stared dumbstruck at the famous skyline as it came closer and closer.

"The final leg of our journey," Cormac said. "Welcome to New York."

A voice reached him from below his shoulder. He turned and found himself looking down at a pleasant and familiar face atop a short, sturdy body.

"Mr. LaGuardia," Cormac said.

"Aha, you remembered."

"I could never forget what you did for me," Fiona added.

"We are indebted to you, sir," Cormac said. "Indeed, you have an extraordinary memory to remember us, considering all the people ye must come into contact with in a single day."

"Yeah, that's true. True. I am pretty amazing, come to think of it. I don't forget a thing. Ever."

Cormac grinned at his new friend.

"You must admit, though," LaGuardia said, "after Miss O'Hara's little escapade today, who could forget?"

Fiona blushed and Cormac chuckled.

"So, first of all, call me Fiorello, no Mr. anything. Where are you two headed?"

"Ahh." Cormac pulled out a piece of paper from his coat pocket. "63 Orchard Street."

"And 57 Essex Street," Fiona chimed in.

"Oh yeah? Know the streets well. What's there?"

"My cousin," she said and blushed. "Sorry, I don't mean to be so forward."

"Nonsense, it's refreshing," LaGuardia said. "I, for one, like women with some spunk."

Fiona blushed deeper.

"And you, sir? What's on Orchard Street?"

"I have secured a flat, that is, my uncle, Sean O'Flaherty did that for me in advance of my arrival."

"He lives here?"

"He does. He's a member of the city's finest police force."

"NYPD? No kiddin'? You too? A cop?"

"That's right. Constable in Ireland, Cop in New York."

"Well, well," LaGuardia said.

Fiona just stared at Cormac with something like awe in her eyes and he felt a little taller.

"Now," LaGuardia said. "Let me show you the way to Orchard and Essex."

"No need to go out of your way," Cormac said.

"My pleasure. Anyone in the NYPD gets my personal attention. Gotta keep track of you boys in blue."

Cormac winked at Fiona.

"So, you have a cousin waiting for you in the lower east side?" La Guardia turned to Fiona.

"I do, although I barely know Patricia."

"Well, what better way to get to know someone that to live in a cramped flat together. Not easy to find flats these days."

LaGuardia pulled out a small notebook and a pencil and began scribbling. "Before I forget, if ya ever need anything, here's the way to contact me. Ya know how to use a telephone? If not, send a messenger boy or come yourself to this address. Can't let ya go running around loose in my city."

Cormac watched Fiona chew her lower lip, no doubt to keep from grinning.

A horn blew and the ferry slowed into the dock.

"Follow me," LaGuardia said.

Cormac followed in the rear, keeping his eye on his new friend. He guessed LaGuardia to be at least six inches shorter than Fiona and a full foot shorter than himself.

How could a man be so short in stature but so long in charm and personality?

From the Whitehall Terminal at Battery Park the three boarded a trolley uptown to the Lower East Side. LaGuardia provided a running commentary on the streets and buildings they rode by.

"It's a most invigorating place," LaGuardia said. "Although it has its ups and downs like any big city. You know trash pickup is spotty at best, sometimes the sewers get backed up. Buses and trolleys run occasionally on time. Crime, of course. That sort of thing."

"The city is much like Dublin," Fiona said.

"That right?" LaGuardia said with a wide grin. "Gritty and grungy, you mean? Full of concrete and brick, smoke and noise. Ahh, nature."

Fiona giggled.

"And filled with people," Cormac added as he stood holding a hanging strap, the baggage at his feet. "Lots of them."

Fiona followed his gaze and twisted in her seat to watch the street vendors hawk their wares on Houston Street. Their voices collided as a hundred languages competed with each other. Was that Greek? Russian?

New smells wafted into the trolley car. Pungent and sweet, like her mother's sweet potato pie, acrid and spicy like, well, nothing she'd ever known. Smells that reflected the multitude of cultures.

Just then LaGuardia jumped up and pulled the bell cord. "This is it."

Cormac grabbed the bags and he and Fiona waited for the trolley to stop then hopped down the steps after their new friend. They rushed to catch up.

"63 Orchard Street." LaGuardia pointed. "And Essex Street is around the corner two blocks that way."

Fiona lifted her head and shielded her eyes from the sun. Towering above them six stories was a narrow brick building with dirty windows that glared down like the eyes of unfriendly ghosts.

"This is where a two-room flat awaits me," Cormac said.

"Not bad, not bad, for a tenement," LaGuardia said, clucking his tongue.

He turned to LaGuardia. "Well, sir, I thank you for your most welcome assistance. It would have been considerably more difficult without your guidance."

"And a lot less interesting without your narrative," Fiona said.

"My pleasure, my pleasure." LaGuardia tipped his hat. "Are you all right now on your own?"

"I believe we are." Cormac gave a slight bow.

"Don't forget now, you have my card." With a wave, LaGuardia was off at a fast clip and around the corner before they could blink.

Both of them looked at each other and beamed. Then they gazed up at the tenement.

"I've heard many stories in Ireland about the dreadful conditions of this city," Fiona said. "But in many ways New York exceeds my expectations."

"Well, I guess that's a good thing." Cormac examined the grimy brick façade, broken tin moldings and rusted wrought iron fire escapes.

"It's lovely," Fiona said.

Cormac's eyes popped. "Hmm. I see your expectations are rather low."

"Don't you see, Cormac, it doesn't matter what the place looks like. I'll make it beautiful. I will scrub the rooms and paint the walls and hang curtains--" She stopped. "I'm being foolish aren't I?"

"Not at all, Fiona. I just hope cousin Patricia appreciates what she's getting."

They looked at each other, both realizing that they had each used their given names for the first time since meeting that day.

"I still don't know how I will ever repay you," she said, a blush rising up her neck.

"Ach. This is nothing. There is something even more important we must do."

She looked at him.

"We have to get you a job."

Chapter 5

March 21, 2011

9:00 p.m.

Frank decided to skip the subway and walk home. He needed to think about what his mother said and the evening air helped de-fog his brain. He tried to draw what little he knew from memory about his great grandfather. Cormac. Arrived from Ireland around 1900-something and joined the NYPD, first of the Mead cops. Married an Irish girl. Fiona. What did he know about her? Just that she died very young. Not unusual for that time.

Was Lizzie crazy or just whacked out on meds? She insisted Fiona was murdered and that Cormac investigated the case. Hard to believe. Frank could see hours of research ahead of him, but he didn't mind. After all, it was history and it was family.

He arrived at his Prince Street apartment on the south edge of the Village sooner than he'd expected. His mind was elsewhere so he'd forgotten momentarily what he'd be greeted with.

A loud, shrill squawk pierced his head and he nearly jumped out of his shoes.

"Jesus, Dexter, what the hell."

"What the hell, what the hell. Awwp."

Frank flipped the lights on as a familiar ache started to blossom behind his eyes. The apartment looked like two Sumo wrestlers had had a pillow fight. How could one lousy bird make such a frigging mess?

Before he could take another step into the room, he felt a strong breeze as wings, a span of nearly three feet, flapped exuberantly in front of him. Frank held out an arm and a large blue and gold macaw landed on it. The two stared at each other, the bird tipping his head, first left then right, as he gawked at his owner to gauge what kind of trouble he might be in.

"Awwwwk." Softly.

"Yeah, right. Trying to get on my good side now." Frank sighed and the bird jumped to his shoulder. "It's a good thing I'm not Mr. Clean or you'd be in a world of shit. Come to think of it, we're both in a world of shit."

He grabbed a handful of paper towels from the kitchen and started wiping up the white sticky piles. Not for the first time, he considered keeping the bird in a cage. Then the guilt set in. How could he keep this magnificent creature in a cage? He should be out in the freakin' jungles of Central America where he belonged, for God's sake.

Dexter nuzzled his cheek as if he could read his mind. There were times Frank swore he could. As he moved toward the cabinet containing the bird food, he could sense Dexter's excitement. First one leg rose, then the other, then a quick ripple of wings, then a few head bobs and the ritual repeated.

"All right, already. Here." Frank took the box of feed and moved across the living room to a huge brass cage. He opened the door, pulled out a food bowl, filled it and set it inside. Dexter jumped in and dove into the food.

Frank watched him in awe. Dexter was selective. He'd pull out the nuts, spit out the shells, push aside certain seeds he didn't like and devour any fruit morsels like a starving predator. Which he was.

Frank left the bird to his meal, walked around, and absently scooped up feathers around the room. All in all, the room wasn't all that trashed. Still, he'd have to find a home for this crazy bird.

This'll teach him a lesson--next time don't rescue animals in need. Unless it's a dog. Then, maybe.

At two in the morning, Frank woke. He stared at the window, diffuse yellow light filtering in from the lamppost on the street. He tossed, threw the covers off, pulled them on. Hell. Too much on his mind--he knew he'd never go back to sleep. He donned a sweatshirt and jeans over his naked body, went into the kitchen, and chugged a bottle of water. Dexter was quiet now, secure in his cage with a towel covering it. Frank wondered if the bird really slept or was merely in meditation.

He wandered over to his desk and fired up his laptop. The image of the young reporter kept flashing in his head. It brought to mind his daughter, a newly-minted reporter for the Times. He hadn't even been invited to her graduation ceremony.

ugh

Frank grabbed his cell phone to check--maybe Amanda had texted him. He'd left her a message after his visit with Lizzie. Nothing.

He leaned over, picked up a photograph of Amanda that Irene had given him. Twenty-two, journalism major at NYU and now a cub reporter at the *New York Times*. He whistled. *Times*. That was some coup. The other girl was at the *Post*. Not nearly as prestigious.

His mother's words came back to him. Amanda was helping Stephanie with research. How well did his daughter know her? He prayed they weren't close friends.

While he waited for his computer, he opened the file on Stephanie Brandt, the start of his own murder book. A good deal of the handwritten notes were from Will Jefferies. Comments on time, date and location. No autopsy report yet. Five witness interviews. Frank skimmed through those. Four students, each corroborating the other's story, had heard the scream from the hallway, ran back into the room and saw no one. Someone pushed her and managed to escape. Which door did the killer exit? Not the door that led to the hallway. He would have bumped into the students. The door that the professor went through or the other door? Where did that lead?

Frank turned the page over and saw the sergeant's sketch of the classroom and where each door led. One door led to the hallway. One to a side hallway where the restrooms were, the door that the professor used. And a third, which opened into another classroom. Had there been another class in there or was it empty? He made a note to check. He also made a note to follow up on Dr. Schueller.

Would he have any motive to kill the girl?

Finally, he shuffled through the photographs. Shots of the Brown Building, looking up to the ninth story open window. Shots of the street beneath that window. And shots of the dead girl. Frank sighed and Dexter responded in kind with a ruffle of his feathers.

Stephanie Brandt had once been a very pretty blond with her whole life ahead of her. Now she resembled a waxen mannequin. He couldn't help thinking of his daughter. Time was slipping away and he hadn't spent enough time with her. Another sigh. Another ruffle of feathers.

He glanced through Jefferies' notes again. Thorough, neatly written, legible. Who was Will Jefferies? He knew little about the man except that he'd been with NYPD for nine years. Made sergeant two years ago. Widower, no kids. Rented a studio two blocks from the station. Didn't appear to socialize with the other men. A loner? Married to the job? What did the other men think of him? What did Jefferies think of the other men? Two questions he could ask about himself.

Frank slipped the photos back in the file and turned to his computer. He clicked on Google and typed in Triangle Shirtwaist Factory fire. Bingo. A long list of websites appeared. He clicked on one. Pages and pages of information. He started with "Eyewitness at the Triangle" by William G. Shephard. Two short pages but powerful prose. He read a paragraph.

"I learned a new sound--a more horrible sound than description can picture. It was the thud of a speeding living body on a stone sidewalk. Thud-dead, thud-dead, thud-dead, thud-dead. Sixty-two thud-deads. I call them that, because the sound and the thought of death came to me each time, at the same instant. There was plenty of chance to watch them as they came down. The height was eighty feet."

Eighty feet, Frank thought. Or ninety. That's about how far Stephanie Brandt fell. How long would it take? Ten seconds, twenty? Every second speeding through your life, knowing it was about to end. He shivered.

He moved on to another story. *"The fire broke out on the top floors of the Asch Building. By the time the fire was over, 146 out of 500 employees had died."*

The New York Times printed, *"Street strewn with bodies, piles of dead inside."*

Frank scanned further. *"Coroner declares building laws were not enforced--building modern--classed fireproof."*

Fireproof, eh? Like the *Titanic* was sink proof. He slumped back in his chair.

So what's the connection between the Triangle disaster a hundred years ago and Stephanie Brandt's murder? Did she stumble onto some information she wasn't supposed to? And what about his mother's allusion to Cormac's murder case? Was Fiona really murdered or did she die in the fire? Did that tie into the fire and the murder today?

The Brown Building today was owned by New York University and used for classrooms. In 1911 it was the Asch Building and the top three floors were occupied by the Triangle Shirtwaist Factory.

Who were the owners and what happened to them after the tragic fire? More to research.

The fact remained. Someone killed Stephanie Brandt. If there was a connection to the past, maybe his great grandfather, Cormac Fergus Mead, would be able to shed some light on the matter.

Chapter 6

March 22, 2011

6:00 a.m.

63 Orchard Street. The place he grew up. The home his mother had lived in much of her life. A century old, five-story gritty brick tenement, badly in need of renovation. Three storefronts--a tiny dress shop at the first level and two below ground; a dry cleaners and a shoe repair inhabited the lower spaces. Above, ten units, ten sets of occupants. Some families, some couples. The lower east side was developing a new caché since the Tenement Museum had opened down the street.

He looked around at similar buildings on the street. Quintessential tenements built in the latter part of the nineteenth and early part of the twentieth century. Prior to central heating, these places were freezing in the winter and broiling in the summer. And before electricity, they were always dark, particularly in the hallways where there were no windows. Water was always cold and sometimes had to be obtained from an outdoor pump. Water closets were situated on each floor, not in each flat.

Must have been quite a trip to live here back then.

Three generations of Meads had inhabited this building, starting with Cormac and Fiona. The neighborhood had definitely gentrified since their time. Building was probably worth a small fortune now. Someday, he'd be part owner of this structure, along with his sister, Irene, and his brother, Thomas.

Thomas. Another headache he didn't want to think about.

Frank started up the front steps and opened the entry door. Chipped black paint speckled the threshold and the doorknob was rust-encrusted. A loud squeal caused him to flinch.

Inside, flowered wallpaper had been his mother's attempt to beautify the hallway, but its corners now curled and the smell of grease clung to its surfaces. Since she'd become ill, she hadn't the energy to keep up the place.

His mother's apartment was on the second level and consisted of two units, combined thanks to his dad, to provide more space and light.

He fiddled with the key and the door clicked open. Frank stepped into another century. This is what it must have looked like when Cormac and Fiona lived here.

Irene would kill him if he said that out loud.

His stomach gurgled with angst and he popped a couple of Tums. He bought them by the ten-pack these days.

His mother had suggested he ask his daughter about Cormac. He and Amanda hadn't been in touch lately, hadn't been in touch much ever, if truth be known. He tried her cell again, left another message.

Right now he was here to find the box Irene had told him about--a box of Cormac's papers stored on a shelf in his mother's bedroom closet. He headed there just as his cell rang.

"Mead here."

"Jefferies. I was wondering if I should call this early."

Frank looked at his watch. 6:30 a.m. "I'm always up early. Whatcha' got?"

"Some background on the Brandt girl."

"Why don't we meet for coffee?"

They arranged a meeting place and Frank clicked off. He felt a spurt of optimism that he could swing Jefferies to his side. Maybe the rest of the men would follow. Time would tell.

In his mother's room he stood a moment, looked around. Pink chenille spread on the bed must have been at least forty years old. He thought he remembered it from his elementary school days.

Knick knacks everywhere. His mother had a hard time throwing anything out. On the nightstand and dressing table were statues, decorative boxes, calendars, candles, and photos. Lots of framed photos. He picked one up. A photo of his mom and dad. Lizzie and Frank, Sr. She was a looker back then.

Frank sighed and went to the closet. Irene was right. On the top shelf was an aged brown cardboard box. He pulled over a chair from her vanity and stood on it. The box read, Cormac Mead, 1909-1918.

For a second, Frank wondered why those particular years and why it ended at 1918?

Mysteries were like old houses. Once you started working on them, new questions exposed themselves, new leads were revealed. Kind of like brushing a long-haired Irish Setter. The layers of fur just keep shedding.

Frank brought the box down and set it on the bed. He only had a few minutes before meeting Jefferies. He lifted the lid. The first thing he saw was a photograph, framed in elaborate gilt-edged painted cardboard. *Paradise Studios, New Lots Avenue, Brooklyn, New York.*

He turned it over. Cormac and Fiona, wedding, St. Joseph's Church, October 18, 1909. Frank calculated in his head. They had arrived at Ellis Island in April of 1909, so they only knew each other six months before they got married.

Life was short back then. No time to waste.

Frank studied the picture of Cormac. Handsome, tall, thick hair, parted to the side, not slicked down as it was in those days. Full mustache. Was that a twinkle in his eye?

Fiona, quite a beauty. Slender, long hair, red, no doubt? High, finely chiseled cheekbones. Elegant.

Looks a little like Maggie, Frank thought.

Don't go there.

His phone vibrated and he snatched it off his belt.

This time he looked at the number. His brother Thomas. He sighed and let it go to voice mail.

Katz's Deli was a New York City icon. At 7:00 a.m. it was humming with rush hour crowds. Situated nearby on Houston Street, it was especially popular with the cops in the 6th, 7th and 9th Precincts. Will Jefferies was already seated, drinking a Dr. Brown's Cream Soda when Frank entered. Hard to find Dr. Brown's outside of the City.

Frank slid into the booth and ordered coffee. He watched the sergeant stuff the last of a corned beef on rye with sauerkraut into his roomy mouth.

"What?" Jefferies said, barely swallowing the load.

"Isn't it a little early for that?"

"You mean corned beef?" Jefferies cracked a smile. "Hell, it's seven in the morning."

Frank grinned. He called the waitress over and ordered two crullers. "I'll stick with breakfast food for breakfast. I'm a little old-fashioned that way." He sipped his coffee. "So, what do you have?"

Jefferies pushed his plate away and pulled out a notebook from his jacket pocket.

Frank observed that Jefferies' jacket was worn thin and had threads dangling around the edges. He realized how much he had to learn about the man.

"Okay. Dead girl is indeed Stephanie Brandt. Parents identified her late last night. They live in Queens. Stephanie lived in the

Village, Broome Street, with a roomie named Betsy Cohen. Cohen's out of town--we're trying to reach her."

Jefferies slurped down his soda. "Vic was twenty-three, had been working for the *Post* for two years, since she graduated from NYU as a journalism major. I'll check at her office, see what I can find out."

"I think my daughter knew her," Frank said.

"Yeah?"

Frank explained the connection. "Haven't been able to reach her yet. Amanda."

Jefferies looked at him.

"What? You'll be the first to know when I talk to her. I doubt she knows anything."

Jefferies said nothing.

"Did her parents have any ideas who might have done this?" Frank asked.

"They swore she was a great kid, honest, hard-working, wanted to get ahead in the newspaper business, such that it is these days. Was also working on a book, some kind of true crime, but they didn't know what. I'll check with the *Post*."

"I'd like to check her apartment," Frank said.

"Here's the address, oh, and the key." Jefferies reached into a battered inside pocket.

"Where's her computer?"

"Missing. Killer must have gotten it. I mean, what's a reporter without a laptop? She must've had it with her."

"Shit."

"We did get her cell phone, though. It was in her pocket. Forensics downloaded all of it and it's back in her apartment now so you can have a look-see."

"I wanted to see that computer. Damn. We need to know about the story she was writing and whether her book was on the same subject."

"You mean the Triangle Factory fire?"

Frank nodded.

"You think there's a connection?"

"What do you think?"

Jefferies chewed his thick lower lip. "Kind of a weird coincidence. Her going out the ninth story window."

"You know the history?" Frank asked.

"Some. Most New Yorkers do. I know it was the biggest disaster in the City until 9-11."

Frank sipped his coffee. "Still, that fire happened a century ago. What's the deal today?"

"Good question," Jefferies said.

"What about cause of death?" Frank said.

"Haven't heard from the M-E yet. "You thinking drugs, maybe?"

Frank shrugged.

"I'll let you know when I know."

"Other physical evidence?" Frank said.

"No prints on the windowsill. Doorknobs too smeared with all the students. As for the witnesses, no one saw anything unusual."

"They didn't notice a new student in the room?"

"Nah. Happens all the time. People sit in for various reasons, audit classes, whatever." He waved a hand in the air.

"Let me know what happens at the newspaper. I'm going to stop off at her apartment after I pay a visit to the Medical Examiner. I'll head into the office later."

"How's your mother?"

Frank blinked. "How'd you know?"

"Word travels." Jefferies looked at him with no expression.

"She'll be okay. I think. Thanks for asking."

Jefferies untangled his long legs, rose, and threw a couple of bills on the table. Frank couldn't help but think Ichabod Crane.

"Happy hunting."

With a nod the sergeant was off.

Chapter 7

September 10, 190**9**

Cormac hummed as he walked his beat that evening, his thoughts on Fiona and their upcoming wedding in October. He still remembered her at their first meeting, fists in the air, pounding that poor purse snatcher.

Listen to me, then. Poor purse snatcher.

A smile touched his lips, as he ambled down Sixth Avenue. He stopped to check his reflection in the glass windows of C.O. Bigelow Apothecaries and shook his head in wonder at the assortment of ladies cosmetics on display.

"Officer Mead." A uniformed cop tapped him on the arm.

"Good evening to you, Officer Briggs."

"Are you thinking about wearing makeup on your puss?" his comrade said.

"Wouldn't that be fittin' then? And what color scheme would ye suggest, peach or mauve?"

"Oh mauve, fur sure."

Both men chuckled.

"Wedding's coming up, ain't it?"

"That it is."

"I betcha yur gettin' nervous right about now."

"I try not to dwell on it too much."

"Ah, well, marriage has its good points."

"Remind me not to tell Fiona about this dastardly conversation or I'll truly be in hot water."

Briggs tapped his cap with his club and went whistling off, turning the corner at Waverly Place.

Cormac looked back in the window. For Fiona--peach.

He breathed in the scents of the city. Rotting garbage, leftover cooking smells. . . and urine. Ripe. Still, above that he could detect the fragrance of lavender in the last throes of life lining window boxes along the street. The city that never slept seemed unusually quiet tonight. Street vendor carts were buttoned up, horses stabled, only an occasional passerby.

He tucked his hands deeper into his pockets as he wandered the deserted streets. Eventually he found himself, as he did every night, across the street from the Asch Building on Greene and Washington Place. He ran his eyes up the row of signs on its corner: *Harris Bros, Cloaks and Suits, Men's Clothing, Clothing Specialties, New York's Crown and Wallach*. Finally at the top: *Triangle Waist Company. Triangle*. The company where Fiona worked, slaved, really.

It angered him, first, that his wife-to-be had to work at all. Second, that she had no choice but to do menial labor for menial dollars under shoddy working conditions. Cormac recalled the grim stories she had related, when pressed, for Fiona wasn't a complainer.

He halted his step along with his musings. He thought he'd heard something. Yes, there it was again, men's voices, then thuds, groans, glass breaking. A woman's cry. A loud crash of a metal can striking a hard surface like the side of a building. He sucked in his breath and took off down the street, turned the corner, ran again.

Two men dressed in oversized raggedy jackets and trousers, caps pulled low on their heads, stood over a bundle on the sidewalk. Repeatedly they lifted their arms and brought down clubs and fists, beating the bundle that now lay still.

"Hey, stop. What're ye doing there? I say, stop. Police," Cormac shouted and sprinted toward the men. They looked up, spied him and took off down the alley way. Cormac raced after them but stopped short when the woman cried out.

"Please, come back. Help me," she said.

He went to her aid.

"Good God, woman, what happened? Are you all right? You need a doctor, let me--"

"No, no, just help. . . help me to my feet. Please."

"I could've caught those men, if--"

"It's better that you didn't," she said.

He stared at her face and neck, red welts swelling before his eyes, cuts seeping blood, a nose bent out of shape, cheeks bruised the color of blueberries.

"Miss, you need to get to the hospital," he said.

"I need to get home." She turned intense brown eyes on him and at once she looked familiar. He couldn't place her. A small but solid young woman in her twenties, curly brown hair pulled back severely, Cormac was certain he'd seen her before.

"Will you not help me get home?" she said.

"What? Of course, if that is what ye wish, but--"

"I am perfectly fine. Nothing that a few cold compresses won't cure." Her grimace belied her words as Cormac helped her stand. She doubled over, clutching her chest.

"Aye, you may have some broken ribs there."

"Nothing to be done for them, now, is there?" She straightened and felt gingerly with her fingers around her face.

"What in the name of God happened?" he asked.

She thought a while before answering, shook her head, looked at him again. Something about him, perhaps, made her speak while Cormac believed she had no wish to.

"Some thugs grabbed me, did this. Tried to teach me a lesson, I guess."

He opened his mouth.

"You needn't say anything. It's enough that you helped me, rather than leave me lying in the street. What's your name? I don't believe we've met."

"Officer Cormac Mead, ma'am. Why *would* we have met?"

She shot him a bewildered look, then a half-smile. "How do you do, Officer Mead. I'm Clara Lemlich. I've met many police officers, sir, and none of them would have treated me thus." All those words made her breathless.

"I don't understand. It's my job."

"Tell that to your comrades." She took a few steps to steady herself then began limping down the cobbled road.

Cormac suddenly knew who she was and exactly what she referred to. Clara Lemlich: one of those so-called unionists working with other like-minded women to improve conditions in the garment industry. Conditions, he knew, that badly needed to improve. As Fiona could testify. But his colleagues at NYPD, in fact, the whole of the Tammany machine, turned their backs on Miss Lemlich and her movement. Socialists, they were called, as if improving poor people's lots was a bad thing.

He followed her at a slight distance, knowing she wouldn't want his escort, but fearing another attack on her person. When they reached her building, she walked up to the front door and swung around to face him.

"You are a kind man, Officer Mead, not like your compatriots at all." And she was inside.

Cormac stood watching her door for many minutes. He felt very cold of a sudden as if the hand of death had reached out and touched his heart. It wasn't a good sign of things to come, not a good sign at all.

The Eighth Precinct, or Mercer Street Station in Greenwich Village, appeared calm and desolate at four in the morning when Cormac returned to clock out. Inside told a different story. Two patrolmen struggled with a drunk, shouting in a gravelly voice, "I demand my rights, I'm a *gen-you-wine* 'pax taying cizithen'. I have rights, I say."

Cormac wound his way past another cop ushering a woman dressed in a gown of torn imitation silk and a crimson boa around her throat onto a wooden bench.

"Now, Meg, my lady, you know you can't just punch out the bartender at the Village Tavern whenever you feel like it."

"Yeah, well, shit on you. He grabbed me by my hair. Look what he did to my new hairdo, just had it done 'n all, too. Goddamn son-of-a-bitch. I'll not take that from--"

"This way, Meg." The cop led her out of the room.

Business as usual.

Cormac headed directly for the time clock, reached for his card and slid it in the slot. Just as the loud pop of the punch sounded, a hand grabbed his shoulder.

"Cormac."

"Sergeant Devine, good to see you."

"Can I have a word?"

Cormac looked at him. Devine turned and walked into a small office out of bedlam's reach. Cormac followed.

"Do you know a Miss Clara Lemlich?" Devine asked.

"What?" Cormac couldn't hide his astonishment.

"Word gets around pretty quick in this big city, ya know, my man. You met her tonight, din't you?"

Cormac hesitated for an instant, the significance of what this meant not fully sinking in.

"I met her tonight on my watch. Two men were beating the life out of her, so I stepped in and stopped them," Cormac said.

"Let me give you a bit of advice, seein's as how you're new 'n all. You'd best stay away from Miss Lemlich or you'll find yourself in an unpleasant situation."

"What do you mean? The lady needed help. These men were pummeling the crap out of her, for Christ's sake."

"That's not our business."

"That's exactly our business. What would you have had me do, then? Let her be beaten to bloody death?"

The sergeant stared at him. "You don't get it, do you?"

"Get it? Get what? I know what my job is. Is that job different here in New York than in Ireland, in the rest of the world, then?"

The sergeant chewed his lower lip. "Officer Mead, ya got a lot to learn. There are some in this town who do not warrant protecting. Doing so will only get you into trouble."

"Well, let me tell you something, Sergeant. Even if I wasn't a policeman, I would have helped her. When someone's in danger of their life, you help them. And what would you have done?"

"Cormac, you don't--"

"And another thing," Cormac said, ignoring the sergeant's words. "How did you know about that incident tonight? It only just happened. There was no one--" He stopped. "What? Hell. Are you following me? Do all new officers get tailed to see if they can do their job?" Cormac's anger surfaced in a sputter.

Devine put a hand on Cormac's arm. "Think about what ya just said, man. Think."

Cormac stood red-faced.

"I'm tellin' ya this as a favor," Devine said. "But I'll tell ya only once. Keep clear of that woman and her companions." With that Devine turned on his heel and moved fast out of range of conversation.

Cormac watched his superior's back as he reflected on his words. *Think.* Think about what? That he was being followed, watched by his own colleagues? His mind tried to grasp the sergeant's meaning. Was this how things were done in New York?

A shudder ran through him as if he had swallowed a snake. The whole confrontation had an ominous overtone that made his skin clammy.

Who was Clara Lemlich in truth and why was she such a threat to them? Cormac was not so naïve to pretend he wasn't aware of City politics and corruption, but violence like this, against a woman? That was going too far.

He slotted his time card as he mulled over the sergeant's warning to "keep clear of that woman and her companions."

There was no way Cormac Mead could do that now.

Chapter 8

September 28, 1909

"Fiona, me love, do ye not think we should find a roomier, more suitable apartment for our wedded life?" Cormac said. "I've been inhabiting this one since we arrived in New York and it is a bit, er, cramped."

Fiona smiled. "I think this is perfectly fine, for a while at least."

"Well, when, I mean, when there are more of us, it will be too small, fer certain."

"More of us? Are you planning on the O'Flahertys moving in with us, then? Or perhaps my cousin Patricia?"

"Ach, don't be so flippant, my little lass. You know very well what I mean." He paused. "But there is something I've wanted to talk to ye about."

Fiona looked at him.

"Your job."

"What about my job?" she said.

"I would very much like you to quit when we get married."

Fiona looked down, smiled. "I know that's what you'd wish."

"Well, then?"

"I have two things to say." She slowed her words, choosing each with care. "First, although I certainly am not enamored with working at the Triangle, it does give me, us, extra income. Money we can use for our wedding, our new life together."

Cormac opened his mouth. "Fiona, you shouldn't concern yourself with money. That is my responsibility."

"Cormac, dear, I've been concerned with money most of my adult life. My mother and my father had no head for it, so it fell to me."

"But this is different. We're to be married and it's my job to--"

She held up a hand. "Second, while I very much care what you would like me to do, I am my own person, therefore, I would like to make my own decisions."

His face turned red.

"Please, my love, don't take this the wrong way. I know you only have my best interests at heart. But understand. This is something I need to decide on my own."

"I see," he said quietly. "And when do you intend to make this grand decision?"

"When the time is right I will know. Trust me. I need to do this for my own peace of mind."

"Very well. But let it be known I am not pleased."

"You've made your point." Fiona took a breath and reached for his hand.

"You are one headstrong woman. I hope ye realize--"

A soft knock on the door took them by surprise.

"Saved," Fiona said in jest.

Cormac swung the door open and found himself facing Clara Lemlich. Sergeant Devine's words rushed at him like floodwaters.

"Miss Lemlich?"

"Officer Mead, I'm sorry to bother you at home, but I beg you, may we talk? It's rather important."

She pushed her way past him. "Please excuse me, but I would rather not stand in the hallway."

"How did ye know where to find me?" he asked.

"I live not far from here, you see, and I have chanced upon you returning home from work." Her face reddened. "Please, sir, give me a few moments to explain."

Fiona drew up to the woman's side. "Forgive Cormac's manners, Miss--?"

"Lemlich, Clara Lemlich, but do call me Clara." Clara turned intense brown eyes on Fiona first, then Cormac.

"Your husband--"

"Betrothed, not married yet," Fiona said with a smile.

"Oh, sorry," Clara said. "Officer Mead was very kind to help me some weeks ago, when I was in a bit of trouble, you see."

Fiona raised an eyebrow. "Trouble?"

Clara turned to Cormac who turned to Fiona.

Fiona suddenly took Clara by the arm. "First things first. Clara, I'm Fiona O'Hara. Won't you sit down? Can I get you some tea or coffee? I even have Dekafa, if you prefer decaffeinated coffee."

"Dekafa would be quite wonderful. That will give me a fighting chance to sleep tonight." Clara smiled and brushed back stray curly hairs that had come loose. She sat down on a green velvet divan.

While Fiona prepared the coffee, Clara apologized about her late intrusion, commented on the pleasant apartment. The women conversed through a glassless window into the kitchen.

Cormac regarded the bruises on Clara's face, which seemed to have faded, making her skin look pale, almost translucent. His mind puzzled on this unexpected visit and he trusted the tingling sensations in his limbs that were always a sign of foreboding. He knew he would not like what Clara Lemlich was about to tell him.

"Here we are, then." Fiona set down a tray with cups and a plate of butter biscuits. She poured the black liquid and handed the cup to her guest, then did the same for herself and Cormac.

"You mentioned some trouble, Clara," Fiona said. "What kind of trouble?"

"I was attacked by some men on the street while walking home. Officer Mead happened by at that same time, lucky for me. I am most grateful to him. After he chased them away, he was kind enough to heed my wishes and take me home, rather than to the hospital."

"You should have gone to the hospital," Cormac said.

Clara smiled and shrugged. "Perhaps. Still, it is because of what you did for me that night that I feel I can trust you now."

"Clara, please," Fiona said. "You keep us in suspense."

Clara set her cup on the table in front of her and folded her hands in her lap. "I came to thank you for your help but also to give you fair warning, Officer Mead."

Fiona shot a glance at Cormac who stared at Clara.

"What happened that day?" Fiona asked, her voice almost a whisper.

"Let me begin first by telling you who I am. I'm a draper at Leiserson's." Clara paused. "Funny how one defines themselves by their job rather than by their personal characteristics. You know, she's a *draper*, not she's a *mother*, or she has a *sense of humor*. Listen to me go on." Clara drank some of her coffee.

"You know of Leisersons?" she asked Fiona.

Fiona nodded. "One of the finest suit makers in the city."

"Well, that day. . . it had been a grueling week with a shipment of suit jackets to get out. Some of the seamstresses worked sixteen-hour days with little rest for meals. A friend of mine, Sarah, told me that she and the women in her row worked a hundred hours that week."

"Eye numbing work," Fiona said.

Clara shrugged. "They expected to receive five dollars each for their efforts. Instead they were told that the owner decided to charge them for the thread and needles they used."

"What? That's outrageous," Fiona said.

Cormac shook his head but said nothing.

"That's not all. Sarah said they were also told that they would owe a fee on the use of the sewing machine. A fee on machines that were not even theirs. This meant each worker's pay would be only three dollars and eighty-five cents." Clara paused, gathering courage.

"Go on," Fiona said.

"Well, I can tell you that it angered me tenfold and while Sarah is a meek little sprite, I am not."

"Really?" Cormac said.

Clara smiled. Fiona didn't.

"I barged into Mr. Leiserson's office and told him a thing or two, and I will say I minced no words."

Fiona's wide eyes rested on her guest.

Clara tilted her head back. "That very night I attended a union meeting at the basement of the Bethel Temple."

"We shouldn't be discussing unions," Cormac said.

"She's only trying to explain what happened," Fiona said. "Please, go on, Clara."

"After the meeting, well. . . it was late and. . . that is the night you found me on the street, Officer Mead."

"You mean to say he, your boss, was responsible for what happened?" Cormac asked. "He hired men to beat you up?"

Clara bowed her head and said nothing.

"Good God, Clara, what can you do?" Fiona said. "There must be some way, some retribution--"

Cormac spoke in a hoarse voice. "You think Leiserson hired street thugs to do this to you, don't you?"

"Yes. . .and no." Clara looked directly at him. "Leiserson is a member of the Business Protection Association, a private organization for the factory owners. Blanck, Harris, Shapiro, Leiserson, others, Murphy probably. They meet at different locations, often at one of their own homes. The BPA has been growing in strength now with the unions making trouble for them, causing them to lose money. They're banded tight together like worms in a bait can." She sucked in some air.

"What about them, the BPA?" Fiona asked.

"They're the ones that hired the hoodlums who attacked me."

"Then why not go to the police?" Fiona said.

Cormac winced inwardly, fearing the answer. He rose and walked to the window, pulled back the curtains to peer out. Leaning on a lamppost across the street was a man wearing a raggedy jacket and trousers. This time he had no cap on and when he lifted his head to look up at the window, Cormac felt his heart rattle in his chest cage.

The women's words blurred behind him as if he were hearing them through a tunnel. Emotions churned in his gut, a mixture of fear, anger, and trepidation. Sergeant Devine's words came back and his meaning became clear. It was not *he*, Cormac, who had been followed that night, but Clara Lemlich.

"This sounds ominous," Fiona said.

Cormac turned to face the women.

"You might take it as a warning, indeed," Clara said, her eyes now on Cormac. "You see, it wasn't hired thugs who beat me to a bloody pulp that night. I'm being watched, followed. My movements are being tracked day by day. Almost as if I'm being stalked."

"But why?" Fiona asked.

"To make sure I'm a good girl, that I don't start trouble."

"You mean union trouble?"

Clara nodded.

"Who did this to you, then, if it wasn't merely toughs for hire?" Fiona said.

Cormac spoke for the first time in minutes. "It was off-duty policemen."

Chapter 9

Frank parked his city-issued Ford Escape hybrid on First Avenue and tossed his official placard in the windshield. 520 First was the Office of the Chief Medical Examiner of New York City. OCME had been at this location since 1960. A few years ago, OCME opened the DNA Building to house state of the art Forensic Biology labs as well as OCME's Administrative unit and Evidence facilities, including a forensic garage to examine vehicles.

As he entered, Frank's stomach did its usual flips and twists. He reached for his Tums as he approached the reception desk. Above the desk was the phrase "Science Serving Justice." He liked that. Science. Reminded him of Maggie. His first real relationship following his wife's death. Maggie. Maybe he'd call her. Maybe not.

He showed his badge and asked for Dr. Oliver.

"Take the elevators to Lower Level 4 and turn left," was a matronly receptionist's curt reply. The New York no-nonsense, abrupt mannerisms still gave him a jolt. After living in D.C. for eleven years, he had grown accustomed to a more southern, genteel approach.

Lower Level 4. The basement. Sub-basement, even. The place he dreaded. For some reason autopsy rooms and morgues were all in basements. Keep the dead underground. As far from the living as possible.

He turned left when the doors opened and walked slumped-shouldered, soft-footed, down the narrow corridor. The smell started getting to him at this point. Or the memory of the smell. His enthusiasm for a new homicide case always waned somewhat at this point.

A light spilled from an open door on the right. The hanging shingle declared: CME, Dr. S. Oliver. He poked his head in. Empty.

"Looking for me?" Serena Oliver exited another room with double doors and called out. She wore a blue gown and a pair of goggles dangled around her neck.

"Yeah, remember me? I'm--."

"Yes, I remember. Lieutenant Mead, right? John?"

"Frank."

"Sorry," she said.

He smiled. "I thought I'd stop by, see if you had any information on Miss Brandt."

She eyed him a minute.

"What?"

"I like that. Miss Brandt. Shows respect for the dead. Rather than call her 'the vic.'"

He waited, taking note of her latté-colored skin and hazel eyes.

She looked back at him. "I usually send the report in when I'm done, you know. But follow me." She spun around and went down the hall at a fast clip, her rubber-soled shoes squeaking on the linoleum.

She pushed through a new set of double doors into a room that Frank was all too familiar with. The autopsy room.

"Here, put these on." She pulled out a yellow gown, a pair of booties and a surgical mask from a bin. He donned them without question.

Then he gazed around at a familiar but unpleasant sight: gleaming stainless tables with holes for drainage, overhead lights and mirrors, sparkling clean counters lined with grim looking dissection tools—everything from buzz saws to tweezers, scales for weighing body parts, light tables for examining x-rays, and bottles filled with liquids of rainbow colors.

On the floor, hoses snaked around the tables. He stepped closer to Oliver who was removing a white sheet from a body. Stephanie Brandt.

"Lieutenant--?"

"Frank."

"Frank, if I didn't know you were a veteran homicide cop, I'd wonder." She smiled.

"Yeah, well, it takes me a few minutes to get my stomach prepared." He looked at her. "The rest of me's okay."

Oliver half-smiled. "I understand." She paused, looked down. "I hate it when young people die needlessly, you know?"

"Yeah. I know."

She picked up a chart and leafed through, reading as she went. "Body of Caucasian woman, Stephanie Ellen Brandt, age 23, brought in, etc., etc., identified by father and mother, James and Louise Brandt, Flushing, Queens, etc." She stopped, looked at Frank. "You'll get the report in a day. Bottom line is lots of internal damage to organs, bones, brain, caused by impact with hard surface from a fall of approximately 90 feet."

Frank grimaced. "Let's forget about her scream for a moment. What tells you this wasn't suicide?"

"She landed a little too far from the building. If she'd jumped she would have been closer. That's not definitive, by the way. I mean I've examined suicides that did an Icarus thing. Arms and legs out, pushed off, like they were going to fly."

"I assume they were on drugs?"

"You assume correctly."

"Stephanie?"

"No drugs, no Icarus."

He walked to the body, looked down.

On the stainless steel table, Stephanie Brandt looked like a teenager rather than a twenty-three year old woman. Her skin was smooth and pale, a sallow white and her lips were bloodless. On first glance, Frank could see no injuries. A step closer showed the damage to the right side of her head. The hair had been shaved and there was a large indentation as if a meteor had landed there.

"She was a pretty girl," Oliver said.

"Yeah," Frank said. "She was." Amanda's face came to mind.

"Did you realize there are two ways you can fall?" Oliver said. She didn't wait for an answer.

"There's a vertical controlled fall, where the person usually lands on his feet. Believe it or not, this fall is survivable and there are reports of people who fell 100 feet and still lived to tell about it. The key is to wind up upright."

"How's that possible?"

"With a controlled fall the initial energy is transmitted through the feet and legs, sparing the vital organs. Oh, there may be broken bones, but still they survive."

"Jesus."

"The uncontrolled fall, however," she continued, "is quite different. Here the person lands on some other part of the body, back, stomach, head. These can be fatal even in short distances. People can kill themselves falling from a ladder."

Frank put his hands on his hips. "Stephanie Brandt didn't just fall."

"No. I don't believe she did. And her landing was definitely uncontrolled." She paused. "I understand witnesses heard her scream?"

"That's right. Not typical for a jumper. Unless it was an eee-ha!"

"Hmm."

"And why would a young woman with everything to look forward to in her life jump anyway?"

"That's a philosophical question for another time," he said. "For now, did you notice anything that wasn't in line with death from the fall?"

"Not a thing. As I said, blood work shows no toxins, alcohol, drugs of any kind. The damages to the body—well, that's hard. The impact would have destroyed any physical evidence like a blow to the head. Besides, she screamed, so she was conscious when she went out that window." Oliver touched her forehead with long slender fingers. "God, what must she have been thinking in those last few seconds of her life?"

Frank shook his head. "I wondered the same thing." He turned and looked down at the dead girl. The thoughts that streamed through his mind surprised him, flashbacks to his mother's words. Another murder. Another time. Same place. The Triangle.

So who killed you, Stephanie? And why

Chapter 10

March 22, 2011

10:30 a.m.

NYPD's First Deputy Commissioner, Sanford Russo, tore his gaze from the window and swung his chair around to face his visitor. His usually red pockmarked face flamed even redder. The stomach pains and nausea came and went but never completely subsided. He reached into his drawer and pulled out a bottle of pills, shook two out, and chugged them with an open can of Coke on his desk.

"Siddown," he said, his voice sounding like a gravel pit after forty years of smoking. "Shut the door."

Frank Mead closed the door and settled into a chair across from his boss.

"You okay?" Frank asked.

"Yeah, sure, just an ulcer. Hey, that's all I got after all these years on the force, count me lucky."

"I guess so."

"Been a long time since we worked together, eh?"

"Yup."

"How long, Frank? How long's it been?"

"Since 2000."

"Glad to be back, I bet? I mean D.C.'s okay, but this is New York. No comparison, right?"

Frank gave a weak smile.

"You see some of the other guys I brought back in? Vincenzo

from L-A. Oh, and Oquendo from Baltimore. Remember him?"

"I do. Good man."

Russo sank back into his chair and exhaled. "So, how're things goin'?"

"Well, if you mean, are the men fucking with me because I'm an outsider? Yeah. They are. But I expected it. They'll come around."

Russo bobbled his head. "This is important to me, Frank. The department is important to me. Important to this city. It's bad when the people don't trust us, know what I mean?" He swiveled in his chair, waved his hands in the air, swiveled more. Abruptly he stood to his full 6"3" height and gathered control. An impressive man despite his bulging gut and 64 years on the planet, Russo had been fidgeting nervously since Frank arrived. Steady now, he turned to his Lieutenant.

"I get it," Frank said.

"Nah, ya don't." He wiped a bead of sweat off his forehead. "The last two years've been like shit. The Rodrigo murders, the Janine case, the riots in Bed Stuy. The whole NYPD is goin' down the friggin' tubes. People don't have respect for men in blue, the whole city goes to hell. See what I'm saying?"

Frank nodded, shifted in his chair.

"So, what I'm tellin' you is this. Get the men on your side. Get that investigation of, what's'er name, the jumper, resolved. And fast. Press is having a field day. Soon people are goin' to think some crazy fucker out there is gonna push them outta window too." He stuffed his oversized hands in his pockets and walked to the window, gazed out.

"This is a great city, Frank. My city. Your city. And the department is what keeps it together. Now the department is in trouble, see? It's up to me to clean the whole mess up. Get rid of the corruption--ha--and start new, ya know, like cutting out the cancer and chemo-ing the shit out of the force. That's why you're here.

You and a half dozen other veterans from departments around the country."

"I know, I know."

"So," Russo sank back into his chair. "So, where are you in this case? What's her name again?"

"Stephanie Brandt."

"Yeah. What's the latest? Any chance she was just a jumper?"

Frank shook his head.

"Shit."

The two men looked at each other.

"Fill me in," Russo said.

Frank briefed him and ended with, "The Medical Examiner confirms she was pushed. She didn't jump."

"Awright, get outta here and find her killer."

"I plan on it." Frank stood, headed for the door. He turned. "What does the press know?"

"As little as possible. But you can believe the *Post* is crawling all over our ass."

"So you said." Frank left.

Russo sat there for several long moments staring at the door and ruminating on his new homicide lieutenant. From what he remembered about Frank Mead he was a bulldog. He got hold of an idea, a suspect, a case, and he didn't let go until it was solved. It struck him that life was all about timing. He brings in the best of the best to solve the Big City's homicides and what happens? The wrong girl dies.

Russo took out a handkerchief from his pocket and wiped his forehead and upper lip. No doubt about it. He'd have to keep a close eye on the situation.

Noon

Outside 1 Police Plaza, a chilly wind blew the prospects of rain into Frank's face. He looked back at the huge thirteen story pink structure that housed the most celebrated and notorious police force in the world, amazed that anyone could design such an ugly block of a building for such an important purpose. He vaguely recalled the architectural style as *Brutalist*. That fit. He stared at its hundred windows looking out over the streets of lower Manhattan, a few with a view of the Brooklyn Bridge. It was scheduled for a big expansion next year.

Was he glad to be back? Russo had asked. He asked himself that very question every day. He didn't have an answer yet. Frank's mind drifted unfocused then settled again on Sanford Russo. He remembered him when he was Commander of the 41st Precinct. Soon after Russo had gotten a degree in law from Brooklyn Law. Still he stayed with NYPD. Loyal. What was the word on him? Good cop came to mind. Serious about cleaning up the department? Maybe. Frank would reserve judgment for now.

He unclipped his cell from his belt and pressed a few keys for Amanda's number. Shoot, he didn't even have her in speed dial. He entered her number right there. Then he called for the third time. Got a voice message. He left his number and asked her to call him. Tried to sound like a father instead of a cop. Right. When was the last time they talked, had dinner together, anything? What did he really know about Amanda besides the usual statistics: age 22, 5'4", smart, going for her master's degree in journalism. Writing was always her thing. And gorgeous like her mother.

She did have his dimples, though. On her they looked good. Dimples on a cop? Don't instill much confidence.

His next stop was Stephanie's apartment. He pulled out his notebook to find the address. He climbed into his Ford and drove north from Avenue of the Finest to Park Row to the Bowery. From there he turned left on W. Houston Street and left on MacDougal to a late nineteenth century brownstone that could today be described as yuppie chic.

The front glass-paned door led to two apartments. Out of habit, he rang the bell on the downstairs apartment, which was draped with crime scene tape. He pulled out the key.

The phone was ringing as he stepped into a wide living area with cushy sofas, long-haired rugs and colorful prints on the wall.

The phone stopped and the caller didn't leave a message. Funny. He didn't think many young people had landlines any more.

He touched the message button but heard only a soft hum. The crime team had wiped it clean so even Stephanie's message was gone. He'd have to go to Forensics to hear her voice. He needed to do that, hear the victim's voice, see her photos, feel how she lived, what she was like. Why she died.

Frank threaded his way through the apartment to get a *gestalt* impression first. Roomy apartment as they go in the city--maybe 900 square feet, packed with furnishings. Two tiny bedrooms, each with its own bath, a kitchen, whose refrigerator was stuffed with Lean Cuisines and salad makings, a modest dining room and ample living room. Large windows looked out on MacDougal Street on one side and Spring Street on another. Kitchen and baths had been modernized and upgraded with stainless steel appliances and small Jacuzzis.

He expected the *Post* didn't pay well so Stephanie must have had some of her own money. Or Mom and Dad did.

Slowly he made the circuit, room by room, and examined the contents more closely. The crime team unit had gone through everything so this was probably a waste of time. He spotted her iPhone and scrolled through the contacts. Just as he was about to set it down, he noticed the name. Amanda Mead.

How well did Amanda know the dead girl? Why didn't she call him back?

A minute later his phone vibrated.

"Amanda?"

"No, Frank, it's Irene." Tears blurred her voice.

"Everything okay?" His heart did a nose dive.

"No. Mom slipped into a coma. They don't know why or what. No doubt related to her cancer, not the fall."

"I'm on my way."

"No, no, there's no point. Nothing you can do. They're running all kinds of tests. I just wanted to let you know. Look, I'll call as soon as we know something. Okay?"

"You sure? I mean I can--"

"No, really, go do your job. I'll call you."

Silence.

"Frank? Were you waiting for a call from Amanda?"

"Yes, in fact. I left her a couple of messages."

"Funny, so did I and I haven't heard back. That's unusual for her. Maybe she's out of town or something."

"Wouldn't she have let you know? I mean, maybe not me, but you. She'd call you, right?" Frank asked. It bothered him that Amanda would choose her aunt rather than her own father to contact. But then he hadn't been a father for a long time.

"Um, maybe. I'd have thought so. Don't worry. I just wanted to give her a heads up on Mom. She and Lizzie are pretty tight."

They were close all right and thank God for that. Ever since Jeannie had died, come on, say it: committed suicide-- Amanda had been living with Lizzie. Until she moved out on her own a year ago.

Frank still had nightmares about the day Jeannie died. And guilt. His answer was to run away. From New York, from the past. Worse, he'd run away from Amanda. It still made him crazy. How could he leave an eleven-year-old girl like that? When she needed him most.

"Frank? Frank? You all right?" Irene said.

"Yeah, sure. I'm fine. Call me when you hear something about Mom. . . or from Amanda." He hit a button. Disconnected. The way he'd been feeling all day.

Chapter 11

October 4, 1909

Early morning fog hung in wisps over the city. The sun had barely risen yet the air was thick with tension. Fiona arrived at the Triangle Factory unusually early, as she had for the past ten days. She spotted her friend Ida Janowitz who hurried over to her.

"You can't get in, Fiona. Mustn't even try," Ida said.

"I have to get to work."

"It's too late. There's no way to sneak past those picketers and not pay the price."

Fiona heard cries of "scab" and "union buster" bellowing through the air.

"Forget it," Ida said.

Fiona looked at her friend and noticed gray hairs sprinkled in with the brown. "What are you going to do?"

"I've a mind to join 'em. Them bloodsuckers, Harris 'n Blanck, bleedin' us dry day after day. Come on, Fiona, girl, whatcha' say?"

Ida tugged Fiona's arm.

"No, I can't," she said, even though her heart would have wished her to. Ever since Clara Lemlich's visit, Fiona felt at one with the workers. She could not afford to strike, however. Not unless she was willing to destroy Cormac's career and their relationship.

God, tell me what to do.

A loud rumble halted her words. The hair on the back of her neck stood on end. Picketers marched as a huge wave in front of the main doors of the Asch Building, chanting and flapping signs.

"Oh my Lord," Ida said. "Can you believe?"

Fiona gasped as a crowd of women barreled toward them from the direction of Washington Square Park.

"Who are they?" she whispered. Her mouth dried and she could barely swallow.

"Those gals ain't no unionists, they ain't comin' to join the strike, that's for damn sure. I can tell ya that."

Fiona gaped. "Prostitutes?"

"Ladies of the night, if you want to be more polite-like."

A horde of women closed in on them. They were dressed in glittery gowns accented by ostentatious furs and dripping in paste jewels. Rouged patches on their cheeks matched slick red-painted lips and they sported teased hair and heavily shadowed eyes.

Fiona wondered if she could be dreaming, the scene was so ludicrous.

Suddenly, the picketers stopped and stared at the spectacle of dozens of bawdy women and unconsciously backed up.

One protester shouted, "Don't let 'em get to you, girls, they can't hurt you."

Others screamed, "Yea," in reply.

Fiona stepped backwards, not knowing what to do next.

A whistle sounded behind her then another and she whirled to see uniformed policemen charging toward the building from the direction of the Mercer Street Station.

Please, please, don't let Cormac be there.

Before they arrived, the whores had breached the picket line and attacked the strikers.

"What are they doing?"

Fiona watched, aghast, as one woman punched a worker in her face with her fist, another kicked a girl with her sharp-toed boot, and a third jabbed at the workers with some sort of club. The workers were not idle either. One tried to stab a harlot with her hat pin, another clawed at their garish clothes. There was much shrieking and hair tearing before the police rushed into the melee. Billy clubs were raised and brought down on the workers again and again. Blood spurted from heads and flowed down necks, drenching clothes.

This can't be happening.

Within minutes the cops began rounding up the women—the strikers, not the prostitutes, to Fiona's bewilderment.

"No, not them, not. . .they didn't do anything. . . please, stop."

No one heard her or cared.

Several co-workers were pushed roughly into the back of a paddy wagon along with other strikers. Out of the corner of her eye, Fiona caught sight of one of the owners of Triangle mixed in with the whores.

"Look there's one of 'em freakin' owners, Max Blanck," a woman cried. "A nasty piece of work, that man is."

"And there's Bernstein; gotta get 'im," someone shouted.

Fiona spied the plant manager, Sam Bernstein, dressed in three-piece suit, his waistcoat unscathed. He veered off to the side of the street, trying to avoid confrontation.

"What? Might get your suit dirty, eh?" Ida shouted to him above the fray.

Fiona caught a young girl out of the corner of her eye. A policeman was pounding her with a billy club. Ida pounced on him, trying to claw at his eyes.

"Get off 'a me, you damn whore," the cop screamed.

"I'm not the whore, Copper," Ida screamed but landed on her back with a sickening thud. The cop proceeded to hit her over and over with his club.

Before she could stop herself, Fiona found herself leaping into the fracas, pushing through the women to reach Ida. She was battered and punched, her hair was caught in the grasp of a fat, bloodied woman, hairpins standing wildly on her tangled coif.

She screamed, "Let go of me, you bully. You oaf." She twisted free, fell to the ground and rolled. Feet stomped and kicked her as she crawled to escape. Her hands and knees, even through her long skirt, were abraded and skinned on the tarmac. When she got free from the crowd, she raised herself to a crouch but was knocked down from behind by a whack to the head. She groaned and turned to see who had bludgeoned her. He was burly and balding and wore a dark suit. She knew him from somewhere, but where? God forbid he was a friend of Cormac. Fiona keeled over and threw up.

"All right, into the wagon with yous. All a' yous."

Two cops lifted her by her arms and into the paddy wagon with a dozen or so other workers.

"We're crammed in like pickles in a jar," a woman across from her said, wiping a bloody nose. Fiona giggled hysterically at the image.

The next few minutes seemed a blur. Her one memory of the ride was the sound of soft crying from a young co-worker, no more than fourteen years old. It tore at her heart.

Fiona dozed on and off in shock until they reached the police station. She was roughly yanked out, tripping on the wagon step and falling to her knees.

"Get up, yer li'l beggar," one cop said and poked her with the baton.

She ached now, every muscle in her body sore from the beating and the falls she took. She was pushed and prodded up the steps to the station and shoved down onto a hard wooden bench with several other strikers. Fiona was keenly aware through her daze, however, that not one prostitute was within sight. Only the strikers had been arrested. Anger rose in her chest until she felt she couldn't breathe.

"Fiona?" Cormac was hurrying toward her. "My God, Fiona, what--?"

She stood on wobbly knees and took the hand he held out to her. She stumbled behind him to a desk in the far corner of the room, where a dozen desks and chairs sat scattered around, lost in the huge space. He eased her into a chair and pulled his own from behind the desk to sit close to her.

"Cormac, they were harlots. . . harlots hired to. . . to stop the strikers . . .they attacked us--" Fiona ran out of breath.

"Us? Us? God, Fiona, were you part of the strike?" He looked around, lowered his voice. "What happened?"

His blue eyes caught her green ones and hers unwillingly overflowed with tears.

Cormac pulled a handkerchief from his pocket and handed it to her.

She wiped her eyes, coughed, swallowed. "Cormac, I don't, I only--"

"All right, just take your time."

"I wanted to get to work, nothing more. But when I got there, all those women were marching, picketing. I didn't know what to do. If I entered the building, I would be branded as a traitor to the cause."

Cormac narrowed his eyes.

"Then the police came and those women, the prostitutes. And it all went crazy. The women fought with the workers. God. You'd think they'd have some sympathy. It was brutal. They fought like, like wildcats. And the police. They started clubbing and beating the women. My friends, Cormac. Women I work with every day." Fiona hiccupped into the handkerchief. "I couldn't let them be treated that way. They were all bruised and bloody and. . . I just couldn't. Poor Ida was hurt badly and--" She stopped, straightened. "I had to do something."

He looked down at the floor.

"You see, don't you?" Her anger rose like a flame doused in kerosene. "And stop trying to shush me."

Cormac threw his hands up. "So you joined the strikers? Fiona? You joined them? Do you understand what this means? I could lose my--" He stopped, looked over his shoulder again. "What were ye thinking?" His voice was low and ominous. "Don't you care about me, about what I think, about my job?" He exhaled the weight of the world.

Tears rolled down her cheeks. "Cormac, my love. There are more important things in this world than a job."

"You tell me what's more important than money for our life together. Tell me."

"Honor. Integrity. Justice."

He squeezed his eyes shut.

She reached out a hand and touched his cheek. "I'm sorry, my dear. I don't mean to hurt you. I'm just so. . . terribly angry."

"Fiona, listen to me." He leaned forward and spoke softly. "I'm going to get you out of here, take you home. There won't be any paperwork filled out, so no one will know what happened today. Understand?"

She stared at him. "Haven't you heard anything I said?"

"I have, but this is not the time and place to deal with this. We can talk about it more at home, but going to jail is not going to serve anyone's sense of justice. It won't resolve the situation."

She slumped in her chair.

"Do you understand?"

She chewed her lower lip.

"Please, Fiona, let's go home. We can talk there."

"You mean without anyone overhearing."

He compressed his lips. Then he held a hand out and she took it.

She had trouble standing from the pain in her wrists, palms and knees, but managed.

At that moment, another officer approached.

"Sergeant Devine," Cormac said.

"Officer Mead." He spoke to Cormac but stared at Fiona.

"This is my fiancé, Fiona. Unfortunately, she got caught up in the skirmish this morning on her way to work."

"Ah, she works at Triangle, does she?"

"Yes, sir, I do," Fiona said and straightened to her full height, eyes dry now.

"Bad timing, eh?"

"Indeed," Cormac said. "She just happened to be there at the wrong time and got a bit tossed about, trying to get to work, is all."

Fiona opened her mouth to speak, but Cormac pressed her hand more tightly. She held her tongue with effort.

"I see. Well, then. Perhaps you should get her home, don't you think?"

"My thought exactly." Cormac put his arm around her waist. They walked slowly side by side until they reached their tenement on Orchard Street.

Exhaustion was setting in and Fiona's anger was spent. She just wanted to curl up and sleep.

Cormac faced her. "Fiona, my love. Striking is a dangerous business, you must know that."

She looked at him, eyes so weary they were closing unbidden.

"Are ye all right now, love? Do you need some antiseptic or bandages for those cuts?"

"No." She trudged up the steps to the front door. He followed. In the dark hallway, he took her by the shoulders and looked into her eyes.

"I understand, you know. I understand why you sympathize with those women, the strikers."

She looked up him, anger dissipating.

"Fiona, you have a kind and caring heart. And it will get you in trouble someday."

Tears filled her eyes again.

"Now go upstairs and rest. I will let the Triangle supervisors know you are out sick today. Your job will be secure. For now." He kissed her forehead.

Fiona turned to open the door.

"By the way," Cormac said with a faint smile. "Just to set the record straight. You and I are not so very different in the end. I would have done the same thing if it was my friend being beaten."

She fell into his arms.

Chapter 12

January 14, 1910

McSorley's Old Ale House hummed with activity as it had every night for over sixty years. Established in 1854, the time-weary saloon boasted that Abraham Lincoln once visited following a speech he delivered at Cooper Union that same year. Sawdust covered the worn plank floor and ancient carvings embellished the table tops. Today, as every day, McSorley's served as a haven for the Mercer Street Station, the city's infamous "penitentiary precinct" of the NYPD.

Cormac entered the tavern, blinked into the dim, smirchy, smoke-filled expanse, and made his way to the bar.

Joe Reilly, the barkeep, mopped a spill on the counter surface and asked, "Eh, Mead, how's married life treatin' you?"

Cormac smiled. "It's fine, Joe, jest fine."

Joe, who looked older than the establishment itself, kept his age a great secret and the officers who frequented had a running bet on that number. Although Joe was a bare wisp of a man who might blow away in a strong breeze, no one, not even Fat Al Camarone would risk his ire. "What'll it be that the little woman will approve?"

"Hmph, little woman." Cormac smiled to himself at what Fiona would say about that title. He had a vision of her pounding the purse snatcher at Ellis Island.

"I'll have an ale then, what else?"

McSorley's sold only ale and hard liquor. Like his father and his father before him, the owner, Aidan McSorley, III, wouldn't hear of serving beer. Too plebeian, Cormac assumed.

Before he downed his first gulp, he felt a hand grasp his shoulder. He turned to look down at smiling eyes.

"Fiorello, hello."

"Hello, my friend, and congratulations on your nuptials."

"Me what?"

"Nuptials, the wedding, ya know?"

"Oh, yes, yes. It was a small affair, just a dozen or so people at St. Joseph's. I wish you could have been there."

"Likewise. But out of town business beckoned and who was I to say no to precious greenbacks? I must say, however, I feel I had some part in your romance. Both of you meeting at Ellis Island, me helping you out in the big city, that kind of thing." He winked then turned to Joe and ordered an ale.

The two men drank in companionable silence when they were jarred by a loud voice.

"Hey, boys, that who I think it is? Yes, Jesus, Mary and Joseph, it's the little wop, LaGuardia." A man with eyes as red as blood and a pockmarked face staggered over, sloshing whiskey out of his glass.

LaGuardia set his ale down and swiveled about. "And who are you, sir?"

"Sir? Sir? My name is Michael J. Sweeney and I don't talk to no wops,'specially no midget wops."

Cormac stood to his full height and loomed over Sweeney by at least four inches. "You've had too much to drink. Watch yer tongue, man." He kept his voice low and measured.

"Oh, yeah? That so? And what are you gonna do about it?" Sweeney turned back to LaGuardia. "Did ya know this copper here," he hiccupped, "is a friggin' bumpkin from Ireland? Wops and

Micks, what a fucked up world, it is."

LaGuardia bunched up his forehead. "Sweeney, Sweeney, seems like that's an Irish, er, Mick name as well."

"I am American, born on this soil in this city," Sweeney said. "Ain't no Mick here."

"I've heard about you," LaGuardia went on. "You and your brother, a cop too, right? No wait a minute. You aren't cops any more. You got kicked out, right? Could there be hard feelings, maybe?"

Sweeney slammed the glass down on the bar. "Who got kicked out? No one kicks me out, you wop pig son-of-a-bitch."

LaGuardia stepped back and Cormac moved in. He grabbed Sweeney by his shirt collar and the smaller man squirmed under his grip. He was too drunk to break away so he just dangled at the end of Cormac's large hands.

Suddenly a shot rang out and everyone froze. The bartender had pumped a round into the ceiling, not the first from the look of the holes in the copper tiles.

"Take it outside ifn' yur gonna break his neck, Mead. And I wouldn't mind if you did. Sweeney, get the hell outta here before I shoot you with a mouth fulla lead, which might be the only way to shut yur trap."

Cormac loosened his grip and Sweeny yanked himself away. He sneered at Cormac, then spat on the floor, just missing LaGuardia's shoe.

LaGuardia smiled. "Go play with the make believe cops, Mr. Sweeney. That's all you'll ever be."

Sweeney lunged at LaGuardia, but Cormac grabbed him by arm. He shook himself free and spat again, not aiming for the spittoon.

"This ain't over yet, Copper," Sweeney said. "Not by a long shot."

"Outta here now," Joe shouted and Sweeney stomped off. On his way, he bumped into a large man, dressed in a gray wool suit, bow tie and spats.

"Pardon me, my good man," the stranger said and paused. "Don't I know you?"

"Fuck you." And Sweeney was gone.

"Indeed," the man said watching the crimson-faced Sweeney push through the door. "Pleasant chap, hmm. Looked familiar somehow."

"Al, Al, good to see you." LaGuardia took the man's hand and pumped. Let me introduce you to a good friend. Al Smith, Cormac Mead, a member of New York City's finest."

"That so? Always a pleasure to meet our boys in blue." Smith shook Cormac's hand.

"You know Mike Sweeney, then?" Cormac asked.

"Al knows everybody," LaGuardia said. "He's Assemblyman for our illustrious State of New York and a leader at City Hall."

City Hall or Tammany Hall? Cormac wondered. Both the same it seemed.

LaGuardia went on, "Al's a fine man despite being a Democrat and far too liberal for my taste. I myself am a Republican, you see, Cormac."

"Well, I, for one, will never forgive you that." Smith grinned. "And calling me liberal is like calling Attila the Hun a gentleman." He turned to Joe, "I'll have your best ale, Joe."

"Yessir, you bet," Joe said, snatching a mug from under the counter.

Cormac wondered at the atypical respect the bartender showed this man named Al Smith.

"Who was that rather coarse gentleman that you had in your grip, Mr. Mead?" Smith asked.

"I'm sorry to say he was a countryman. Mike Sweeney. Drunk, angry and obnoxious, a common state of affairs for him, I'm afraid."

"As I recall, didn't he and his ne'er do well brother, what's his name, I forget, get thrown off the police force?" LaGuardia asked.

"Ahh, that's how I know him. The Sweeney brothers. Now they're dabbling in, uh, what's it called, private security, I believe."

"Hmph. Private security, in a pig's eye." LaGuardia spat.

Smith faced Cormac. "So, you're here from Ireland? How did you manage to land such a prestigious job?"

Cormac nodded. "Contacts. My uncle is a sergeant at NYPD."

"Ah, it's always about who you know, isn't it? And who might your uncle be?" Smith asked.

"Sean O'Flaherty."

"I know Sean O'Flaherty." Smith took a swig of his beer. "He's a good man. Honest. Hard to find that in anyone these days."

"Yup. Particularly in politicians." LaGuardia grinned at his friend. Then he gulped down his ale and the three fell silent, each into his own thoughts.

A moment later angry shouting at the far end of the bar snapped Cormac out of his ruminations. He vaulted from his bar stool to determine what the ruckus was about, if Mike Sweeney had returned. Before he could take two steps, the situation became clear. A man with skin the color of brown shoe polish argued with Joe, whose voice was an octave higher and a volume louder than normal.

"We don't take yur kind in here, mister. Din't you read the sign in the window? Now get the hell out of my bar."

"It's not *your* bar. I believe the owner's name is McSorley and yours is not," the colored man countered. "I have every right to be here. You can't throw me out."

Several officers stepped forward but none of them spoke a word or lifted a hand to the black man. Strangely, they all seemed at a loss.

"Get him outta here," Joe said to the policemen.

Cormac took a step closer to the commotion, wondering why the officers didn't escort the colored man out. McSorley's did, indeed, have the right to serve whomever they chose, although he himself couldn't see why a black man couldn't drink ale as well as a white man. Then he saw the reason for the officers' hesitation. The black man wasn't any ordinary man. Cormac hadn't registered the fact before now but he wore a cop's uniform just like his own.

Cormac hadn't met the man personally, but had read a story about him in the *Times*. The man in question was Samuel J. Battle. The first colored police officer in the NYPD.

Cormac weighed his options. His first notion was to defend the colored man -- why? Because he was a police officer? Because coloreds had rights too? Maybe both.

He walked over to Battle. The policemen nearby waited, ready to act, but torn. Should they throw Battle out or defend one of their own? Cormac understood their quandary completely.

There was no need. Cormac leaned over the bar and talked to Joe quietly in his ear. Eyes popped a minute later when Joe tapped cool frothy ale into a new mug and set it in front of Samuel Battle. McSorley's had gone dead quiet.

Battle tipped his head at Cormac, lifted the mug and drank. He did not put the glass down until the liquid was gone. Suddenly the men cheered and relief filled the atmosphere. Battle wiped his mouth delicately with long slender fingers, nodded again at Cormac, and left the bar.

Cormac felt a surge of emotion he was unfamiliar with. Pride? Gratification? Honor? It came to him. The blue uniform was what mattered, not the color of the skin of the man who wore it.

He also realized at that moment, how alike he and Fiona truly were. It made him smile.

Al Smith put his hand on Cormac's shoulder. "That was a fine thing to do, my good man. No matter the color of a man's skin, he is a sworn police officer and deserves respect." Smith held out his hand.

"You've done the uniform proud."

Chapter 13

March 22, 2011

1:00 p.m.

Rain started with a spatter outside Stephanie Brandt's living room window, picked up with ferocity and jarred Frank out of his daydreams. He looked at his watch. The search of the murdered girl's apartment was taking longer than it should.

He moved into the first bedroom and realized this room belonged to her roommate, Betsy Cohen. Wooden letters spelled out B.E.T.S.Y on her vanity mirror. Jefferies had reached her by phone at her parents' house in Bangor, Maine. She was shocked at the news of her friend, but had been out of town for over a week and could offer no new information.

Frank browsed through the living room, its walls dotted with prints of famous art that even he could recognize. Degas' ballerinas, Van Gogh's flower vases, Renoir's pastel girls. Rugs of minimalist patterns with soft, cushy chairs and sofas to match the palette. End tables held an assortment of framed photos, mostly of Stephanie and her parents in different places. One looked like Hawaii, one a ski resort, maybe Stowe, Vermont?

The kitchen looked and smelled like lemons, all soft yellows and sunflowers. The refrigerator, surprisingly, held a variety of foods from broccoli and lettuce heads to chicken packages and salad containers. A full wine rack sat on the end of the granite countertop. Everything he saw confirmed that Stephanie had all intentions of returning home that night.

Wind whistled through the vents and rattled the windows as Frank strode into her bedroom. He went straight to her dressing table, which was decked out in the color of ocean waves in the Bahamas. There on the mirror were taped photographs. Stephanie with a young man in an NYU sweatshirt, one with a handsome older couple, the same as in the other photographs. And two with a beautiful redheaded young woman with brooding green eyes, a blush on her cheeks and a smile that could stop traffic. And dimples. His dimples. My God. He'd known from Stephanie's cell that Amanda and the dead girl were friends. But from the picture they appeared to be good friends. He had his answer.

Did Amanda know about her friend's murder? Had she sunk into depression as she had on and off since Jeannie died?

Visions of his daughter at eleven came to him unbidden. He could see her in bed rolled up tight like a pill bug armored against pain, buried under a lavender comforter, staring into nothingness. He suppressed a shudder. Her mother's suicide had devastated Amanda and it was months before she could function. It had also created a rift between them, one he wanted to bridge but didn't know how. So, he had bailed. Typical response when things weren't going well.

Frank yanked the picture of his daughter and Stephanie from the mirror and examined it. She'd never lost that deep-rooted sadness, even years later as an adult. He could see it in her eyes, in the downward-turned crinkles around her mouth. His concern deepened. Why hadn't she called him back? He'd been in New York over two weeks and he had talked to her just once. Not a good try at reconciliation, was it? Maybe she didn't call him back because she didn't want to talk to him. Or, was she curled up like a fetus again in her bed because of her friend's death?

He tucked the photo in his pocket and shot out the door.

Stephanie could wait. She was dead.

Amanda was not.

2:00 p.m.

Twenty minutes and eight blocks later, Frank ran up the steps to a small three-story apartment building on Greene Street. He buzzed the apartment from the front door. Surprisingly there was an answering response in the call box.

"Who is it?"

"Amanda? It's Dad."

"Amanda's not here, Mr. Mead. This is Connie."

"Can I come up?"

A buzzer clicked the door open.

"Connie?" Frank said to a tall woman, so slender it looked as if light could shine through her.

"Come on in."

It had been almost a year since he'd visited Amanda in this apartment, when she first moved in, and recalled now how comfortable it was. How comfortable she'd made it. All the furnishings belonged to Amanda. She enjoyed decorating and the apartment was nothing like you'd expect a recent college student to have. No cinder block bookcases in the living room, no Formica table and plastic chairs in the dining room, no shag rugs. This was designer décor. Good taste. Like Jeannie.

He swallowed the rock in his throat. "Have you seen or heard from Amanda? I've been trying to get hold of her."

"Not since early yesterday," Connie said. "I'm, well, kind of worried myself. She usually lets me know where she's going, you know, so if she comes in late, she doesn't disturb me or anything. I've tried calling her but there's just a message. Also--" She paused.

"Go on."

"She didn't show up at work today. She's working on an article about *WhizBang Computers*. They've got the latest apps on -- never mind. Anyway, her editor at the *Times* called. She missed a meeting this morning."

Frank rested his hands on his hips and said nothing. His gut ached, a trusted sign of bad things to come.

Connie shook her head. "I'm glad you came. I was going to call you. Amanda mentioned you're a cop, um, policeman."

"Tell me the last time you saw her and what happened."

Connie waved him into a chair but he remained standing. Adrenaline fizzed through his body.

"Okay, yesterday I saw her about nine-thirty in the morning. She was having a piece of toast and a cup of coffee, standing up in the kitchen. Kind of like you, now." She smiled.

"Did she go to work?"

"No, she said she was working at home. Sometimes she worked here, sometimes at the newspaper office."

"Can you show me her computer?"

"Sure."

Frank followed her into Amanda's bedroom, a riot of bright colors that made him feel edgy. He wandered around the space, noting the neatness--her bed made with a bright pink and turquoise coverlet, several colorful rugs and large framed photos of famous scientists on the wall. He recognized Einstein, Sagan, Galileo but there were several he couldn't place.

Frank picked up little dog knick knacks and remembered how Amanda always wanted a dog, any kind, but a yellow lab in particular. He riffled through her closet, finding mostly jeans, sweaters and shirts. Only a few dresses. He guessed she didn't need dresses in her line of work. That got him wondering if she dated and who? Getting to know this stranger that was his daughter.

Frank turned to see Connie watching him.

"Did she know about Stephanie?" he asked.

"Stephanie Brandt? What about her?"

"She's dead. I'm sorry."

"Oh my God. What happened?"

"She was pushed out of a window," he said.

Connie's face drained of blood. "What?"

"Sorry. I didn't mean to blurt it out. Did Amanda know, do you think?"

"Not as of yesterday morning when I saw her. Was it on TV? We never watch." Connie touched her fingers to her forehead as if forcing this new information into her brain. "I don't believe this. Someone killed her, I mean, on purpose?"

Frank just looked at her. "Did you know Stephanie?"

"Only through Amanda. She was a reporter, too. Of course, you know that. God, this will shake her up."

"Was that how they met? Through their jobs?" he asked.

"I think so. Yeah. It was at a writer's conference at the Plaza about three years ago, maybe four. They were both still at NYU."

Frank sat down at Amanda's desk and flipped open her laptop. At least the computer was there. Unlike Stephanie's.

Fortunately, it was booted up as well so he didn't need a password. He clicked on her e-mail, scanned through, but didn't find anything relevant. Then he called up her documents and perused the most recent. One was titled, *Triangle*. He double clicked, read her notes:

Steph doing story on 100th anniversary of Triangle fire.

I recalled stories of Cormac and Fiona from same time.

Checked with Lizzie. She flipped me out with an amazing tale about Fiona. True?

Searched through attic at Orchard Street.

Incredible cache! Photos, letters, news stories, clothes, odds and ends, demanding closer inspection, when have time.

Found notebook hidden in trunk lining that appears to be notes Cormac wrote on a murder investigation in 1911-- Fiona's? Put in safe place for now.

Must show Frank.

She calls me Frank? Why did that surprise him? He was a stranger. He went back to her notes.

So much junk in attic, accidentally dropped a framed photo and a piece of paper flew out—a letter from 1911 (scanned in separate document). Mysterious. Why save it? Who hid it? More for Frank?

All great background for Steph.

Big question: If Fiona was murdered, by whom? And why? Was it tied to Triangle Factory fire?

So when Amanda wrote this she didn't know Stephanie was dead. He checked the date on the computer. She must know by now.

Where the hell is she?

Chapter 14

Frank swiveled back in the desk chair, contemplating Amanda's notes. He was about to open the scanned letter from 1911, when his phone vibrated. He checked the caller.

Thomas. Shit. He had to face the music eventually.

"Hello, Thomas."

"Frank, we need to talk. It's--"

"How's Mom, any news?"

"Uh, no. Still in a coma. That's why we need to talk. About the tenement."

Frank's anger began to fill his chest like an inflated airbag. He felt stifled. Through the rage he could envision his brother, impeccably tailored and groomed, like an Esquire model. Except he was a stockbroker and his whole life was spent playing with money.

"Frank? Look, this is the perfect time to sell that old building. The Lower East Side is booming and lots of yuppies are--"

"So, Thomas, tell me. How come when they were passing out feelings, you never got in line?"

"Very funny. Listen. I'm serious. I've been talking to a realtor about the property. We can make a mint on this baby. Mom can move into an apartment, lots of those in the same neighborhood, she'll be living high on the hog."

Frank worked his jaws. "Mom will be living high on the hog? You know Tom" -- his voice was now perilously low -- "you are one cold, heartless bastard. Don't you think you can even wait to see how she does? Whether she comes out of the coma or not, before you cash in on another one of your deals?"

Frank could visualize his younger brother sitting in his black, white, and chrome office on Wall Street, feet propped up on a massive Strato designer desk.

Thomas said nothing.

"Thomas? I don't think I want to talk to you right now." Frank hung up.

"Everything okay, Mr., I mean Lieutenant, Mead?"

Frank had forgotten Connie was standing nearby.

"Sure, yeah." He stood up. "I'm going to print this out."

"Whatever."

He clicked a few keys and the printer whirred. He printed the scanned letter that Amanda had chanced upon to review later as well.

"Right now, I'm just going to check a few things in her room, if you don't mind." Meaning privately.

"Okay." Connie left him in Amanda's room, closing the door behind her.

Frank began opening desk drawers, bureau drawers. He scanned under the bed, in the closet, even behind the furniture. He stood taking in the room. Where were the things from the attic? Where was the murder book? Was the original letter that she scanned tucked inside, hidden in the apartment somewhere? Did she take it with her? Maybe she had a safe deposit box at a bank. Christ, he didn't even know these little things about her.

Before he stepped out of the bedroom, he noticed a small framed photograph on the night table. Frank picked it up and stared at it. He could recall exactly when and where it was taken and it took his breath away to think that Amanda had kept it. It was 1998 in Kennebunkport, Maine. He, Jeannie, and Amanda at ten years old, had rented a cottage on the water. It was possibly the last time they all smiled together. After that vacation everything fell apart.

Frank set the picture back on the night stand and walked into the bathroom. His head pounded and he wondered if there were any Advil in the medicine cabinet. He checked out the tiny room and opened the cabinet above the sink. Sure enough, there were Advil. He chugged three down with a palm full of water.

Besides Advil were toothpaste, Scope, and a big bottle of Tums. Evidently his daughter suffered from the same maladies as he.

Weary, he moved back to the living room.

"Connie, do you mind if I look around the rest of the apartment?"

"No, no, go ahead."

He did a quick search of the living areas and kitchen. When it came to Connie's bedroom, she nodded before he could even ask.

"What do you do, Connie? Not a reporter, too?"

"I'm a computer analyst for an insurance company."

"Ahh," Frank said as he searched her room. He found nothing.

"Did Amanda ever mention a notebook to you? Where she might have put it? Or a box of stuff she collected from her grandmother's house on Orchard Street?"

"No, I don't think so. I'm sorry."

"It's okay. If Amanda gets in touch with you, call me right away." He handed her a card.

She stared at it, eyes watering. "She's, I mean, you do think she's okay, don't you?"

"We'll find her. Thanks for your help, Connie."

"Please let me know if you find out anything."

He nodded and swung the door open then asked, "Was she seeing anybody?"

Connie paused. "Not really *seeing*. There was one guy she dated a few times. Just in the last few weeks."

"Yeah? Name?"

"I'm sorry. I don't remember. Never met him either."

Frank stopped what he was doing and looked at her.

"No idea what he did, whether he was a reporter too?"

"No. She only saw him a few times. Too busy with work and all. You know her."

Frank smiled faintly as if he did. He didn't.

Connie chewed her lower lip and abruptly sank down on the sofa.

Frank leaned over and touched her shoulder. "You all right?"

"Not really. I mean it's just sinking in about Stephanie. Now Amanda is--"

"Why don't you call a friend to keep you company? Keep your mind off all of this. I'll be in touch."

He headed for the door and this time went through it.

3:30 p.m.

Luis Hector Santiago stepped into his office, closed the door and leaned his back against it. His face burned red hot and his heart only now began to slow.

Damn that bitch.

That bitch was Deputy Commissioner for Public Information, Jane Magliatti. His boss. She'd scheduled a press conference for the next day on the Stephanie Brandt murder. Too soon. He wasn't ready for this. Shit. He'd have to deal with it. Reporters. Ass-sucking vultures and all their questions.

"Do you have any suspects?"

"What was the actual cause of death?"

"What was Brandt working on? Could that have had anything to do with her death?"

Oh yeah. It had plenty to do with her death.

Santiago paced in front of his window on the fourth floor of 1 Police Plaza. He'd come a long way since his days as beat cop. Not far enough for him, though. He pulled out his cell phone and checked messages. Junk. No doubt, First Deputy Commissioner Russo would be calling any minute. Word traveled at warp speed inside the tomb. The big man would want to meet.

He opened built-in cabinet doors to a small bar, yanked a glass, and filled a quarter of it with scotch. He caught a glimpse of himself in the mirror behind the sink and realized his hair was tousled and his eyes blazed. Calm down, man.

His cell rang, startling him and causing him to slosh the amber liquid out of his glass. He checked the number. Russo's private line.

"Deputy Commissioner, what a surprise. What can I do for you?"

"Meet me at McSorley's in an hour."

Santiago opened his mouth to respond. There was no one on the other end.

Chapter 15

4:00 p.m.

McSorley's Bar hadn't changed significantly in a hundred years and still served as a popular police respite. Santiago and Russo studied each other across a table tucked away in a back corner of the pub. Outward appearances were not deceiving; there was nothing but disdain between them.

"I assume you want to talk about the press conference tomorrow," Santiago said. He leaned forward and lowered his voice. "It's under control. Trust me."

"Trust you? You want me to trust you." Not a question. "I'm gonna ask this question and you better be straight with me." Russo kept his voice low. "Did you kill that reporter?" His eyes darted around although there was little chance that anyone might recognize them at that early hour.

Santiago compressed his lips into a thin smile. "What do you think?" He held up a hand as a stop signal. "Hey, you asked me to kill the story. I did. I'm telling you, there's no connection to me, to us, in any way. It's a dead end. No trace, no prints, no nothin'."

Russo stared into his club soda. "You know Frank Mead?"

"Sure. I heard a' him."

Russo thrummed his fingers on the table.

"What? He's going to manufacture evidence? There is no evidence. There's no connection."

"Are you just freaking stupid or am I missing something here? Stephanie Brandt was doing an article on the Triangle fire, the--"

"Yeah, yeah. Big fire in New York, blah blah."

Russo took a deep breath. "Not just a big fire. *The* fire. The fire that killed 146."

"So?"

"Many of those were young girls, like Brandt. They jumped out of the same window on the ninth floor. You don't think there's a connection? You don't think the press will get it? You don't think Mead will get it?"

"Kind of poetic, actually," Santiago said.

Russo's red face deepened to purple.

"Just kidding, Boss, just kidding. Look. It was an unfortunate coincidence. The Brown Building being the Asch Building, that is. Who knew? But it's done and a story about a fire a hundred years ago dies with her. Big deal. Who the shit cares what happened back then?"

"Jesus. Her *death* is going to make people care. That's the point. There's a goddamn group out there, some union league of women, planning memorial services on the hundredth anniversary, that's who. Dozens, maybe hundreds, of citizens who want to keep that memory alive. *They* care. They've gotten all kinds of press. Where the hell've you been?"

Santiago rolled his eyes. "You made your point. Now, let me make mine. I talked to the reporter. Used all my Latin charms on her like you suggested. She didn't buy it. Hard to believe." He chuckled. "In fact, just the opposite. Made her more eager to investigate." Santiago paused. "Is that what you wanted? You wanted me to let her dig deeper into the story?"

Russo said nothing.

Santiago played with his glass. "I did what had to be done. You should be grateful, not sitting here giving me shit. The story's dead.

The Post isn't going to pursue. And Mead--" He shrugged his shoulders.

"Mead is relentless. He will not quit until he knows what happened."

"Sounds like a real Super Cop, this Mead." Santiago smiled.

Russo wiped beads of sweat off his upper lip. "Did you really have to kill her?"

"I told you I tried reason. She wouldn't listen."

"How did it happen?"

"How?"

"Tell me exactly how you killed her."

Santiago sighed. "You sure you want to go there? This gonna make you sleep any better?"

Russo waited.

"I had a couple of chats with her. Told her the story would open a can of worms that would hurt some people, an old lady. You know, play on her sympathy. Did she really want to do that?"

Santiago swirled his drink. "She just got more and more riled up. Wanted to know what old lady, what people would be hurt, why. Accused me and the NYPD of wanting to bury the news. She just wouldn't quit."

Russo watched him.

"I followed her coupla' times. See where she was gettin' her information. Wound up at the Brown Building. She was meeting with some of the professors at NYU to get their take on the Triangle fire, I guess. There she was, waiting in a room on the ninth floor."

"And?"

"I surprised her. She started getting pretty snippy with me. Told me to get out of her face. . . that she wasn't going to drop the story. In fact, she was going to do even more research. Just to spite me. Jesus. What a bitch."

"Go on."

"What? You want me to draw you a picture? She pissed me off. She turned her back on me, went to the window. Opened it. Leaned over to look down."

Russo shook his head, eyes squeezed shut.

"Guess she wanted to see the view those other women had before they jumped. It was so easy." Santiago stared into space. "So damn easy."

Russo stared at him.

"I stepped up behind her and, and, the rest is history, so to speak." Santiago grinned.

"You sick son of a bitch. Killing is easy for you, isn't it?"

"I've done it before. Only in the line of duty, you understand. I'm a cop remember? Like you." Santiago swallowed more of his drink.

Russo leaned back in his chair, face drained.

"Hey, Commish. I can see the wheels spinning in there." He pointed to his own head. "What are you thinking?"

"I'm trying to remember why I got you this job."

"Oh, you remember very well. You owed my father. Big time. He still thinks very highly of you. Even in that stinkin' home where he rots like a worm-ridden apple."

Russo sat up, balled his fists. "Now you listen to me, you little piece of shit. Your father is a good man. I owe him my life."

"And that's exactly why we're in this together."

Russo sank back in his chair, the wood braces creaking.

"It's a little late to be changing your mind about me now. After all, if it comes out what a badass I really am, you've got another scandal on your hands. Exactly what you don't want." Santiago wiped the smile from his face. "Look, Boss, let's come to an understanding here. I was doing your dirty work and it didn't turn out exactly like planned. It's done. We move on."

"You're out of your frigging mind, Santiago."

"Probably."

"The press conference is tomorrow. I want you to defuse this situation. Steer them clear of the story she was writing. Give them something else as motive." He rubbed his nearly bald head.

"And what do you think Frank Mead will say to that?"

Russo clenched his jaws. "Who's handling the questions, you or Jane?"

"Jane doesn't know fuck-all about this. It's me." He leaned over the table. "I said it before and I'll say it again. Trust me on this."

Russo stretched his neck and breathed out a long heavy sigh. "You better be right. Otherwise, this is not over by a long shot."

He stood, looked down at Santiago then headed for the door without another word.

Santiago slugged down the last of his scotch and thought about what lay ahead. Russo was right and that fucker didn't know the half of it. It was not over by far. What he'd found on Stephanie Brandt's computer proved it. There was one more person to deal with. But he already had the ball rolling. That problem would soon be taken care of.

Chapter 16

June 12, 1910

Fiona and Cormac stepped off the streetcar as the sun was setting and followed the general direction of a swarm of carriages unloading their passengers--women in long gowns, men in tails and top hats.

"Oh my," Fiona said. She looked down at her long dress, the fanciest one she owned, and frowned.

"Now, sweets, ye look lovely," Cormac said. "Not one of those fine ladies can hold a candle to you."

Fiona felt shabby despite her husband's praise. She lifted her skirts to avoid the muck in the road from the long periods of rain that had soaked the city.

They arrived a few minutes later at their destination, an elegant narrow, two-story brick townhouse, its majestic front doors opened, allowing light and music to pour out.

Fiona hesitated again. Cormac put his arm on her waist and escorted her up the steps to the soiree. Mr. and Mrs. Edward Robinson hosted this political fundraiser for Al Smith's election to a second term in the State Assembly and LaGuardia had maneuvered an invitation for them. Cormac had been looking forward to this and Fiona, feeling guilty, wanted to make it up to him. Why did she feel guilty? She tried to make him happy. But Cormac wanted her to quit the Triangle, stay home and be a mother. He certainly wanted her to have nothing to do with the union movement.

But how could she help how she felt? She saw the grievances every day. The unfair, sometimes cruel, treatment of the workers-- women, her friends. Fiona saw the safety hazards, the dangerous working conditions. So why couldn't she make Cormac understand? Perhaps because she herself wavered. One day she wanted to change the world, the next she just wanted to keep her husband happy. Her body, blossoming with child, fought her mind every step of the way.

Tonight, however, she would not think on it. She thrust her chin out and stood tall.

Cormac reached into his jacket pocket and pulled out his invitation for inspection as the servant at the door checked. They were ushered through into a large marble-floored foyer and down three steps to the main living room. Side tables were skirted with red velvet and piled high with food, the likes of which she'd never seen in such abundance.

"Do you see that, Fiona? More shrimp on those platters than in the whole of the ocean. And grapes enough to make wine for an entire country."

Fiona's eyes were elsewhere. While Cormac had been focusing his eyes on the food, she was ogling the women's dresses.

"My God, Cormac, look at those gowns. Silks, taffetas, voile, colors rich enough to match Mother Nature. It takes my breath away just looking."

"Mr. Mead," a voice boomed out. "How wonderful you could make our little get-together." Al Smith reached his arms out and pulled Fiona into a gentle hug. "Ahh, Mrs. Mead. I better be careful how I manhandle you, right? Fiorello tells me you are expecting. How splendid."

She grinned and blushed. "How are you, Mr. Smith?"

"With an event like this in my honor, how could I be?" He turned to Cormac and slapped his arm. "How are you, my good man? Still at NYPD, protecting our good citizens?"

"I am, indeed."

Al looked at him steadily. "That's fine, really fine. And that was a splendid show at McSorley's I might add. I respect a man that stands up for what he believes, for what is right. Particularly, if I believe it too."

They both laughed.

Fiona looked at him with a question in her eyes.

"What incident is that?" she asked.

"Oh, it was nothing. I'll tell you later."

Fiona made a note to follow up. Al Smith's comment on *standing up for what is right* intrigued her.

Smith went on. "In truth, I've heard nothing but good about you, Mr. Mead. You'll go far. Mark my words."

Cormac reddened under the praise as Al spun about to face a woman walking toward them.

"Officer Mead, Mrs. Mead, may I introduce you to a very special lady -- Miss Frances Perkins, one of very few women who can boast a Master's Degree in economics. Frances, this is Cormac and Fiona Mead. Cormac is a member of our NYPD."

Frances stepped closer and Fiona looked upon a plain but comely face, sans make-up, dark brown hair pulled back in a simple chignon, wearing an elegant flowing gown in a deep russet.

Cormac took her hand.

"How do you do, Mr. Mead," Frances said. She smiled and her eyes lit up.

Fiona could detect a fire behind the dark brown color.

"It's a pleasure, Miss Perkins. My wife, Fiona."

Frances turned to Fiona. "I feel as if I know you both already, thanks to my friend, Clara Lemlich. She has nothing but good things to say about you. About both of you, in fact."

"Ahh, well," Cormac stuttered.

Frances smiled. "And Mrs. Mead, you work at the Triangle factory, I understand."

"I am merely a seamstress."

"Never belittle your occupation," Frances said. "Being a seamstress takes patience, great skill and talent. Indeed, I was wondering if you designed your dress."

Fiona glanced down. "I, er, yes, I did, but--"

"Actually, I noticed how well it is made, with the double stitching on the collar, the tiny buttons painstakingly in perfect line, the spot of lace—just enough, not gaudy. Lovely." She grinned.

Fiona's spirits lifted.

"Oh yes, I notice these things."

"I can see you do." Fiona grinned back. "Thank you, Miss Perkins, you've made me feel a good bit better." She paused.

Cormac lifted two glasses of a burgundy wine from the tray of a passing waiter. Al Smith carried a tall glass of dark amber liquid as he strolled back to them after chatting with other cliques. He stood next to Frances.

Frances smiled at him but continued her conversation with Fiona. "So, did you take part in the little strike at the factory?"

Fiona blushed but said, "In a way, I suppose I did."

Frances pursed her lips. "Oh yes, I know all about it."

"Were you there, then, Miss Perkins?" Cormac asked.

Before Frances could answer, Al said, "Frances is everywhere. She's a watchdog, bulldog, I should say, for the garment industry. And a necessary one at that. Always keeping an eye on the working conditions of the factory laborers."

"And well I should," Frances said. "Someone needs to watch over them, my dear Al. I will remind you that it's these same laborers, as you put it, *women* workers, whose votes shall put you in office one day. As soon as women *get* the vote."

"Aiyiyi, dear lady, don't get your feathers all ruffled. I was only teasing you," Al said. "Excuse me. The Robinsons beckon. Mr. Mead, please, I'd like to introduce you." He nodded his head to the ladies and whisked Cormac off to the other end of the room.

When the two women were alone, Frances leaned into Fiona's ear. "I would like to get your opinions on the working conditions at Triangle some time, if I may."

"Well, of course, Miss Perkins. I must tell you, though, that Cormac is eager for me to quit once the baby is born."

"Ahh, congratulations. I didn't realize."

"Thank you. Yes, it will be a merry Christmas this year."

"Your husband would like you to, er, retire?"

"He would. However, I rather like having the extra income."

"Indeed. A close friend of mine, Mary Drier, is the head of the Women's Trade Union League. She might be interested in your help if you do decide to leave the Triangle."

"Help doing what?"

"Clara has told you about the organization, I believe?"

"Word certainly gets around, doesn't it?" Fiona said.

"We women need to stick together, or we'll be bullied for all eternity." She drank her wine. "Mary has mentioned she needs help in the office. Getting out flyers, pamphlets, things like that. She'd pay you, of course."

Fiona looked around to see where Cormac was. "Hmm. I'm sure my husband would not like that at all. Perhaps even less than the factory."

"I understand both your position and his." She stopped, pulled in a breath. "Mrs. Mead, we are accomplishing things no one had ever dreamed. We have already seen small but significant improvements in working conditions. Someday--" She stopped, her eyes unfocused.

"Yes?"

"Someday factories will be safe and comfortable working environments for all women. It is up to us to make sure that happens and soon."

Fiona looked down at her drink.

"Please, I would not presume to force our ideas upon you. This is just a friendly conversation. You needn't feel obligated to do a thing."

Fiona couldn't resist a smile. "We live at 63 Orchard Street, apartment 2A."

Frances nodded. "Good." She held out her hand and the women shook. "I'll be in touch. Please say good night to your husband."

And Frances Perkins was off, drifting toward a coterie of society matrons gathered in the other room.

Fiona sipped her wine and fretted about what Cormac's reaction would be. If he found out. But how would he, unless she told him? Then again, she always confided everything in him. Still, this was different. She was her own person. Her eyes took in the gay surroundings and her spirits lifted. Here was a chance to do something good, something right for the women she worked with. She would not back down. In a far corner of her mind, she could hear her father's voice.

"Do what is right, me lass, always, no matter the circumstances. And when yer head tells ye one thing, and yer heart another, tis important to respect both. But in the end, listen to yer heart."

Listen to your heart.

Fiona spotted Cormac heading back toward her. She decided to ignore her father's advice. . . for the moment. She would not mention this conversation with Miss Perkins to her husband. Not just yet.

The wine suddenly tasted sour in her mouth.

Chapter 17

September 5, 1910

The Triangle Shirtwaist Factory was gearing up to full speed production following a slower than usual summer season. Now, however, the new Paris line was out and design changes forced all manufacturers to follow suit. This year the shirtwaist blouse would have new nips, tucks, and pleats.

Fiona had only just returned to work after a two-month seasonal layoff with her co-workers and was eager to earn some income. She had much to buy for the new baby.

On her third day back, she received what she hoped would be good news. Sam Bernstein, the factory manager and brother to Bertha, wife of Max Blanck, one of the owners, asked to see her in his office. Fiona hadn't forgotten him standing at the sidelines during the strike, but she had her own interests to look out for right now. She prayed they wouldn't conflict.

She tidied her hair and rubbed her damp hands on her skirt, then took the elevator to floor ten.

"Oh, Miss Mead?" Bernstein waved to a chair.

"Mrs."

"Whaa?"

"Mrs. Mead."

"Of course, of course. Let's get down to it. You've done some temp work in the office here, haven't you? Typing, filing and such?"

"Yes, I--"

"Dinah tells me you have good reading and writing skills."

"She does?" Fiona raised an eyebrow. Complimented by Dinah Lipschitz?

Bernstein ran on. "We've just lost one of our clerks and need help. Is that something that would interest you?"

"Very much, sir."

"Good, good. The pay would be the same as now but the work would be, well, the work would be different, as you know. Less, er, physical, at least."

Does he know I'm with child?

"Yes, of course," she said. "That would be most satisfactory."

"Good, good, tomorrow report to the office here at 7:30 and see Dinah."

Fiona nodded and left, her feet skipping lightly on the wood floor. She bounced out to the floor and twirled in circles as she waited for the interminably slow elevator to take her back to the production floor, hopefully for the last time. When the bell sounded and the lift arrived, the doors opened and two men stepped out. Fiona couldn't help but notice them, since they didn't walk as much as swagger across the floor and nearly knocked her over on their way.

One was thin and short with a paunchy middle and beady eyes. The other was taller and athletic but had a mean look to him like he had stones in his kidneys. His hair was slicked back and his face was pockmarked and ruddy. Fiona couldn't see his eye color, but when he aimed a glance at her, she felt naked, vulnerable, as if her clothes had fallen off her body.

She dismissed the emotion and watched them enter the outer office, the tall one keeping his cold eyes on her. Then he smiled and her stomach flipped. Fiona blinked and forced herself to look away.

Before she could escape, Mr. Bernstein stuck his head out the door.

"Oh, Miss Mead? Will you come back here a minute?"

Why now? Fiona's breath stuck in her throat.

She walked back to the office, trying to avoid the sinister man. He brought back memories from her childhood of a neighborhood voyeur who was, finally, after three horrific crimes, arrested for rape and murder.

"Say, here's that sweet little lady we saw here before, Billy. Ain't that right, Miss? Wasn't you here in the office before? Remember me, Michael J. Sweeney?" Sweeney leaned his face into hers.

Fiona backed away from his foul breath. "Sorry, I don't remember."

"Hear that, Billy boy? She don't remember. Well then, mebbe we should get better acquainted, eh?"

Fiona wheeled around.

"Now where you goin', darlin'?" He reached out to grab her arm.

She darted away and tried to skirt around him to Bernstein's office. She wasn't fast enough. He seized her in his arms and pressed himself up against her. She struggled to get free.

"Let's go, Mike, come on," the man named Billy said.

"I just want to dance with the little lady, thaa's all, what's so wrong with that? Eh?" He pulled her closer and as he hummed a tune, shoved the lower half of his body into hers.

"Let go of me," Fiona hissed.

"Come on, Babe, you're actually quite a looker, you are."

She managed to squirm out of his grip and with her free hand slapped him hard on the face.

"Jesus Christ, you little whore bitch, wha'd you go and do that for?" He rubbed his cheek but kept a grip on her arm.

"Get away from me, you pig."

"Mike, fer crissakes, let 'er go, we got work here."

Sweeney's face turned a blood red and he stared into her eyes. "You're gonna be sorry you ever did that to Michael J. Sweeney."

The words were spoken so quietly that Fiona found herself shuddering when he finally let her go. The man was the devil incarnate.

Bernstein burst out of his office. "Sweeney, get in here. Quit fooling with the help. Miss Mead, here's an application to fill out formally for the position."

Fiona snatched it from him, afraid he would see her hands shaking. "I'll bring it with me tomorrow, sir."

"Right." Bernstein strode back to his office.

"See you again soon, darlin'." Sweeney gave her a leer before the door closed.

Out in the hall, she flew into the elevator and fairly shrieked at the operator that she wanted the ninth floor. The doors closed. Her body shook. The good news of the day was ruined.

Dusk had fallen when Fiona left the Asch Building. She pulled her light coat around her tightly even though it didn't cover her thickening middle. She felt chilled even now, hours later, from her encounter with that fiend, Sweeney. What was a man like that doing at the Triangle? What sort of business would Mr. Bernstein have for the likes of him?

Fiona thought back to the strike. Had she seen Sweeney there? Was he instrumental in organizing the prostitutes? She wouldn't put it past him to associate with women of ill repute.

Her steps were long and quick and she barely lifted her eyes off the sidewalk as she started for home.

God, will I see him every day in the office? I must find a way to deal with him.

She caught the streetcar just in time and breathed a sigh of relief. A gentleman offered her a seat and she took it, relieved to get off her feet and force her heart to slow.

She looked around. Mike Sweeney hung onto a strap at the end of the car. He was staring directly at her. She averted her eyes and looked out the window across the aisle.

He's trailing me. What should I do? If I get off at my stop, I have four blocks to walk. If he follows, he'll find out where I live.

Thoughts clamored in her head. She had to get off sooner or later. Would he follow her no matter where?

Her stop was fast approaching. She glanced out the window behind her on the off chance there was someone she knew, someone that might help her. And there was. Samuel Battle, a police officer and friend of Cormac's. If she hurried she could catch up with him.

Fiona jumped out of her seat and made for the doors at the back. Her eye had caught Sweeney and he was moving toward her.

She rang the bell.

When she got off, Sweeney exited as well.

She stopped to get her bearings. Where was Samuel?

She felt someone touch her shoulder and a male voice speak, "Miz Fiona?"

She spun around, fully prepared to confront Sweeney. But it was Samuel Battle, in blue uniform. Her legs nearly buckled.

"Say, you all right?" Battle said. "You look a little pale."

Fiona did a scan up and down the street. Sweeney was gone.

"Hi Samuel," she said, breathless. "Sorry, I didn't realize it was you."

"Need an arm?" He held it up for her to lean on.

"I'm fine, really. But I wonder if you'd be kind enough to walk me home."

"You bet. I was gonna suggest exactly the same thing."

Her spirits lifted immediately.

"There's the smile I remember," he said. "Now what's going on? Wanna tell me?"

She shrugged. "I met this man today, who, well, I didn't meet him, actually, just sort of ran into him and--"

"And?"

"He frightened me, I guess. I, uh, please don't mention it to Cormac. I don't want him worried."

"Should he worry? Who was this guy?" Battle asked.

"No, I mean, he was coming out of the elevator and he just, just upset me is all." She stopped. "I thought I saw him on the trolley, but. . . never mind. It's really nothing. My nerves are getting the better of me, you know. Probably because of the baby, I'm all out of sorts."

"You let me decide if it's nothing. Who's the guy? You know his name?"

"Sweeney, Michael Sweeney."

Battle came to an abrupt halt.

"What?" she said. "You know him?"

"Stay away from him, Fiona."

She stopped on the street and faced him.

"Samuel, I feel foolish. I'm making much too much of this."

"Well, maybe yes and maybe no. That man, he's not one to take lightly."

"Why? Who is he?" Fiona asked.

"He's trouble. That's all you need to know. Big trouble."

"Really, I can take care of myself." She could still feel Sweeney's hand burning her arm.

They kept walking, not paying any mind to several heads that turned at the sight of a colored policeman in uniform walking side by side with a white woman.

"Listen, Fiona, I want you to tell me if you see this guy again."

"Why?"

"Just tell me."

"I think I will see him again. I've run into him at the Triangle. He and this other man, Billy something or other, were in to see the manager, Mr. Bernstein."

Battle frowned and furrowed his brow. "Billy Sweeney, his good-for-nothin' brother."

She stopped and looked at him.

"Samuel, tell me, who is Mike Sweeney?"

"All's I know is that he works for a private detective company. Not a reputable one, neither. They're usually hired to, uh, strong arm folks, if you get my meaning."

Fiona nodded.

"Used to be a cop but got hisself kicked out."

"Why?"

"Taking bribes, gettin' in fights all the time, drinkin'. Who knows what else? Takes a lot to get thrown out of NYPD." He paused. "He's a bad man, Fiona. Always in some kinda' trouble. And mean, you know? Like somethin's twisted inside him."

"What's he doing at the Triangle?"

"Don't have an answer to that."

"Don't you think it's strange? That someone like him would have business with the Triangle?"

Battle gave a faint smile but didn't respond.

They walked on.

"Look, Samuel, I was just, um, promoted today. I'm going to be working in the office from now on."

"No kiddin'? That's great. How'd you manage that?"

"I can read and write." She blushed.

"That's real fine, Miz Fiona. Real fine."

"But it means I may run into this Sweeney person again." She paused. "What do I do?"

"Duck out to the Ladies' Room or into another office."

Her mind churned. "Hide? Well, that's a fine thing. I'm a newly promoted, well-skilled office clerk and I'm quaking in the Ladies Room."

"Maybe you can talk to your boss, tell him that--"

"Maybe," Fiona said, "I can find out what Sweeney's really doing there. What business he has at the Triangle. Then I can talk to Mr. Bernstein and--"

"No, don't go pokin' around in stuff like that. I mean it."

She looked at him.

"If Sweeney, in fact, if this Bernstein, finds out you're nosin' around business that don't concern you, well, I don't know."

"What's the worst that can happen?" she said. "I can lose my job?"

Battle looked at his feet.

"What?"

"Yeah, you'll lose your job, for sure."

They found themselves in front of 63 Orchard Street.

"Thanks for walking me home, Samuel."

"It's my pleasure, Miz Fiona. Say hello to Cormac for me."

"I will."

"And remember," Battle said. "Keep your distance from Mike Sweeney. A mile's probably too close."

Fiona entered the hallway, hesitated in the dim light before climbing the stairs. Should she mention this to Cormac? It was risky. He might demand she quit her job immediately--at the very least, refuse the office job. Fiona didn't want to give that up; it was such a coup.

Then again, if she knew her husband, he'd probably go off half-cocked, find Sweeney and beat him to a bloody pulp. He'd lose his job and then where would they be?

Fiona giggled, surprising herself. The image of Mike Sweeney beaten to a bloody pulp was a most agreeable one.

Chapter 18

March 22, 2011

9:00 p.m.

The apartment was dark when Frank arrived home. He'd forgotten to leave a light on. Dexter was particularly unhappy about that and gave him a loud screech.

"Okay, awright. Sorry, Dex." He flipped the switch on and groaned at the latest mess.

"Awwwwwwwp," the parrot screaked as he landed on Frank's outstretched arm. "Awwwwwp," meaning where the hell were you and where's my dinner?

Frank went straight to the bird food and fed his pal. He shook his head at the bird feathers, pillow stuffing and shit piles around the living room. Then he got busy cleaning them up.

He opened the refrigerator and happily saw one last Corona. In two minutes, half was gone. He wiped his mouth with the back of his hand and went to his desk. He booted up his laptop and while he waited, he checked his cell phone for messages he might have missed. None. Still no word from Amanda.

He polished off the rest of the beer more slowly as he thought about his daughter. Amanda and Lizzie were pretty tight, not surprising since *his* mom had been *her* mom for the last eleven years. God, had it been that long since Jeannie's death? He sat on the couch, laid his head back, just for a few minutes. Just to have a breather from the day. Only a few minutes.

He'd staggered dead tired into his house. The day had been one of relentless frustration, following up on zero leads on a brutal child murder case. His body was in knots, his brain numb. As usual he'd forgotten to call home. Jeannie would understand, especially about this case. But it had been like that for every case. So many forgotten calls.

It was payback time. The house was dark when he'd arrived. She'd often leave a light on for him or for Amanda in case she woke up in the middle of the night and wanted a drink or something. Wasn't she too old for that sort of thing?

That wormy sensation started up from his gut to his throat but he ignored it. He didn't bother turning on the light, just felt his way up the stairs. Tripped on the way, thumped his shin hard and stifled a curse.

At the top he stopped at the sound. Water dripping. That annoying persistent sound that would keep him awake. Why didn't Jeannie hear it and turn it off? Monotonous. Drip, drip, drip.

He stumbled over a rug in the bedroom. The first thing he noticed was that the bed was empty. How could he tell that in the dark? It was as if an unseen spotlight lit up the bed from behind him. The covers were untouched, the bed still made.

Then the drip became louder. . . Huge heavy droplets falling like golf balls on a tin roof. Bam. Bam. Bam. Gotta fix that.

He followed the noise into the master bathroom. Just like before. Always the same. The room was burning white, searing into his eyeballs. The black and white floor tiles scintillated in the fluorescence. And the heat. Radiating upward, the air seemed to undulate in waves.

Jeannie lay in the tub, eyes glazed, open but lifeless, a tiny smile on her lips. An empty pill bottle sat on the tub's shelf. He dropped to his knees, as he did every time, his lungs ready to implode. His eyes caught a note, the same note each time. It rested under the pill bottle. "I'm sorry."

That's it? You're sorry?

A clamor of emotions beat at him. He crawled to the toilet and threw up his last three meals.

At that moment, Amanda entered the room. He pulled his head up, eyes red and swollen, face sweat-smeared. The look in her eyes ripped a hole in his heart. His heart was rife with holes.

"What did you do to Mommy, Dad? What did you do to her?"

Then his daughter morphed into a wisp of white vapor and disappeared through the closed window. She never returned.

Frank wrenched himself awake with a howl. "Amanda, where are you? Amanda?"

Dexter shrieked in surprise.

Frank dropped his head in his hands and shook himself into consciousness. Damn dream was back again. He hadn't had it for two years. He wasn't surprised. Amanda was missing and Lizzie was in a coma. It seemed the gods had targeted him once again.

Frank looked at the clock. 6:00 a.m. He stood and stretched then went into the bathroom and threw cold water on his face and head. He dried off and walked into his office.

A soft "brrp" and Dexter landed on his desk, waddled up to his computer and eyed him first with one eye then the other. "Brrrp," the bird said again softly, nodding his head to encourage conversation.

Frank held his finger out and rubbed his chest. Dexter moved into the massage, cooing like a lovebird.

"Yeah, for a bird, you're okay," Frank said.

"Ohhhh-kaaay," was the reply.

"Sorry, Dude, but I've got work to do."

He scooted the parrot out of the way and clicked on his keyboard.

"Awwp, Dude, Awwwp." Dexter took the hint and flapped over to the couch.

Frank pulled out the printouts he made at Amanda's apartment. First, her notes. Next the scanned letter she'd found hidden in a picture frame in the attic. The copies were in color and the letter appeared to have been written on paper the color of sand. At the top was a letterhead embossed in garish gold leaf. The body of the letter was typed in black ink. When *were* typewriters invented he wondered.

Soames and Slatten Private Detective Agency

15 West Broadway

New York, New York

March 19, 1911

Mr. Max Blanck

Triangle Shirt Factory

Asch Building

New York, New York

Dear Mr. Blanck,

Pursuant to our discussion of last week, this is to confirm our upcoming business arrangement. As in past contracts, we will be sure to execute the plan at the close of factory business. The said venture will involve only certain floors and will take place on Saturday next.

In working with Arches Insurance Company, any damages will be reimbursable to the full extent of the inventory as well as the hard costs of building repair.

As mentioned, I will handle all arrangements personally. I look forward to a successful enterprise and to working with you on future projects.

Sincerely,

Michael J. Sweeney

March 23

6:30 a.m.

A knock on the door. He opened it to Will Jefferies.

"Jefferies, hey. Come in. Don't mind the mess. Dexter's a lousy housekeeper."

"Dexter?"

"Awwwwp."

"Oh. Dexter. *Killer* bird, eh?" Jefferies shook his head as the bird launched himself across the room and landed on Frank's arm. Frank carried him to the cage, set him inside and closed the door.

"Sorry, Buddy. Take a rest." To Jefferies, Frank said,

"Can I get you something, beer, oh, no beer, I drank the last one yesterday--soda maybe?"

"Beer? It's 6:30 in the morning."

"To go with your pastrami sandwich."

"Corned beef," Jefferies said but smiled.

"Sit."

"I knew you'd be up early so thought we could catch up on the Brandt case."

"Good. I'm glad you came." Frank filled Jefferies in on his suspicions regarding Amanda and her connection to the murdered girl.

"Jesus. You think your daughter may be missing?"

"I don't know. She's been out of touch close to two days now."

"Is that unusual?" Jefferies said. "I mean, do you talk to her every day or anything?"

"No nothing like that. But with her friend just murdered and this link to the Triangle fire, well, it's just too much of a coincidence." He paused. "Look, everything I'm reading points to the fact that the Triangle fire was arson. And, yeah, it was a hundred years ago, but someone today may not want this uncovered." Frank handed Jefferies the photocopies. "Read this."

Jefferies read Amanda's notes, then the letter.

"Interesting letter. You think this Sweeney was hired to set the fire?"

"Looks that way."

"I'm not really surprised that the Triangle owner actually committed arson," Jefferies said. "If so, it sounds like this wasn't the first time. Maybe this one just got out of hand."

"Out of hand, right," Frank said. "In the end, 146 died, mostly women and young girls, all for the insurance money."

Jefferies groaned. "Things never change."

"Check this out." Frank went back to the computer. He clicked on the Internet, scrolled through information sites and read out loud, "Max Blanck was co-owner of the Triangle Factory with Isaac Harris. Not long after the two set up shop at their big modern factory, the fire department was called to the ninth floor of the Asch Building at five o'clock in the morning. They arrived too late to save the contents of the company. Luckily no one had been at work so early in the day. And luckily for the owners, they had insurance to cover their losses."

"I bet they did," Jefferies said.

"About six months later, also early in the morning," Frank went on, "another fire broke out. Similarly, the owners collected insurance to cover the damages. Between the two fires, Blanck and Harris collected over thirty thousand dollars."

"A fortune in those days," Jefferies said. "So how come those fires were set at five in the morning and this big one wasn't? I mean, the letter says at the close of factory business. Why take a chance that anyone would be there?"

Frank shook his head. "Interestingly, both fires occurred around the end of the twice-a-year busy season, which was always a risky time for the owners of garment factories."

"Convenient." Jefferies flipped through the photocopies of Amanda's notes and the letter.

"Why don't you let me do a little digging here?" Jefferies said. "Into Soames and Slatten, and this Mike Sweeney. See if there's any connection today."

"Right. In the meantime, I've got to find my daughter. Would you put a trace on her cell?"

"No problem."

Frank gave him the number. Then he paused, looked at Jefferies. "What?"

"Why was this letter hidden in our attic?"

"Where did she find it again?" Jefferies asked.

"Amanda accidentally dropped and broke a picture frame in the attic at our family tenement on Orchard Street."

"And voilá?"

Frank nodded. "So, the big question is, who originally found the letter and hid it?"

"Sounds like one of your ancestors."

"Yeah. Getting more and more interesting by the minute."

Jefferies stood. "Let me also see what I can find out about boyfriends of Stephanie Brandt. What about your daughter?

"What about her?"

"Any boyfriends?"

"I asked her roommate, Connie. She said Amanda dated someone a few times in the last coupla' weeks but she had no idea who."

"You two aren't close, huh?"

Frank walked from the couch to the dining table and back again. "Truthfully, I've been a lousy father. Ever since my wife. . . died, I kinda left my mom holding the bag when it came to raising Amanda."

"Fathers sometimes do that."

"But to answer your question about Amanda's boyfriends, my mother might actually know. Unfortunately she's in a coma."

"Jesus, sorry about that. She gonna be okay?"

"I hope so. The fall was one thing. She also has cancer."

Jefferies rubbed the stubble on his chin. "Yeah, I know about that." He didn't leave room for question.

Frank raised his eyebrows.

"Anyhow, what about other family or friends that might know of your daughter's beaus?"

"I can try my sister." Frank ran his hands through his short blond hair. "I'll also see if I can find that notebook that Amanda mentioned."

"Yeah. What's that about?"

"Believe it or not my mother claims it's my great grandfather's murder book."

"Whaa?"

"Cormac Mead, NYPD beat cop. He was called to the scene of the Triangle fire, but mom insists he discovered a murder."

"At the fire? No kiddin'?" Jefferies smiled. "Talk about cold cases."

"If there really was a murder at the time of the fire," Frank said. "Maybe that's the answer to our question about timing. The big fire was set when there were still workers around. To cover up a crime."

"Helluva deal. Kill 146 for one target."

Frank gave him a faint smile.

"Okay," Jefferies said. "Your job is to find the murder book and the motive. Mine is to find the boyfriend . . . and the killer."

Chapter 19

March 23, 2011

10:00 a.m.

Later that morning Frank sat across from his sister at the Village Starbucks and noted new lines etched in her face. At thirty-five, Irene seemed to have aged in the last week. She and Lizzie were close. Their mom's illness had taken a toll on both of them, but Irene especially. This morning, however, the lines were softened by her smile.

"She's going to make it, Frank. Do you believe?"

He reached out and took her hand. "That's great, Reeny, really great."

She lifted her Vente Mocha and sipped through the plastic top. "God, I thought that was it, you know? She was just a goner. The doctors couldn't figure anything out. Jeez. But she pulled out of it. Just woke up. Surprised us all. She's a tough old girl."

"She won't die until she's good and ready. I hope that's not for a really long time," he said. "Mom has a lot to live for, what with me home now to boss around." He grinned. "What do the doctors say at this point?"

"They don't have a flippin' clue, pardon my French. Probably related to the cancer, although all her test results look positive." She sighed, drank. "Just happens like that, I guess. But lemme tell you, she's her old feisty self. You should have heard her ream out Thomas, that asshole."

"Oh yeah?"

"She told him, 'Tommy, quit trying to sell my house out from under me. You're putting me in the grave too damn early. I gotta long way to go.' Something of that sort."

Frank laughed.

"So what's with Amanda?" Irene said, turning serious.

He shrugged. "Don't know where she is. I'm worried. I mean, well, you know we're not exactly close."

"I know."

"But she usually calls me back."

"She's pretty darn independent, that girl. Still, I expected her to call me about Lizzie. That's unusual, especially since I left messages that she was in a coma." Irene looked at him. "What about her job at the paper? Have they heard anything?"

"Not according to her roommate who got a call from her editor," Frank said. "I left messages with a co-worker and her boss as well."

"Yikes. Not good." She sat back and played with a spoon.

He leaned forward. "Irene, do you know of any boyfriends, someone Amanda was seeing?"

"No. I wish I did. I wish she was seeing someone, but--"

She stopped.

"What?"

"You know, come to think of it, Mom said something about that. About Amanda having a date with someone recently. She wasn't happy, Mom, that is. The guy was Hispanic, maybe. Yeah. Now I remember. Luis something or other. Not an Irishman at any rate."

"Anything else? No last name?"

"I don't think she said."

"Damn," he said.

"Hold on, the more I think about it . . . he worked for NYPD. A cop, yeah, right. Mom said Amanda joked about not being able to get away from the department. Cops surrounded her. Something like that."

Frank's mind churned. How many cops named Luis were there? Could be hundreds. He'd do a check and see what came up.

"Any ideas?" she asked.

Frank was on his feet. "Maybe. Gotta go, sweetie. I'll stop by and visit Mom later today." He was out the door.

11:00 a.m.

His next stop was Orchard Street where he wasted an hour searching in vain for Cormac's notebook. He took apart boxes, suitcases, trunks. Pulled books out of bookcases. Even checked for loose floorboards. He felt sure Amanda had hidden it back where she'd found it in the attic.

Where the hell could it be? A safe hiding place.

Frank wracked his brain trying to figure out where the murder book was as he drove the few miles back to the hospital to see Lizzie. He wasn't looking forward to telling his mom that Amanda was missing. Maybe he wouldn't tell her, at least not exactly in those words.

Lizzie was awake when he entered the room.

She smiled and he leaned down to kiss her cheek.

"Glad to have you back."

"You don't think I'd leave you kids to your own devices for long, do you?" She waved to a chair. "Sit."

He pulled the chair close. "What do the doctors say?"

"Ah, phooey, doctors. What do they know? I'm alive. I'm doing fine. That's all that counts, right? Ach. I needed a long nap. Now I'm recovered."

"I just--"

"Let's not talk about me. I'm telling you, I'm okay. I want to hear about the case."

He blew out a long breath. "You know I can't tell you much, Mom."

"So, don't say much. Say a little. You got the killer yet?"

"No. We will." He paused, gauging how strong Lizzie was for the next question. "So, tell me about Cormac's murder book."

"Is it connected to the killing?" she asked.

"Might be. Might not."

"That's a no-answer."

"Mom, the book, where is it?"

"I told you. Amanda has it." She stopped. "By the way, where is she? I was hoping to see her now that I'm back in the world of the undead."

"I'm sure she'll be by soon. Say, what do you know about her boyfriends?"

"She doesn't really have any."

"None?"

"I remember she had a couple of dates with this Puerto Rican guy, Raoul, or Luis, or something. Maybe Sanchez? San – something. Why the hell can't she find a nice Irish boy?"

"Beats me. What else do you know about him?"

"Let's see, maybe he's a cop? I don't remember. Sorry. Is it important, Frankie?"

"No, no. Get back to Cormac's book," he went on. "Any idea where she might have it?"

Lizzie squinted at him. "No. If it's not connected, why do you need to know?"

"We're kind of playing a little game, me and Amanda. She told me she hid it in a safe place. But being a lousy detective, I can't figure out where. It's not at Orchard Street, by the way. First place I looked."

"Hmmm," she said, warming to the mystery. "Well, let's see. Where would I hide something like a notebook?"

"I give up."

"In plain sight. Always a good hiding place."

Frank did not want to tell her that plain sight didn't include Amanda's own apartment since he had searched there.

"Okay, where in plain sight?"

She rattled off some possibilities as his eyes took in the hospital room. On the side table were a stack of books, hardbacks and paperbacks.

"Mom, are those yours?" He pointed.

"Yeah. . . they. . . are."

He got up and picked them up one at a time. Autobiography of Teddy Roosevelt, a mystery by P.D. James, and a thriller by Daniel Silva. The fourth one down was unusual. Untitled.

"That's not mine. Amanda," she whispered.

The blood churned in his veins. The leather bound notebook was soft, darkened by human oils and well worn, but the pages inside were legible and orderly. They included diagrams, sketches and notes, copious notes. At the back of the book was an envelope, aged, lumpy with photographs. From a quick glance, he could see they were images depicting a human body lying on a table in the morgue.

He let out the breath he didn't know he was holding. He hadn't really believed this book existed. Somehow this moment seemed sacred. This was history yet it was possibly connected today to Stephanie Brandt's murder and Amanda's disappearance. No, not possibly. Definitely. He felt it in every molecule of his body.

He looked down and clutched the leather tighter as if it would vanish if he loosened his grip.

He held it up and nodded to his mother.

Cormac Mead's murder book. Fiona Mead's murder.

12:30 p.m.

Ten minutes after he left the hospital his cell rang.

"Mead."

"Jefferies. Any luck on the murder book?"

"Plenty, but I'll tell you later. I did find out something about a possible boyfriend. Amanda evidently dated someone named Raoul or Luis San-*something*, like Sanchez, who works for NYPD but isn't a cop."

"Luis?" Jefferies said. "I hope it's not Luis Santiago."

"Why? Who's he?"

"Jane Magliatti's assistant, a beat cop turned public relations man. Fits, if you know what I mean."

"No, tell me," Frank said.

"Early thirties, dark, oily. Gleaming white teeth like a shark. News anchorman type, you know. Women like him. Go figure."

Frank's gut roared and he popped three Tums. "Shit."

"Let me do some more digging. In the meantime, I found out some dope on Soames and Slatten," Jefferies said.

"Go ahead."

"They were a private eye firm of lesser repute in the early part of the 1900's. Apparently most of their work centered on the garment industry. They worked for a number of the drapers and blouse factories. No definite proof, of course, but they seemed to be connected to fires at these factories," Jefferies said. "At least their contracts were timed to match fires that broke out at the factories. Soames and Slatten also had ties to a few insurance companies. It would take quite a bit of research to track anything more down."

"Let's hold off on that for now."

"You were right about the Triangle," Jefferies said.

"Yeah?"

"Uh, let's see. Blanck and Harris, the Triangle owners, engaged these bozos five times in three years. And five times they had fires break out at the factory."

Frank was silent for a moment. "Any connection today?"

"Dead end there. Harry Soames died without leaving any kids. Jeremiah Slatten had two kids but no grandkids. So, there's no living descendants of Soames and Slatten today." He paused. "Sounds like the world's a better place."

"What about that guy, Sweeney? Mike Sweeney."

"Still working on that. The name was a common one with all the Irish immigrants landing in New York at the time."

"Right. Keep at it, though," Frank said. "I have this feeling Sweeney's the man that's going to be the link from the past."

"So you have psychic abilities?"

"I have this little worm in my gut that talks to me. I'm usually sorry when I don't listen."

Chapter 20

March 23, 2011

1:00 p.m.

Luis Santiago hated to sweat. It made him look like his low-class, good-for-shit brothers and cousins. He worked hard at distancing himself from them and his abusive father. As early as ten years of age, he'd made up his mind to make something of himself. Not to make his family proud. No way. He'd become a success so he could gloat, show them up, thumb his nose at them.

Yeah, he hated to sweat mostly because it made him feel out of control. He needed to get a grip on this situation, one that Russo made him acutely aware of. He wiped his face with a paper towel and ran his fingers through his hair.

In ten minutes, he would open the door of his office to Lieutenant Frank Mead. He'd never met the man, but thanks to Russo felt he knew him intimately. Santiago was not looking forward to this first encounter especially since Mead would be asking questions about his daughter.

Mead's daughter. Shit. How was he to know that Amanda Mead was related to *that* Mead? An NYPD homicide lieutenant's daughter.

So what? He'd tell him the truth, that's all. Just not all of it.

Santiago shot over to his desk, spun around to his computer and called up personnel records. What dirt could he find out about Mead? He clicked keys. Frank Mead, Frank Mead. There it was. Worked for NYPD ten years then moved to Metro D.C. eleven years ago. Top resolve rate in the department there. Re-recruited back to NYPD about a month ago. No wonder Russo wanted him.

Santiago whistled between his teeth. No way could he let Russo find out the truth. He'd have to take care of this situation personally.

He dug deeper into Mead's file. Commendations, stacks of thank you letters from victim's relatives, and what, wait, several notes of chastisement. Santiago read them. . . *inappropriate actions of. . . further actions warranted. . . use of unnecessary force. . .*

"So, Frankie boy, evidently you lose your temper once in a while, eh? Got you in trouble a few times. Hotheaded cowboy, eh?"

He scrolled further. Coroner Report on Jean Alice Mead, age 33, died July, 2000, overdose of barbiturates. Holy shit. Mead's wife committed suicide. Then it struck him. There'd been rumors of Sanford Russo having an affair with some cop's wife. Could it have been Mead's wife? Whoa. Did Mead know? Nah, spouses were usually the last to know. Did their daughter know? Maybe wifey offed herself because of the affair. Christ. He couldn't imagine any woman killing themselves over Russo. Who could figure women? Maybe that's why Mead bailed out of the city. Timing coincided. All very interesting. He'd have to look into that one. Never know when information like that can come in handy.

Santiago clicked off and leaned his head back on his leather chair. In accordance with the laws of physics, this ball was spinning in motion and there was no stopping it now.

The door opened and Marta announced Frank Mead.

Frank walked in and stood across the desk from him.

"Lieutenant, nice to meet you. Please, sit down."

Frank walked over to a wall decorated with framed objects.

"So what brings you to my office?" Santiago asked.

"Impressive. All these plaques, awards, photos with celebrities. Isn't that the mayor? And the governor, hey. You're quite a celebrity yourself, aren't you, Luis?" Frank asked.

"I've met a few important folks in my line of work."

"I bet. What is it you do, exactly?"

"I handle things for the Deputy Commissioner, Ms. Magliatti. Press, in particular."

"Like the press secretary for Obama?"

"Uh, I guess." Santiago watched as Frank studied the photos and certificates on the wall.

"How is the investigation of the reporter going?"

"You mean Stephanie Brandt?" Frank said. "I hate it when no one uses her name. She may be dead but she still has a name."

"Yeah, sure. It shows no respect for the dead. Sorry about that." Santiago paused. "That why you're here?"

"Indirectly. I wanted to ask you about my daughter."

"Your daughter?"

"That's right. Amanda. I believe you've dated her?"

"Amanda? Amanda Mead? Is your daughter? No kidding. It's a small world." Santiago smiled. "What about her?"

"You did go out with her?"

"Sure, sure. We met at an NYU basketball game. I took her on a coupla' dates. Just dinner, a movie, you know. Nice girl."

"That's it? Dinner, movie?" Frank said.

"Yeah, why? We didn't sleep together if that's what you're worried about."

"Who said I was worried?" Frank paused. "When was that?"

"When?"

"Yeah. When did you date her?"

"Umm, a week ago, maybe, two. Why?"

"Have you seen her in the last few days?"

Santiago shook his head. "No. I've been really busy with all the press about this repor--uh, Stephanie Brandt."

"Did you know that Amanda and Stephanie were friends?"

"Ah, so that's what this is about. Amanda is linked to the dead girl and you're tracking their movements. Right?"

Frank didn't answer.

"To answer your questions, I didn't know Stephanie and Amanda were friends. No." Santiago sat up and began to push papers around on his desk. "I wish I could be of more help, but--" He held his hands out, palms up. "Anything else, Lieutenant? I've got a lot of work to do."

Frank sat.

"I really am busy. Why don't you tell me why you're really here."

"I already have. Just a few more questions, if you don't mind. This is a homicide investigation."

"Of course, of course. However I can help."

"What did you and Amanda talk about on your dates?"

"Is this really relevant to the investigation?"

"Everything is relevant. Tell me what you and Amanda talked about on your dates."

Santiago sat up taller. "I don't know how this can help the--"

"Did you talk about your job, her job, what?"

"Yeah, yeah, the usual."

"What is her job?" Frank asked.

"What?"

"You said you talked about her job. What did she tell you about her job?"

Santiago blinked, acid reaching up into his throat. "She's a reporter. Hence the connection to Miss Brandt."

"For what paper?"

"*Post*, no, *Times*. Right?" Santiago forced himself to smile.

"What story was she working on?"

"Sorry. That I don't know." Santiago leaned forward. "Look, Lieutenant, is this just a father concerned about his daughter's boyfriends or is something else going on here?"

"I didn't realize you were a boyfriend. Thought you just went on a few dates."

"Now we're getting into semantics. Come on, get to the point. If you want, I'll promise never to see her again. She and I didn't really, well, this was just a friendship thing, you know? Not a romance."

Frank stood.

Santiago stood as well. "I'm sorry I wasn't able to help. Let me know if there's anything you need from this office. And please keep me informed on the case. I often have to answer to the press when Jane's tied up."

Frank gave a barely perceptible nod. "I'll find out, you know."

He left.

Santiago sank down in his chair and blew out a breath.

How they hell did he find out about me and Amanda so fast? Not through Amanda anyway. His hands shook. *I'm gonna have to accelerate the timeline.*

2:00 p.m.

Frank drove back to the 6th Precinct on West 10th Street. His mind roiled on the conversation he just had with Luis Santiago.

"Hoo-ey, lookout," Jefferies said, as Frank nearly ran him over as he headed into the bull pen. "You don't look too happy, boss."

"You were right," Frank said.

"Yeah?"

"Slimy creep, dancing around on the balls of his feet."

"Ah, you must be talking about our friend Luis."

Frank looked at him, hands on his hips. "He's one slick s-o-b. But dangerous. I don't trust him."

"What'd he say?"

"That Amanda was a reporter, but he had no idea what story she was working on. Wasn't even sure if she worked for the *Post* or the *Times*.

"Did he say anything about her friendship with Stephanie?" Jefferies asked.

"He said he didn't know they were friends, but you better believe he knew. For all I know, he dated Stephanie too."

"Think so?"

"He's hiding something." Frank didn't give voice to his question of whether Santiago could be covering for his boss Jane Magliatti, or someone higher up the ranks.

That worm in his gut was singing now. A veritable opera. He popped more Tums.

"Maybe you should buy some stock," Jefferies said.

"What?"

Jefferies pointed at the bottle. "Never mind.

Frank smiled as he walked to his office.

Several of the cops looked up. They were watching him, not openly, but under cover of paperwork, answering phones, talking to each other. It was confrontation time. He couldn't put it off any longer.

"Listen up, everyone," he shouted. "I want you all in the conference room in ten minutes. We're going to go over a few things. Pass the word."

He turned and grabbed his mug. Too bad he couldn't have a beer. Courage was what he needed to drink right now.

In ten minutes, seven men and four women were sitting and standing around the small room. Several out in the field would miss this. Besides a few tables, there were magnetic white boards at the front and a tray with markers and erasers. He began placing photographs on the board with magnets.

He could hear conversation, but tuned out the words. He didn't want to know what they thought of him. At least not until they got to know him.

Finally he turned. The room went dead silent. But the faces were not friendly.

"First, I want to thank you for being patient with me. Seems like someone arranged for a murder to take place the minute I got here, so I wouldn't be at a loss for what to do."

A few faint smiles.

"This isn't any easier for me than it is for you. I know some of you think it's bullshit that I waltz in here from another city and take over. Even those of you I worked with when I was here before." He folded his arms across his chest.

"Some of you probably think that one of you should be standing here instead of me." He avoided eye contact with Jefferies.

"Well, all that may be true. The fact is, this is what it is, for better or worse. So we may as well live with it. Another fact is, I'm a New Yorker like most of you, grew up on the Lower East Side. Just because I lived in D.C. for a while, doesn't mean I'm no longer a New Yorker." He paused, walked the front of the room.

"Is that a good thing or not? I don't know. But maybe you'll feel better knowing I'm not a total foreigner."

A few more faint smiles.

"I'd like to get to know you all as individuals. Find out what your strengths are so we could use those to help us resolve open cases. But that's going to take time. I'm asking you for your patience. In the meantime, we've got a killer to catch and a case that's turning out to be more complicated than we thought."

Frank moved to the board. "Before we begin working, are there any questions or comments on what I've just said?"

Silence.

"Fair enough. Let's get to work."

For twenty minutes, Frank went over the details of the case as they knew them to date.

Next to Stephanie Brandt's photographs were two of Amanda. Frank explained why he thought Amanda might be missing and how she was involved. He left out any word of Luis Santiago for now and Jefferies added none of his own.

"Lieutenant?" a woman named Collins asked. "Do you really think there's a connection to the Triangle fire a hundred years ago? That's pretty weird."

"I agree. But Stephanie Brandt went out the same ninth story window that scores of workers at the factory did almost exactly a hundred years ago. We have to check out all possibilities." He'd made notes on the board and now put the marker down.

"You all have your assignments. Get busy and report back to me or Sergeant Jefferies. Thanks."

Frank headed back to his office and stood over his desk.

When he looked up, he saw Jefferies heading toward him.

Frank grabbed his jacket, intercepted him and waved him toward the elevator. Jefferies followed and said nothing.

Outside the building, Frank told him his concerns about Santiago and why he didn't mention him at the meeting.

"If he is involved, it will be hell for the department. If he isn't, we don't need to make it hell."

Jefferies nodded.

"Listen," Frank said. "I'm going to stick my neck out big time on this. My visit to Santiago scared him. He seemed jittery even before I opened my mouth."

"Santiago? Jittery? Hmm."

"Like a poodle in a cage with a Dobie."

"That's not how I'd describe him. He's an arrogant little prick. Nothing ever seems to ruffle him."

"Well, he looked pretty ruffled just now. Ruffled and sweaty."

"What do you wanna do?" Jefferies asked.

"If he's hiding something, he's going to have to make a move. . . and soon."

Jefferies nodded.

"I want to follow him tonight, see where he goes, what he does."

"That a good idea?"

"Fuck no. But it'll make me feel better."

Jefferies half-smiled, the most he ever did. "Want some company? I'm sick of *NYPD Blue* re-runs. And I know where the asshole lives."

Chapter 21

February 20, 1911

On a Monday two months into the New Year, Fiona hummed a tune as she typed on her new Underwood. Funny, she already thought of the machine as *hers*.

"You are surely learning that new contraption rapidly, aren't you?" Dinah Lipschitz said, exiting her tiny office next door.

Fiona smiled. "It's just fascinating."

"Well, I couldn't be less interested. Glad to see someone can." The bookkeeper left the room without a smile or backward glance.

Fiona enjoyed working in the office despite Dinah, and despite the fact that some of her former fellow workers on the production floor were envious. Some even snubbed her, although not her friend Ida. Fiona didn't care. She hoped she could stay here forever. Well, at least for a year.

Da, you'd be proud of me.

The door crashed open. Her hands froze on the keys as Michael J. Sweeney stormed in. Her mouth went dry.

"Where is he?" Sweeney growled.

"Who?"

"Bernstein, your boss, who'd ya think?"

"He'll be back in a moment," she said and tried to resume typing with her hands shaking. This was the first time she'd seen Sweeney since she'd been promoted. Now, Battle's words came back and she wondered if she should try to make an escape. The doorway, however, was blocked.

Sweeney rubbed his hands together and moved to the side of her desk. She jumped to her feet and grabbed a folder. Then she moved to the file cabinet trying to put as much distance as she could between Sweeney and herself.

"Playin' hard to get, now, are ya?" He laughed and her stomach coiled into a knot. "I'm glad to see you're still here. Must be doin' a good job, then, eh?"

She opened a file drawer, thumbed through to find the correct space then dropped the file in.

Sweeney came up behind her. Close. So close, he wriggled into her back. His arms came around her and he reached into the drawer.

"Now what's this? *Soames and Slatten.* Is this the file yer lookin' for?" He pulled it out.

"Put that back." Fiona twisted and ducked from out of his embrace. "Those are private. You've no right to be going through the--"

"But this isn't private. This is my file, ain't it?"

She said nothing.

"I'm talkin' to you. It's not polite to ignore someone who's talkin' to you. Don't you agree?"

She said nothing.

"Have you read my file, little lady? Are you familiar with the business agreements between Triangle and *Soames and Slatten*?"

His grin was more like a leer.

"Of course not. I don't read the files."

"Your face is all red. Does it get all blushy pink like that whenever you lie?"

"What is it you want?" she said. "I'm busy." Fiona pushed her way to her desk and tried typing. Her hands shook.

"Well, of course you are." He leaned over her. "You didn't answer my question. Did you read this file?"

"I told you I did not. Now please leave. I have work to do."

"What would happen if you didn't get your work done? Would the big man fire you?"

Her face burned.

Sweeney burst out laughing, a nasty sound, even nastier in the quiet room. It sent chills down the ridge of her spine.

Suddenly his hands were on her shoulders and he was lifting her out of her chair.

"Stop it. Put me down." She thrashed at him but he was touching her, grasping, pinching, rubbing her belly. How could he be so strong? Or she so weak?

"Say, where's the bulge? Baby born already? How sweet." He had pinned both her arms behind her back and brought her up close to him. He rubbed his body against her breasts and she squirmed. Then he licked the side of her face. Sickened, she shrieked and with all her strength, pulled her arms out of his grasp and lashed out at his face. Her nails tore a deep rent in his cheek and blood bubbled out.

"Ouch, you bitch." He pushed her away and touched his cheek. His hand came away bloodied. He stood there wiping the blood. Then his eyes caught hers.

Fiona darted for the door. She wasn't quick enough. He grasped her wrists and threw her backwards onto the desk. Papers, pens, ink bottles, wire baskets of folders flew to the floor. Her shoulders crashed into the typewriter and pain shot into her neck.

"You are a little wildcat, aren't you? I like my women spirited."

Fiona screamed and Sweeney covered her mouth with his hand. He had leaped up on the desk and pinned her with his knees.

Please God, please God. Fiona cried silently.

"What the hell is going on here?" Sam Bernstein burst into the room. "Sweeney?"

"Just having a little fun, Mr. B. This little vixen here was flirtin' with me, is all." He released his grip on her and Fiona rolled off, barely able to stand. "I didn't know you hired such fast and easy girls here." He glowered at her, licked his lips.

Fiona felt nauseated, her eyes on the floor.

Bernstein looked from her to Sweeney. "You can go for today, Fiona," he said. "It's almost quitting time."

Her hair ruffled, her clothes out of order and her face stained with tears, she nodded and ran out.

"Wait," Bernstein called.

She turned, her hands holding her top buttons closed.

"You need to clean up this mess first." Her boss spun around and pushed Sweeney into the inner office. He left the door open a crack.

Mortified, Fiona stumbled back to the desk and started picking up papers, folders, pens and anything else that had toppled to the floor. While she straightened, she listened to the men's voices in the other room.

"Quit worrying. Have I ever let you down?" Sweeney said.

"I always worry. Things can go wrong." Bernstein said. "When? We've got a particularly slow season this year. It's got to be soon."

"Tonight. That soon enough?"

No answer from Bernstein.

"Relax. All will go well. You worry too much."

"After hours?"

"Of course. I said, just like before."

Suddenly the voices stopped and the door to Bernstein's office slammed shut.

Fiona was on the floor behind the desk. They didn't know she was still there. She'd overheard a conversation she wasn't supposed to. What did it mean? What was going to happen after hours tonight?

She spotted a folder that had blown under her desk in the fracas. *Soames and Slatten.* Sweeney's company. She was about to open it when she heard footsteps moving to the door in the inner office.

Quietly, she rose, tucked the folder under her Underwood and scurried from the room. This time she did not wait for the elevator.

The next morning, Fiona arrived at the Triangle to find a crowd of workers milling about outside the main doors.

"What's the problem?" Her heart plummeted.

"Fire," one woman answered. "Last night on the eighth floor."

She looked up and could see a murky brown haze hovering outside the windows two stories below the roof. She recalled the conversation between Bernstein and Sweeney. Last night when everyone was gone. That was the plan. A fire during a slow season, unusual in the winter. Insurance money, what else?

Bernstein came out of the front doors and shouted, "No work today. Come back in a week to check." That was all.

A collective groan from the workers. They would be short cash now and many supported large families.

Fiona turned and started for home. She noticed Ida a few feet away.

"Ida," Fiona said.

"Jesus God, what next?" Ida said. "Now we'll have to make do with broth and stale bread for a while."

"I'm sorry."

"Ain't yur fault, Dearie. Yur in the same boat as the rest of us poor lot."

No. This is my fault. All my fault. If I had spoken up, maybe I could've prevented this.

Ida patted her arm and trudged off down Sixth Avenue.

What should she do now? Fiona wanted so badly to tell Cormac. She had no proof, only her word that she'd overheard the deadly conversation. He would believe her. Or would he? He'd been unhappy with her talk of unions recently, her friendship with Clara Lemlich, and, of course, the strike she'd gotten herself involved in.

Now this? Even if Cormac did believe her, it wouldn't be enough. He was a cop. He would need hard evidence.

Fiona stood outside the Asch building, feeling frustrated and helpless. What evidence, how? One thing she knew for certain. She was the only one who could get that hard evidence for him. And get it she would.

Chapter 22

February 22, 1910

Fiona took the streetcar, strolled the half block to Washington Square Park and sat on one of the benches. The day, Sunday, was bright with sunshine and unseasonably warm. Cormac was at work, baby Patrick was with Mrs. Odermeyer for a few hours, and she needed to talk to someone.

The factory had been shut down after the fire and Fiona wasn't sure when she'd be getting back to work. She *was* sure about one thing -- Mike Sweeney set that fire.

"Fiona."

She looked up to see Clara Lemlich standing over her.

"Clara. I'm so glad you could meet me. Sit down." She patted the bench.

Clara sat at the edge so she could turn and look at her friend comfortably. "You're troubled, my dear. I hope I can help."

Fiona smiled. "Just talking to someone will help."

She fell silent. Clara didn't push.

Finally, Fiona said, "Did you realize that right beneath our feet, 20,000 poor souls are buried?"

"I recall something about that. A public burial ground. How like New York."

"It was used mainly for burying indigent people. And, when New York went through a yellow fever epidemic at the beginning of the nineteenth century, many of those casualties were buried here as well."

"How utterly gruesome," Clara said. "I, for one, am glad that it is now a place for the living."

They relaxed and watched a juggler toss balls and bats in the air.

"When do you return to work, Fiona?"

"You know about the Triangle fire, then?"

"Word travels."

"I don't know when the factory will reopen. Maybe a week, maybe a month. It depends on how much the insurance covers."

"What do you mean?"

"The fire was deliberately set, Clara. For insurance money. The season is slow, the owners aren't making money. So, they set a fire."

Clara blinked, looked around to make sure no one was in earshot. "Do you know this for a fact?"

Fiona hesitated before answering. If she didn't tell someone, she'd explode.

"Clara, what I tell you must be kept between us. I will tell Cormac, but in my own time. Please. Do you understand?"

"Of course."

Fiona divulged what she had heard in Bernstein's office.

"So you think this Mike Sweeney set the fire?"

"Or his company."

"At the behest of the Triangle owners."

"Deliberately. For the insurance money. When I return to work there will be a new insurance claim to file, I am sure." She shifted to face her friend. "I feel responsible, Clara. If I had revealed this two days ago, the fire might have been prevented."

"There was nothing you could do, Fiona. If it didn't happen then, it would happen next week or next month."

Fiona said nothing.

"Being a whistle blower is a dangerous business." Clara shook her head. "It makes me angry that they can get away with it. Now you really see our dilemma and why the union is so important."

Fiona stared ahead at nothing.

"Can you confide in Cormac? Trust him not to do anything rash?"

"Cormac would be outraged. I don't know what he'd do. That worries me." She turned to Clara. "You see, Cormac has a fight going on within himself. He wants to get ahead, get promoted someday to sergeant, maybe higher eventually. He's so proud of his job. Proud of the NYPD. He wants to succeed, not just for himself, but for us, for his family. For me."

Clara nodded.

"But he knows things." Fiona stopped, looked down.

"Things?"

"I'd rather not talk about it."

"You mean things that happen in those smoke-filled back rooms? Bribery, payoffs, corruption, those things?"

Fiona looked into her friend's eyes.

"Yes. He won't be part of anything illegal or immoral, but he sees things. And they disturb him. So much so that his dreams are. . . well, he calls out in his sleep and he's. . . never mind."

"Your husband has an admirable sense of justice."

"He knows what's right and believes that it's his job to uphold the law. But if his own colleagues--"

"Yes. He's caught in this Tammany Hall-City Hall conundrum. And, how can he do what's right if he's thrown off the force? So he tows the line." Clara sighed. "I understand."

"Clara, that's why I can't tell him about this. I don't know how he'll react. He may get so angry, he'll do something he'll regret."

Clara shook her head. "I'm sorry, Fiona. I know how difficult this must be for you. For you both."

They fell silent and watched the jugglers.

"Mike Sweeney. . . scares me, Clara."

"And rightly so. You must keep away from him."

"How? Why?" Fiona threw her hands in the air. "No, I won't be intimidated by this, this monster. I can't go running from the man every time he steps into the office. I just have to deal with it."

"Have you mentioned Mike Sweeney to Cormac?"

"No." She shook her head in a way that left no room for argument. "I don't plan to either."

"You sure that's a good idea?" Clara said.

"I don't want Cormac going off half-cocked. God knows what he'll do to Sweeney. I'm not sure he has many friends on the force, either, who will back him, to be honest."

"There's Samuel Battle."

"You know Samuel?"

"Everyone knows how Cormac defended him."

"Yes. That and all this union stuff has isolated him from the rest of the force."

"I'm sorry," Clara said.

"No. It's still the right thing. And I'm not going to back away."

Clara patted her friend's hand. "Fiona, you're a lot like Cormac. Fighting the injustices of the world. Pretty soon we'll recruit you to fight for women's right to vote."

"Hmm, the Suffragist movement. Well, if women can work, take care of families, why can't we have a say in government?"

Clara grinned. "Let's leave that conversation for another time. In the meantime, let me know what you decide to tell Cormac, so I don't put my foot in my mouth. And please, please, stay away from this Sweeney fellow."

Clara stood, smoothed her skirts. "Now I have to get back home. My father expects his Sunday dinner. . . on time."

She gave Fiona a peck on the cheek then hurried off.

Fiona reflected on Clara's words. Stay away from Sweeney. Same advice as Samuel gave. She knew they were right. Sweeney was dangerous. But he also was the key to the fires. And no matter how she tried not to, she did blame herself.

If she wanted to get rid of Sweeney for good, she had to find evidence of his crime. Hard proof of arson that Cormac could use.

Working in the office would provide her with an opportunity to find that evidence. Perhaps an insurance policy, perhaps some written contract with that damnable Michael Sweeney. Suddenly she remembered the file on Soames and Slatten. Mike Sweeney had pulled it out of the file drawer and now it was under her typewriter. A good start.

As soon as she could safely enter the building and get back to work, she'd go through the file and see what she could learn. If she could trap that devil at his own game, it would be worth the danger.

The more she pondered, the more promising it sounded. She'd not let Sweeney or Bernstein bully her. The very moment the factory re-opened she would search the files from top to bottom and find the proof she needed.

Chapter 23

March 23, 2011

6:30 p.m.

Dexter alerted Frank to his visitor before the knock.

He opened it to Jefferies, loaded down with a large paper bag and a six-pack.

"Let me guess. Corned beef on rye from Katz's?"

"You are a helluva detective, Lou."

Dexter tested out his wings over Jefferies head.

"Jesus F. Christ, bird." Jefferies ducked.

Frank laughed.

Dexter landed on the kitchen counter, visible from the dining room table and squawked. "Kee-rist, Kee-rist, Awwp."

"Quit teaching him new words. I'll have the religious fanatics on my ass now."

Frank popped two beers and brought out plates and napkins.

"So let me take a look at this murder book," Jefferies said.

"To be honest, I'm not ready to tackle that just yet. Besides, I'm not sure how much, if any, bearing it'll have on the case."

Now why did he say that, Frank wondered. He wanted very much to dive into Cormac's murder book. Just not with Jefferies. Not right now. Maybe it was stupid, but this was between him and his great grandfather. And Amanda.

Jefferies eyed him with a scrunched brow and pulled the oozing sandwiches out of the bag.

"Tell me," Frank said. "Any news from trace?"

"Techs found nothing. Well, they found a lot, but mostly debris from the victim's landing on the pavement. Not surprising. The killer probably just put his palm on her back and gave a shove."

"Which answers the question of whether Stephanie was already at the window," Mead said. "And the killer, who must have been tailing her, took the opportunity when it arose."

"My guess is she was looking out the window as part of her research. She probably opened it, maybe was going to take a picture--"

"We know that no prints were found on the window, just lots of smears. Wait. What did you say about pictures?" Frank said.

"What do you mean?"

"If Stephanie was going to take a picture for the article. You know, 'the last view the victims of the Triangle saw, etc.', then where's the camera? Where are the photos?"

"Shit, her phone." Jefferies snatched his cell and dialed. "Katie? Jefferies. Did you ever check the reporter's phone for photographs?" He waited, listened. "Thanks."

"They did check the phone. Photos, but none taken that day. They're dated digitally. Maybe she didn't have a chance. Or, if she had a camera, the killer stole it with her computer."

Frank crunched on a pickle. "So Stephanie opened the window to get a look at what the factory workers faced when they were locked in," Frank said.

"The killer creeps up behind her and bingo. Perfect opportunity." He drank some beer.

Frank nodded.

"So what if the opportunity didn't present itself?" Jefferies asked.

"You mean, would he have killed her another way? Or was murder not the original intent?"

"Maybe he just wanted to scare her into quitting the article," Jefferies said. "Still doesn't make sense that the article would motivate murder."

"According to what you found out from her boss at the *Post*, that's the only story she was working on."

"He thought she was going to draft a book on the same subject too."

Frank finished his sandwich and pushed his plate aside. "What about this Dr. Schueller?"

"Clean as a whistle, well, except for egg stains on his tie, that is," Jefferies said. "Nah, he checked out."

Frank polished off his beer. "What about the *Post*? Had Stephanie sent them any part of the story?"

"What do you think? Nope. She was waiting until the whole thing was done. They've decided not to do the story now, just a short blurb from the archives."

"Why?"

"Too late to get a writer, do the research. Whatever."

"Too bad," Frank said. "That plays right into the killer's hands. Dead girl, dead story. End of story. What about Sweeney?"

"Got our best working on it."

"Officer Collins?"

"How'd you know?" Jefferies asked.

Frank smiled. "She seemed interested in the historical connection." He said, "So how did the troops respond to my speech yesterday? Any blow back?"

Jefferies took a long swig. "Mixed review, if you want the truth. Most of them will get over it. A few won't."

"The ones who had a chance for the position?"

"Yeah."

"What about you? How do you feel about a stranger coming in and taking charge?"

Jefferies looked at him. "I'm one of them who wanted your job. But I'll get over it too."

"Kee-rist, Kee-rist," came the soft reply from the kitchen.

Both men smiled.

"So tell me about Will Jefferies," Frank said.

"Most of it you probably read in the files."

Frank shrugged a shoulder. "I'd rather hear you tell it."

"Born in Brooklyn, thirty-eight years ago, Park Slope to be exact. No sibs. Parents dead. No other family. My wife died three years ago. No kids."

Frank realized the homicide squad was Jefferies' family.

"How'd your wife die, if you don't mind me asking?"

"Hit and run driver. She was cut off and forced into the oncoming lane on the Belt Parkway. Lousy shithead. Can't believe it's three years ago now." Jefferies twirled his empty beer bottle. "Sometimes it seems like yesterday. Sometimes it seems a lifetime ago." He stopped then started to speak, stopped again.

"Never found him?"

Jefferies shook his head. "Funny thing is we were in the middle of a divorce when she was killed."

"Sorry," Frank said.

"Yeah, me too. Your wife is dead too, right?"

Frank paused. "You know, don't you?"

Jefferies looked down. "Hard to keep that a secret."

"Yeah. Was a secret, in a way. Never saw it coming although I probably should have. If I'd've paid attention."

"Cop's life. Tough on the spouse. I always--" Jefferies stopped.

"You always what?"

"I always wondered why a woman marries a cop then gets pissed when he's not around, or he drinks, or he's depressed 'cause of all the shit he sees every day. Why don't they get it?"

"Mystery of life? She falls in love, thinks it will be different with them. He'll change for her. I don't know."

"That what happened with you?" Jefferies asked. "Never mind, none of my business."

"It's okay. Yeah, I guess that's what happened with Jeannie. In the beginning, she seemed to understand. I was gone a lot. She worked, kept busy, took care of Amanda. Then the last year or so something happened. I don't really know what." He stopped.

"Yeah, I do know," Frank said. "I think she was seeing someone. She seemed different. Distant. Even distant from Amanda." He stared into the empty bottle."

Jefferies turned to him, said nothing.

"I don't know for sure. Never had the courage to ask. But I could tell. She'd be flying around on high for weeks, then crash."

"Maybe she was manic-depressive?"

"New pieces of jewelry began appearing. New clothes. She'd be out sometimes until the morning, even later than me."

"What about Amanda?"

"She was nine or ten by that time and mom always baby-sitted. Amanda noticed the changes in her mother too. We never really talked about it, just exchanged those 'knowing looks.'"

"You mean like, what's up with Mom?" Jefferies said.

"Yup. Instead of confronting it, I pretended it didn't exist. Only made it worse."

"Do you know who the guy was?"

"No. Again, I'm not positive there really was a guy."

"Jesus. That why you left New York after she died?"

"Partly. Partly because I had a great opportunity."

"But you came back," Jefferies said.

"Another great opportunity. And a chance to make it up to my daughter."

"How long ago did all this happen?"

"Eleven years," Frank said. "Shook us up, I tell you. Amanda, well, she had a really hard time. Blamed herself. Mom didn't love her enough to stick around."

"And you?"

"Yeah. I'm still having a hard time."

"What happened to Amanda when you left for D.C?"

"Left her here with my mom. Nice, huh?"

"That why you moved back to New York? Enough time for both of you to heal?"

Frank thought about that. He wasn't sure of the answer.

"I guess. I was always so married to the job I didn't really think of myself as having a family. But coming back to New York gives me another shot at it. My mother, sister and brother are here too. And, well, there's nothing, no one for me in D.C. anymore."

"Ah, a lady friend?"

"Used to be." Frank paused. "What about you? Lady friend?"

Jefferies looked at him for a long minute. "No. No lady friend. I think I'm a perennial bachelor. *I* wouldn't want to marry me. Too difficult to live with."

Frank gave a half smile. "In what way?"

"Well, see for yourself. Corned beef on rye at 6:30 in the morning? What woman could put up with that?"

"Don't sell yourself short."

Jefferies raised an eyebrow. "Remember, I too, am a cop. Tough hours, tough cases, see the world through a dark-colored lens. Hard on the softer sex."

"I guess."

"At least you have a kid to remember your wife by."

Frank's smile was wistful. True, he had a kid. There was just so much distance between them. That would change once he found her--if she was willing to bridge the gap. He promised himself that.

Frank stood, put the plates in the sink and grabbed his jacket. Will followed suit.

"Sergeant," Frank said. "What do you say we see what our friend Luis Santiago is doing tonight?"

Chapter 24

March 23, 2011

9:00 p.m.

The night was clear with a full moon. Ideal surveillance weather. Frank sat in the passenger seat of Jefferies' 2006 Yukon. They'd been watching Santiago's house in Forest Hills, Queens, for two hours and four empty coffee cups. He was getting to like his sergeant. They both enjoyed Starbuck's black and strong and Jefferies had thought to get a large cardboard container filled with enough for twelve cups to keep them going through the night.

Luis Santiago had gotten home around seven and hadn't gone out. Yet. His house was a 1940's brick duplex, typical of the area. Every borough in New York was individual unto itself. While Brooklyn had older and more residential neighborhoods, Queens was packed with apartment buildings.

All was quiet, most people at dinner or home relaxing. He could see the light from several big screens in two or three windows. Other than the occasional jogger pacing by, a dog walker, a flower delivery truck, and a UPS truck were the only action so far.

Jefferies nudged him and Frank turned his attention out the windshield. A man was walking in the direction of Santiago's house. Big, white, nearly bald, about 6'3", 240 pounds, a lot of it around the middle. He wore loose sweats and a ball cap. Sure enough he hopped up the steps and rang the bell. Santiago opened the door and let him in.

"Classy company Luis keeps. Does he look familiar?" Frank asked.

If it's who I think it is, he should be in prison. Let me check." Jefferies rapped out some numbers on his cell and waited.

"Lorraine, it's Will. I'm doing fine, how you doin'? Listen I need to know a con's in or out. Salvatore Espinosa. I thought he bought himself a few years on a robbery." He nodded. "Yeah, I'll wait."

"Who is this guy?" Frank asked.

"A thug usually hired by a smarter thug to do his dirty work." Jefferies held up a hand. "Yo, I'm here. What? He's out, then? Say can you email a photo? Send it right now to Bruno 2 at cyberhome dot com. Thanks."

"Who's Bruno?"

"He was my dog. Chocolate lab. Great dog, labs. Died a year ago. Still think about him."

Frank looked at Jefferies a minute. "Stupid animals get to you, don't they?"

"What's with your bird?" Jefferies said.

"Dumb move." Frank sighed.

"I'm listening."

"Brought my car into a garage out in Canarsie. The bird was in the back of the shop squawking up a storm. Real nasty place, they didn't give a shit about him. He was covered in grease. So I took him. Fifty bucks. They sold him just like that. I figured I'd clean him up and give him away, to some good home or something." His face reddened.

"So?"

"Kinda got used to the company. He's incredibly smart, talks and, well, never mind. Stupid ass bird."

Jefferies burst out laughing.

"You going to get another dog?"

Jefferies looked at him. "You know, I think I am."

"Chocolate Lab?"

The sergeant grinned, actually showed teeth. "Yeah, another chocolate lab. Been thinking of calling this one Java. Nice having someone to come home to."

"No problem leaving him alone?" Frank asked.

"I used to bring him with me a lot."

"To crime scenes?"

"He'd stay in the car. I'd bounce all kinds of ideas off him. He was a great detective, actually."

"I suppose you could always get two dogs. Keep each other company." Frank smiled.

"Yeah. Call one Sherlock and the other Spade."

A chirp on his phone stopped their conversation. The sergeant called up his email and the two of them looked at the picture of Espinosa.

"Definitely him," Jefferies said. "Tough luck for the neighborhood."

"So what the hell is he doing visiting Santiago?" Frank said.

"I don't know, but frankly, I'm surprised."

"What do you mean?"

"Espinosa's a scumbag. What the hell is Santiago doing associating with a known criminal? Letting him into his house."

"Maybe he's family?" Frank says.

"Espinosa? He's not Puerto Rican like Santiago, mostly Italian, I think, but I suppose it's possible. Maybe he's married to a relative.

"Here he comes."

They scrunched down in their seats.

"There he goes," Frank said.

"Shall we see what this asshole is up to? Or do you want to keep an eye on Mr. Slick inside?"

"Let's follow Espinosa. I have this feeling."

"Uh oh, that stomach thing again." Jefferies started up his vehicle.

They watched as the ex-con got into a dark blue, heavily dented 70's Chevy truck and followed several car lengths behind.

Espinosa led them up Queens Boulevard, eventually making a number of right and lefts, the back way into Jackson Heights, a less than spiffy neighborhood in Queens. He pulled into the driveway of a tiny wood frame house, probably built in the same era as the truck.

Jefferies pulled his Yukon across the street and turned off the engine.

"Now what?" Frank said.

"We wait until. . . shit." Jefferies pointed.

Espinosa came flying out of a side door, fists balled up, yelling something incomprehensible. His face glowed crimson and with the extra weight he carried, Frank thought he might keel over right there.

The ex-con was shrieking and coughing up a storm. The only words they could make out were fucking cunt, bitch, and a few harsher swear words in some other language. Then he jumped into his truck and barreled out down the street, leaving a swath of rubber behind.

"What the fuck was that?" Jefferies said.

Frank swung open the door and leaped out.

"Hey. Where you going? Jefferies said.

Frank didn't answer, so Jefferies followed, both running toward the house.

Frank crept around the side and saw the door had remained opened. "Look, Espinosa's inviting us in. We'll just oblige him."

Chapter 25

March 23, 2011

10:30 p.m.

Both men drew their weapons and slowly entered the house.

The place reeked of body odor, beer, urine and Frank hated to hazard a guess at what else. The housekeeper hadn't been by in a while, either. Grease and oil stained the walls and floor and there were damp spots on the ceiling. He didn't want to touch the furniture.

They moved through the living room and came to a staircase.

"I'll go up," Jefferies said.

Frank pointed to a door under the stairs. He headed down to the basement. Two minutes later, he shouted, "Jefferies, get down here. Now."

Jefferies crashed down the stairs. When he reached the bottom, his mouth dropped.

"Holy fuckin' shit," Jefferies whispered.

Frank's eyes took in a cot, complete with a filthy, unsheeted mattress and handcuffs attached to the iron footboard. Scattered around were water bottles, a food tray with something resembling a frozen dinner, and a chamber pot.

"Looks like he kept someone against their will, would you say?" Jefferies said. "I'll get a team down here on probable cause and see if we can get trace and DNA on whoever slept in that bed."

Frank shook his head. "Amanda," he said with a rasp.

"If it was your daughter then where is she? From the way Espinosa came screaming out of here, he didn't give her permission to leave. Which is good news."

"She escaped," Mead said.

"Brave girl."

"Yeah, if I know anything about my daughter, that's what she'd do."

Is that what she would do? Frank thought about Amanda. She'd inherited his genes and if it were him, yeah, he'd try to escape, any way he could. A surge of pride coursed through his blood. His daughter escaped.

He looked at Jefferies. "So where the hell could she be?"

Jefferies was already on his cell calling for the crime lab team, putting an APB out on Espinosa, his truck and Amanda. In the meantime, Frank began examining the basement for evidence that his daughter was, indeed, the prisoner. He found several long reddish-blond hairs on the pillow and he felt a flutter in his chest like Dexter flapping inside him. Under the bed he located a pair of women's two-inch heels, black with a tiny bow. Shit, shit, shit.

"They hers?" Jefferies said.

"Could be. Size six, that'd be about right." Frank ran his hands through his hair for the fifth time in ten minutes.

He picked up the cuffs that were chained to the bed.

"Blood."

"She must have wriggled out of them. Ouch," Jefferies said.

"Goddamn."

"Let's think about this," Jefferies said. "Amanda manages to escape. Where would she go from here? Without shoes?"

"She'd be smart enough not to try a next door neighbor, in case they were friends of Espinosa," Frank said.

"Where's the nearest hospital or police station?"

"I doubt she'd know where they were and in any case, she might be in bad shape to try."

"Could she hail a cab or stop a car?" Jefferies asked.

"How about the nearest busy intersection?"

Before they could pursue this question, sirens blared outside.

"The gang's here. Let me go meet them," Jefferies said. He ran up the steps, leaving Frank to figure out where Amanda might have gone.

He looked around the room.

God, baby, I'm so sorry.

How did she get out? He walked to the bed and slipped some crime scene gloves on. Always had a pair in his pocket. Then he lifted the cuffs gently with one finger. Sure enough there was blood. Jefferies was right. Amanda had wiggled her foot out. Damn. She's probably bleeding and crippled. He wandered around the room looking for some hint of where she might be. Why did she leave her shoes behind if she was running? He checked them again. Heels. Maybe she thought she could run faster barefoot? Maybe she didn't have time. Espinosa was already back.

An idea came to him. Frank took the stairs two at time.

He pushed past the crime scene investigators and ran out to the street. He looked left and right, walked to the corner and back.

"What are you looking for?" Jefferies came up to him.

"A safe place. A place that Amanda may have found to hide for a while until she could get help. I don't think she went far since she left her shoes behind."

Jefferies rubbed the bridge of his nose. He did a quick circle looking at the neighborhood. People were already starting to gather. He went over to several of them.

"Did you see a young woman here a few minutes ago?"

A large black woman shook her head. "I ain't seen nothin'. Been mindin' my own business."

"How about you?" Jefferies addressed a young boy.

The kid, no more than twelve shook his head.

Someone else called out. "What'd she look like?"

"Blond, pretty about--"

The crowd started dispersing in a hurry.

"What the hell?" Frank said.

"They heard blond. Translate, white girl, translate, trouble. No one saw anything. Trust me," Jefferies said.

"So where then?"

"Would she hide in a dumpster?"

"Why not check?" Frank said.

Jefferies gave orders to a few officers, turned back to Frank. "Where the hell else could she find a safe place around here?"

Frank snapped his fingers and shouted to one of the team. "Anyone know this neighborhood?"

An Asian woman walked over. "Yeah, I grew up near here. Whatcha' need?"

"Where's the nearest church?"

"Easy one." She pointed over the tops of some houses. There was a church steeple. Amanda could have seen it too.

"Two blocks east and right one. Church of the Magdalene."

Frank took off at a run. Jefferies followed, calling over his shoulder to the woman. "You know where we'll be."

Frank came to a halt at the church doors. He caught his breath leaning over his knees and then stepped through large oak doors into a dimly lit hallway. Jefferies followed at a distance.

It had been years since Frank had attended mass, decades since he went to confession. A finger of chill wrapped around him as he moved forward. Would God punish him by hurting his daughter? He tiptoed so he could listen, catch any sound that Amanda might make. Then he realized she would try to be absolutely silent in case her abductor came looking for her. The hell with it.

"Amanda?" he called. "Amanda are you here? It's Dad."

A muffled sound from one of the pews.

Jefferies pointed.

"Amanda? Sweetie, I'm here. Are you okay?"

Not a sound.

Frank walked up the aisle, looking left and right. He spotted the top of her head, the reddish strands greasy and dark. The rest of her lay half-hidden under a pew.

His lungs contracted but no oxygen got through as he took in her condition. His daughter was barely conscious, clothing torn, barefoot, blood dripping from her head, her hands, feet, everywhere.

A host of memories shot through his brain in a blink of Dexter's eye. Amanda as an infant, secured in a yellow blanket with rabbits on top--she'd slept through the night at one month old. Amanda in elementary school--winning the national spelling bee and accepting the award in a red-checked dress and patent leather shoes--how she hated dresses. Amanda in high school--long hair tied back with a band, fingers typing furiously on the keyboard as she edited the yearbook. He'd helped her with grammar back then. Amanda in college--not needing him anymore, for grammar or anything else. Maybe never needing him again.

"Lieutenant?" Jefferies said.

Frank didn't answer. Just wedged himself into the pew with his daughter.

"I'll call for paramedics." Jefferies raced out.

"Honey, I'm here," Frank said, his voice a rasp.

She raised her head and looked at him with anguished, brimming eyes.

"It's okay now. I've got you."

Her lips quivered.

He wiped a drop of blood off her cheek.

"Can you get up?"

Amanda sucked in a breath and pushed herself from a curled position to her knees.

"Easy, Sweet Pea."

Her brows furrowed in a quizzical look.

He reached for her but she shook him off.

"No," was all she said.

Blood dripped down the side of her face. He reached in his pocket to get a handkerchief, realized he didn't have one. He yanked off his jacket and unbuttoned his shirt, glad he wasn't wearing a tie. Then he pulled it off and dabbed his daughter's head with it. It came away bloody.

"No," she said again.

Frank's heart dropped. "Let me help you."

She looked into his eyes. "I don't. . . I. . ."

"It's all right."

She allowed him to ease her out of the aisle.

He held her by the waist but her knees wouldn't hold her.

"Oh, honey." He lifted his daughter in his arms, and carried her to the waiting ambulance.

Chapter 26

March 24, 2011

Midnight

Frank caught a break when Amanda was transported to the same hospital his mother was in. It was after eleven p.m. when he snuck past some nurses and into Lizzie's room.

"Frankie, that you? What are you doing here so late? Oh my God, is anything wrong, is it--?"

"Ssh, mom, everything's fine. Just came to see how you were doing."

"At this hour? Don't give me that. What's going on? Have you seen Amanda? She hasn't been by to visit and I'm getting worried."

Frank pulled over the familiar orange plastic chair. "There are a few things you should know." He began to fill her in.

Lizzie said nothing, simply stared at him.

"Mom, close your mouth. Amanda is okay. That's why I came by. I didn't want you to hear it on the news or anything. In fact she's downstairs in the hospital. A few dings and scratches, but fine."

"Why didn't you tell me? I mean that she was kidnapped, my God."

"One, because I didn't know for sure until just a few hours ago. Two, because you weren't able to handle the information in a comatose state."

"What's going on? This is related to her friend's murder, isn't it?" Lizzie said.

"I believe it is. But you know I can't tell you anymore. I'm sorry."

"What've you got to be sorry about? You found her."

Frank leaned his elbows on his knees and wondered about his mother. Most mothers would be angry that his job had placed his family in jeopardy. But Lizzie was not only a cop's mother, but a cop's wife and a cop's daughter. She understood the life.

"Amanda's pretty amazing, you know," he said. "Kind of like you. How many young women would find the courage to escape like she did?"

"I know she's amazing. I'm glad you do. About time." She smiled. "Maybe now you can be the father she'd like to have."

"I'm not so sure."

"What do you mean?" she said.

"I don't know if I've got it in me. I'm still a cop. Still unavailable, emotionally, as Jeannie said. Being a cop and a father are kind of like an oxymoron. One cancels out the other."

"You're a lot like your father," she said.

He waited.

"Job came first, always. Oh sure, he loved us all. Dearly. But his sense of responsibility, of. . . duty, I guess, was even deeper than that love." Lizzie looked out over Frank's shoulder. "It took a while for me to understand. I almost left him several times. In the early days. But then something happened." She looked back at him.

"A little boy down the block was taken. . . abducted. Frank was the lead on the case. Kid was missing, oh, I don't know, maybe a week. Before that two other little boys had been found murdered not far from where this one was taken."

"I think I remember the case. Dad found him alive, though, didn't he?"

"Yeah, he did. I barely saw him that week. He only came home to shower and change clothes. I thought *I can't do this, God, this life isn't for me.* Then he found the kid, alive. And something in me changed. I finally came to realize what was important in life. It wasn't about me. It wasn't even about you and your brother and sister. It was about what was right, what was necessary. And I knew that deep in my heart. Saving that boy's life changed everything."

Frank's face creased into a wistful smile. "I wish Jeannie could have had that epiphany."

"Jean and I talked about that. Before you two separated."

"You did?"

"She heard what I had to say, but she couldn't get beyond her own needs." Lizzie sighed. "She wasn't a bad person, Jeannie. Just terribly needy."

"And I was oblivious to those needs."

"You have a chance now with Amanda."

"I'm not so sure Amanda really wants a relationship with her father. I think she blames me for--"

"For Jeannie's death. Maybe at one time," Lizzie said. "Not anymore."

Frank shook his head.

"Trust me."

"Well, I don't think she's feeling really warm and fuzzy toward me right now."

"That's it?" Lizzie smiled. "First of all, you may be a cop with all the baggage that goes with it. But Amanda's a lot like me. She's descended from a line of cops and, like me, I think she honestly understands what that means. She may not like it all the time, may resent it some of the time, but she knows what it means, for better or worse. She's a good girl, Frank. She loves you. Give her a chance to prove it."

He nodded.

"You, on the other hand. That's another story." Her eyes softened. "Do you want a relationship with her, Frankie?"

He smiled. "I've been giving that a lot of thought these days. And, yes, I do. But--"

"But on your terms. She'll understand. Have a talk with her. Get it all out. Let her know you care. It's easy."

"You are something else, Mom. Did anyone ever tell you that?"

"Everyone tells me that and not always in a complimentary way." She smiled. "You gonna catch the son-of-a-bitch that did this, right?"

"Yes. I'll catch him. Now, go to sleep. You've had a rough time these last few days. But you're going home soon. We need you to be strong. Who else is going to boss around the lot of us?"

"I'm glad you're home. Now my whole family is here."

He stood, leaned over and kissed her cheek.

"Tell Mandy to visit me when she's up to it." She winked then closed her eyes.

Frank felt like an elephant had been lifted from each shoulder. Now all he had to do was catch the killer and remove the remaining one that weighed on his back.

He ran into Jefferies outside Amanda's door.

"Where were you?" Jefferies asked.

"Visiting my mother upstairs. Jeez, it's like old home week at the hospital."

Jefferies chuckled. "Got a guard posted outside your daughter's door. Do you know how long he'll be needed?"

"I think she'll be going home with me this morning unless tests show otherwise." Frank rubbed his chin. "I need to go home, shave, shower and feed my feathered friend."

Jefferies smiled.

"Any news on Espinosa?" Frank said.

"Yeah. That's why I'm here. He's dead."

"What?"

"Uh huh, dead like in bullet to the brain, or whatever soft mush was in Espinosa's skull. Ballistics working on it now, but it looks like a .38 special."

"Jesus. Where was he found?"

"Flushing Meadows Park on a park bench. His truck was parked nearby."

"Must've run into someone who didn't like the botched up job he did as prison guard," Frank said.

"Got that right."

The two men looked at each other.

"You thinking what I'm thinking?" Jefferies said.

"Where was Luis Santiago tonight after we left him?"

Jefferies smiled. "Let me call in a few favors." He strode to the elevator.

Chapter 27

March 24, 2011

1:00 a.m.

Amanda was sleeping when Frank slipped into her room. He figured he'd check in on her before he went home.

Dexter. The bird would be starving and mega pissed. Heaven only knows what the apartment would look like.

Amanda opened her eyes.

"Hi," he said.

"Hey," was the response.

He moved closer to the bed and took her hand in both of his. She pulled it away.

"So, Sweet Pea, how're you feeling?"

She blinked a few times. "You haven't called me that in a long time."

"Do you want me to stop?"

She shrugged, turned her head away from him and winced.

"Neck hurt?"

"Everything hurts, even my pride."

"Why your pride?" he said.

"I feel stupid, letting myself get ambushed like that. God, how could I not have guessed something would happen to me?"

"Listen, Amanda. Don't blame yourself. This wasn't your fault."

"I should have known. When I found out about Steph, I should've known." Tears welled in her eyes. She swiped at them with her hand.

He opened his mouth to speak and she stopped him with, "Whatever."

Frank pulled over a chair. "Amanda, you are an amazingly brave girl. When I found your lock-up and saw you had escaped, I was floored. Incredible."

Her eyes found his.

"Yeah?"

"Yeah. Not many people could've done what you did."

Her lower lip quivered.

He took her hand again and she let him. "Right now, you need to rest. You need to heal. You've been through a hell of a lot."

"You don't have a million questions for me? What kind of cop are you?"

He smiled. "I have two million questions but they can wait. Yeah, I'm a cop. I'm also your father."

She turned her head away again.

"Which is something we'll have to address when this is all over."

She didn't move.

"I'll come back later." He stood, debating whether to kiss her or not. He decided not to risk a rebuff and walked away.

"I saw on the news that you're the lead on Stephanie's murder," Amanda said. "So you know a good deal already."

He watched her and waited.

"I can't rest now. Not with Steph's murderer running around on the loose." Amanda pulled herself up to a sitting position and Frank helped her fluff her pillows.

"It started just a few days ago when Steph and I were working on this story she was doing. You know about the Triangle fire, right? It's the hundredth anniversary, uh, what's the date today?"

"The 24th." He sat back down on the edge of the bed.

"God, it's tomorrow. Hers was a commemorative piece. When Grandma told me about Cormac and Fiona's association to the events in 1911, I thought I'd help Steph with the historical data. I got all jazzed when I found stuff that related to the fire itself." She paused. "We both wondered. . . what if we could get some interesting scoop on that angle, well, it could be more than commemorative. More investigative, you know?"

"You mean from the letter and Cormac's murder book?"

"How do you know about those?" she asked.

"Sorry, when I realized you were missing, I searched your computer, found the documents you wrote and the letter."

"Shoot. Guess victims have no privacy."

"Tell me about the kidnapping," he said. "I know a lot of the rest."

Her face reddened as if it was her fault.

"I was leaving my apartment couple of days ago, going to the office, when a big, fat pig of a guy grabbed me and covered my mouth with some rag. Must have been drugged because the next thing I knew I was in this room, ugh, my foot cuffed to a disgusting bed." She shivered.

Frank burned.

"He wanted to know about the story," she said. "What I knew, where the copy was. I kept telling him I didn't know anything and why did he want that, but he was just a hired gun, I suppose." She looked at her father. "Why on earth was Steph's story so important? I kept asking the creep if he killed her."

"What did he say?"

Her eyes welled. "He said no. He had nothing to do with that." She looked at him. "You know, I believed him too."

She wet her lips. "So what was so important about Steph's story that someone would kill her?"

"There may be a connection to the fire--perhaps the person that set it or set it in motion--is somehow a threat to someone living today. How and who we don't know yet."

"It was more than a fire. It was murder. You know about that?" she asked.

"Fiona. Yes. Lizzie told me."

"Arson and murder. A hundred years ago. Of course there's a connection today." Her eyes stared into space then she focused her gaze on him.

"Let's go, then. We've got work to do."

"Now, now, Miss Marple." Frank said. "There's time for that later. Right now you rest."

She looked at him, her face drawn in a pout.

"Tell me, Amanda, how did you ever manage to escape?" Frank touched her cheek and she backed into her pillows. Her face was drawn as if she'd lost ten pounds. Blue bruises circled her eyes and her lips were pale and chapped.

"Some water?" he said.

She nodded. He filled a glass with a straw and let her sip. He was encouraged when she touched his hand to take the glass.

"The fucker, excuse me, the creep, had me cuffed to the foot of the bed. The cuff was loose, though, and I was able to squeak my ankle through." Her eyes widened. "That's why it hurts so much. I forgot. Repressed it, maybe."

Frank tried taking her hand again. This time she let him.

"The door wasn't locked," she began. "The jerk. . . what was his name, do you know?"

"Salvatore Espinosa."

"He didn't think I was going anywhere. I snuck up into the house in case someone else was around and looked for a phone. Couldn't find it. So I ran out into the street. Then I heard his truck firing up so I just ran into the back yard and over the fence. I didn't know where I was or where to go, so I just kept running."

"Until you found the church."

She nodded. "I was so tired, I had to stop. Needed to call for help before he found me."

She paused.

He squeezed her hand.

"You know," she said. "I don't think he would have killed me. He even seemed a little sorry he got into this whole mess. I really--"

"What?"

"I think someone hired him and he wasn't too keen on murdering me. Maybe he wasn't paid enough."

Frank looked down but didn't respond.

"I guess I was out of it when you found me," she said in a soft voice. "How *did* you find me?"

Frank told her the sequence of events but left out any mention of Santiago.

"Funny. Why'd you figure I'd hide in a church? I haven't been to church since mom died."

"It was a safe house and since you probably didn't know the neighborhood, where else would you be safe?" Frank filled the glass of water a second time and handed it to her. "You are so brave. I'm proud of you."

Tears sprang from her eyes.

He touched her cheek with the back of his hand. "Listen, Amanda. I'm no shrink but I've dealt with people who have been through serious trauma."

"You mean PTSD?"

"You know much about it?"

"Just that after a trauma, you're likely to show some symptoms, mentally, that is."

"And physically. Something about the brain pathways being interrupted or not making connections."

"Why are you telling me this?" she asked.

"Because I want you to be prepared for. . . I don't know what. Bad dreams, insomnia, depression, any number of symptoms." He stopped, rubbed her hand. "And I want you to remember, it's not you, it's normal for this to happen."

"So plan on it, is what you're telling me?"

He gave a faint smile. "Just a possibility."

"You want me to see a shrink?"

"Wouldn't hurt."

She tightened her lips and looked down at her lap. She pulled her hand away from his. "Maybe."

"Good enough." To change the subject, he said, "You up for some news?"

She sat up taller. "What?"

"First, while you were, er, out of commission the last few days, Lizzie landed in the hospital. She fell going up the steps and broke a few bones."

"Oh no, is she okay?" Amanda struggled to sit up.

"Easy now, yes, she's okay." He paused.

"What? You're not telling me something. Is it about her cancer?"

"She slipped into a coma for a day during all of this, but she's fine now. Honest. Doctors say everything checks out okay."

"Oh my God. Grandma." She fell back onto the pillows, tears filling her eyes. "You're sure she's--?"

"She's back to her old fiery self. Asking about you every two minutes."

More tears.

"She's upstairs, would you believe?" Frank said. "You can visit later. Please, visit, or I'll never hear the end of it."

Amanda wiped her eyes and hiccupped a laugh. "I'm so glad."

"The other news is also not bad. Sal Espinosa is dead. Got himself murdered tonight."

Her eyes popped. "Really? Whoa. Someone killed that stupid gorilla. Huh." She looked at him. "I guess that's good news."

"You don't seem so sure."

She shrugged. "Maybe. Do you know who killed him? Is it the same guy who murdered Steph?"

"We think so."

"But you don't know who."

"We have some leads to pursue."

"Mysterious. Just like a cop," she said. "Dad?"

He waited.

"I want to work with you on this case. Now, wait, wait, hear me out. It's not what you think. Don't shake your head until you listen to what I have to say." She wriggled into a taller seat, drank and took a breath.

"I want to help solve Fiona's murder. I know it's connected to Steph's, somehow. Call me crazy."

He didn't say anything.

"Cormac tried to solve her murder, but apparently never did. I found his, what do you call it, murder book, right?"

"Yeah, I know. I've got it. You did a good job hiding it too."

"You found it?" she said. "How did you manage that? I thought I was so clever hiding it in plain sight."

"Hmm. I'm a detective, remember?"

"Grandma never noticed it?"

"Nope."

"Well, good. I put one over on her. Ha."

Frank grinned.

"Please, Dad. I want to do some research and see if I could figure out who murdered her and why Cormac was never able to solve the case."

"How do you know for a fact that he didn't?"

"You haven't looked at the murder book, have you?"

Frank shook his head.

"I know he didn't solve it because he was never allowed to open the case. NYPD wouldn't let him officially investigate. From his notes, though, it sounds like he pursued it on his own. Unofficially."

Frank looked at her, eyes narrowed.

"Well, it couldn't hurt for me to do a little historical investigation, could it?" Amanda said. "It all happened a century ago and yet there are strong connections to today, aren't there? I mean, Steph was doing a centennial story on the Triangle fire and I was helping her with some background and--"

"Okay, okay. Listen, when you get out of the hospital, you're coming back to my place for a few days."

"Am I still in danger?"

"Probably not, but I'd feel better if you were not in your apartment." He paused. "Besides Dexter needs some female companionship."

"Grandma told me about him. You're really a sap for animals, aren't you?" She grinned. "Ouch. My mouth hurts when I smile." She looked down at her hands. "Dad?"

"Yeah?"

"Can I come home with you now? I don't want to stay here. Besides, I want to meet Dexter."

"Amanda," he began.

"Please. I know I'll sleep better there. Please. Take me home with you."

Home. With him. That cinched it for Frank. "I'll go check with the doctor. See what he says."

"Thanks, Dad. Tell him I feel fine."

Frank shook his head.

"Later we'll both look through the murder book. Okay?" Amanda said.

"Okay, okay."

Frank slipped out of the room to hunt for the doctor, feeling good for the first time in days.

Chapter 28

March 24, 1911

Fiona had been back to work for only one week following the factory fire in February. The Triangle had been closed for nearly a month, a devastating blow for most of the women, including office workers.

On her first day back, she immediately looked for the *Soames and Slatten* file that she'd hidden under her typewriter. It was not there.

Could Dinah have seen it, filed it away? Could Bernstein have noticed it? Or Mike Sweeney? That set her heart to thrumming.

Today was Friday and she still had a tremendous amount of catch-up work to do. She hadn't time to do a thorough search, but she knew the file was not in her cabinet, nor anywhere else in her tiny office.

When she arrived, she was greeted as usual by an aloof bookkeeper who said, "All those folders need to be filed." Dinah pointed to a foot-high stack on the file cabinet. "I'll be in meetings for a few hours. See that it's done by the time I get back."

Fiona merely nodded.

Yes, your highness, your majesty, your queenliness.

The outer door closed. Dinah's office was empty. Now might be her only chance. Fiona stole a glance at the door and darted into the bookkeeper's office. She scooted over to the small filing cabinet in the far corner and opened the drawer marked S-T. She heard no noise from the outer hall, so she chanced scanning through the files. There it was. It had been switched from her cabinet to Dinah's.

Why? Do they suspect me of spying?

Fiona yanked it out and almost dropped it, her hands trembled so. *Soames and Slatten.* She opened it, began to read. But time had run out. She heard the elevator doors open and footsteps heading in her direction. Not Dinah's. Heavier. A man's.

Fiona quickly grabbed the most recent piece of correspondence, found the correct place in the drawer and stuck the file back in. She folded the letter, stuffed it into her pocket and closed the cabinet door barely a few seconds before the outer door opened and Mike Sweeney stepped in.

He looked around and spotted her from across the room. He moved slowly to Dinah's office.

"What are you doing here?" he said.

"I work here."

"Not in this office. That ain't your desk."

He marched to the file cabinet in two long strides and pulled open the drawer.

"This what you're lookin' for?" He held up the *Soames and Slatten* file.

"As a matter of fact it was."

Sweeney moved close to her. "Yeah? Why's that?"

"Because when I was filing, I found it in the wrong place so I was going to file it correctly."

"Yeah? Did you find it interesting reading?"

"What makes you think I read it?" Her voice sounded calm even to her ears.

"'cause you seem so curious about me. I think you got a crush on me." He grinned.

"Is there something in the file that's of interest, something I should read?" Fiona asked, unwilling to let him goad her into anger.

"Now that depends on how you look at it."

"How do you look at it, Mr. Sweeney?" Fiona tipped her head, tired of kowtowing to him, to Bernstein, to Dinah Lipschitz. Tired of playing the victim to their churlish games.

Sweeney's smile turned feral. His eyes narrowed, his lips thinned, and his Adam's apple twitched in his skinny throat.

"You know what I think?" He moved in closer.

Fiona did not back away.

"I think you did read the file and you--"

Fiona did an about face and walked out of the office and back to her desk.

"Don't you turn your back on me, you little bitch."

"I have work to do. Please leave."

"If I don't?"

"I'll scream so loud, the whole building will hear, not only Mr. Bernstein next door. And I'll claw the other side of your face, Mr. Sweeney, so it matches the first scar."

Fiona plunked herself down in her chair and began rolling paper in her typewriter.

Dinah Lipschitz walked in.

Thank God, Fiona thought. What would I have done? Sharpen my nails in the pencil sharpener for the attack?

"Mr. Sweeney," Dinah said. "Mr. Bernstein wasn't expecting you."

"No, he wasn't. I'll be back later, though. You can count on it." Sweeney moved to the door and wheeled about. To Fiona, "You and me, Babe, we've got more business to discuss."

Fiona swallowed a few times to moisten her dry throat. She slid her hand in her pocket to make sure the letter was hidden and continued her work. She felt an uncanny sense of euphoria at standing up to Sweeney. Clara would have applauded.

At closing time, she punched out, took the elevator down with the other workers and left the building. A glance around told her Mike Sweeney had not waited.

She hurried toward the streetcar stop, lifting her skirts and navigating mounds of horse dung on the cobbles. Around her, street vendors were packing up for the day, gossiping while their horses nickered and stomped their feet, impatient for their dinner.

People jostled by on their way home for the start of the weekend. She barely noticed, her mind exploding with so many thoughts about the letter in her pocket. When she arrived home, she was disappointed to find Cormac had already gone to work. He left a note:

Dearest,
I'm filling in for Lanahan, which means a double shift. See you tomorrow night. Kiss my boy.
Love,
Cormac

The clock on the mantel chimed six times she and realized she had a few minutes before she needed to pick up Patrick.

Fiona pulled out the Sweeney letter and read it over and over again, trying to make sense of it, not daring to believe, but afraid not to. Written on fine paper with a distinctive letterhead embossed in gold leaf was the title, *Soames and Slatten Private Detective Agency*. But what was in the letter made her heart roar, her legs tremble, even now. It was dated almost a week ago and alluded to something that would happen on Saturday next. Two things put the fear of the devil in her heart. First, it reminded her of the conversation between Bernstein and Sweeney that she'd overheard before the last fire.

Second, that monster Mike Sweeney had signed it. That did not bode well.

She mulled it over later that evening as she fed Patrick, put him to bed and took up her kitchen chores of washing the clothes and the dishes.

Ahh, Cormac, my love, why is it this very night you won't be here? When I need so badly to speak to you. Now that I've made up my mind, I will confide in you everything I know about Sweeney, the fires, the Triangle. Will I have the courage tomorrow?

Cormac needed to know her fears and suspicions regardless of whether she had tangible proof or not. He was her husband, he loved her, trusted her. He would believe her. What he would do as an officer of the law was another matter. They would deal with it together.

She felt immense relief at her decision.

Everything will be all right.

Then her mind flitted to Mike Sweeney and her mood blackened.

Fiona snatched up the letter and started to put it in a drawer. Somehow, she knew by instinct that there was danger there. She had to find a safe place for it until she could share it with Cormac. She looked around the room. First she thought of tucking it under the mattress, but that would ruin the paper. Then she considered the kitchen cupboard, but there were insects and an occasional mouse in there that might chew on it.

Her eyes caught a framed photo of her mother hanging on the wall near the bed. She pulled it down, took the backing off with a kitchen knife and flattened it inside the frame. There. That would do for now. She hung the picture back in its place, and dusted it off with a feather duster.

The next morning, Saturday and payday, commenced with the four a.m. chaos of readying baby Patrick for the sitter. Fiona felt the need to spend extra time with him today and Patrick seemed to understand. He smiled and cooed and didn't fuss as usual. She cuddled him and touched his chubby cheeks and marveled at how much he already resembled his father.

"What will the world be like when you grow up, little man? Will you also follow in your Da's footsteps and become a policeman? Will you go to college and become a lawyer or a doctor, a writer, a poet, a carpenter?"

The baby gurgled and grabbed her finger.

"You've got lots of time to think about that."

A knock and Mrs. Odermeyer poked her gray head in the door.

"Is young Patrick ready?"

"He's ready."

Fiona wrapped his blankets around him. With a smile, she kissed her baby goodbye.

Chapter 29

March 25, 1911

Cormac was summoned to the Asch Building at 4:48 p.m. The sound of alarm bells could be heard throughout the city.

My God, Fiona is working today.

At least eight wagons were at the site or nearby. He pushed his way through the mobs. Engine Co. 72 was parked in front on Washington Place. Streets were in chaos and it took several minutes to discern the situation. Firemen lugged hoses through the building's front doors, hoisted ladders from the wagons. He looked upward.

The three top floors were ablaze, smoke mushrooming out of windows of floors eight and nine. With all the din and confusion, Cormac could not make out whether anyone was trapped inside. It was then he saw a sight that would haunt him waking and sleeping for the rest of his life. Women's faces at the windows, their mouths opened in silent screams, their eyes filled with terror as they stared out. Some, he felt certain, were looking directly at him.

Fiona. Was she up there?

He gathered his wits with great effort, rushed through the main doors and tried to get to the staircase. Battalion Chief Edward Worth put his hands out to stop him.

"There's no getting up there now," he said. "Best go back and help crews with the rescue on the street."

"My wife is up there. I've got to go." He pushed past Worth, but the Chief caught him by the arm and several firemen rushed over to stop him.

"Nothin' you can do now." Worth shouted to be heard above the clamor of fire bells, flapping of water hoses, and the gushing of water.

Firemen held onto him.

"My wife. I've got to do something. Don't ye understand? My wife is up there."

"Pray, man. That's all you can do now."

"We need help here," a fire fighter near the main doors called out.

"Go, sir, please, we need your help outside." The Chief pushed Cormac in the direction of the caller.

Numb, Cormac turned to do as asked. He guided several survivors to ambulances, all the while watching for Fiona. He spied the door to the staircase, now wide open with men running in and out. When he saw his chance he made a dash for the door, bulled his way through and up the first set of stairs. He passed fire fighters on the way, lugging equipment as fast as they could despite the heavy weight.

He made it up to the fifth floor when he was stopped.

"Can't go up," a fireman said, as he struggled to hold onto the giant hose. "Too much smoke." His voice testified to that.

Cormac refused to give up. He leaped around the hose and took the stairs two at a time. Now the smoke and heat reached him and he found his lungs struggling to take in breath. One more floor and he collapsed onto the top step coughing and wheezing. Several men took him by the arms and led him back down.

"No, no, my wife is up there. I can't let. . . I have. . . please, she's. . ." He stopped in a fit of coughing.

Back in the lobby, he leaned against a wall, trying to breathe and calm his racing heart. He dragged out a blackened handkerchief and wiped soot and sweat from his eyes. Or was it tears?

He made his way through the lobby to assist more injured. Once outside on the street Cormac was prevented further entrance into the building by rescue workers blocking the way. Things were going from bad to worse.

Only three minutes had gone by yet the hopes of saving more survivors had severely diminished. Frantic, he hurried up and down the street, pushing his way through throngs of bystanders.

"Fiona," he shouted. He fought his way through the crowds, searching, calling.

He heard a man howl.

"My God, look."

Cormac craned his neck.

Nine stories up and still he could hear the smashing of glass as someone punched out a window. Shards and splinters of all sizes rained down as the watchers below screamed and rushed away from the deadly deluge.

What happened next shook him to the core. A woman climbed onto the windowsill. She stood, looking out as if she were going to step from a trolley. Then she jumped. Rather than be burned alive she shot out into the air and plummeted, feet-first, then head-first, to the sidewalk with a ghastly thud. Another woman leaped, her hair afire. And another. Whump, whump. The sound reverberated in his ears. This could not really be happening.

He kept watching, could not turn his eyes away as one young woman sprang forth from the window, waving her arms and trying desperately to keep her body upright, until the very instant she struck the ground.

Mother of God, this must be a dream, a nightmare. Was there no other way out of that inferno? He heard shouts that doors were locked, that the elevator was out of order, that the fire escape had crashed to the ground.

Cormac's head reeled as he knelt beside one of the jumpers. She had landed on her back and her head had hit the ground so hard, her face was twisted and contorted, barely recognizable as human.

When he turned to another, he could barely contain his stomach and had to crawl away to retch in a corner. He remained doubled over, trying to catch his breath.

Dear God. Where is my Fiona?

His brain couldn't focus clearly enough to comprehend the circumstances and he acted purely on adrenaline. His past experience in no way had prepared him for such a calamity and he foundered. By the time Cormac recovered his senses, he realized dozens of jumpers had made their way to a brutal death, some badly burned beyond recognition, some, amazingly, intact.

In his dazed state, he somehow noted that firemen had attempted to raise a ladder to the building. The ladder was too short, reaching only to the sixth floor. Other firemen rushed over with a life net. Two girls flashed through it, breaking bones beneath it on the sidewalk. He was sure the same ghastly thumps could be heard miles away.

Cormac arched his neck to look up again. Now a young man was assisting a girl to the window sill on the ninth floor. He lifted her and held her out, then, horrors, dropped her. The same young man did it again, three times, four. The girls allowed it and fell to their eternity without a complaint. Then the young man himself was on the window sill, his trousers aflame. He turned back to the building as if for a final look and flung himself into the air.

The whole tragic event was over in less than thirty minutes, the longest minutes of Cormac's life. The flames engulfed the top floors but now had no flesh to consume. The fuel was spent, the humans all dead.

The Chief staggered toward him. "It's over. Over." He pointed to Cormac. "Go to the Pier, man. They need help."

Cormac stumbled through debris and bodies on the wet street. He pulled himself together in order to help facilitate the moving of bodies to the Charities Pier at 26th Street near the East River. On a normal day a long way off; today, an interminable distance.

By the time the convoy of wagons with dead bodies and coffins arrived, the gloomy dock took on a funereal bleakness that was hard to fathom. Cormac shuddered at the sight.

Along with other NYPD officers, he laid the bodies face up in the pine boxes so relatives and friends could identify them–thousands upon thousands of family members, the line continuing down the pier as far as the eye could see.

"Men," the Chief said, "identifying the dead will be no easy task."

Cormac stared down at the coffins. The fire and the jump had mutilated many of the corpses beyond recognition.

"Look to the belongings for identification," Worth continued. "An unusual shoe, a piece of jewelry or clothing that the relatives can recognize."

Dear God.

Wailing, crying, screaming filled Cormac's ears until he wanted to plunge into the river to end the cacophony. Still no Fiona. He prayed that was a good sign and forced himself to tend to his duties. Perhaps she'd escaped early. Is home now tending to Patrick. The longer he went without finding her, the better her chance.

These thoughts in his mind, with a sick heart he propped up the dead girls, trying to be as gentle as possible, for fingers fell off easily as did clumps of hair and skin.

Then the thing he dreaded, his worst fear, lay stretched out in front of him. Her face wasn't badly damaged, but even were it so, he would have known her by her hair. That lovely auburn hair. It was his own love, his dear wife, Fiona.

No, please, dear Lord.

He dropped to his knees. Cormac didn't realize until later that he was sobbing, not until a colleague came and touched him on the shoulder. He waved him away.

Cormac held his wife in his arms and wept, unable to comprehend life without her. And their tiny son. How would he grow up without his mother? His sadness turned to anger. Was the fire chief correct? Had the doors been locked, blocking the workers' escape? Why had there been no fire escape? So many questions.

Finally, spent, exhausted, he reached around her waist to straighten her body for he couldn't bear to see her twisted so. That's when he felt something.

Cormac pulled back instinctively and his hand came away bloody. Was she broken like a doll in a fall? He rolled her over to look, wanting, but not wanting to see. In the small of her back was a large, oblique patch of blood, torn through her dress, as if something had pierced her.

He reached for a lantern to have a better look, all the while trying to block the sounds of despair and grief. He tore at her clothes to see the injury and found himself gawking at a small cruel wound, one he'd been familiar with in the past on many occasions. There were black, sooty dots still visible around the deadly hole. Cormac was struck dumb with the realization of what had transpired. He shook so hard he nearly dropped her. His worst horrors were confirmed.

His beloved Fiona had not died in the fire. She'd been shot to death at close range.

Samuel Battle found him weeping. Nothing could stem the tears and Samuel feared his friend might die of a broken heart.

Some minutes later, Cormac stood up, gently resting his wife in the crude wooden box on the Pier. Samuel held onto his arm and tried to soothe his pain.

But Cormac had stopped crying. There was a new hardness in his features, a coldness in his eyes and a firm set to his chin. His wife had not died in the fire. This was a homicide. Fiona had been deliberately, brutally murdered. And Cormac was, after all, a policeman first. . . by genetics, by instinct, and by aspiration. He had a crime to solve. The most important case of his life.

That was what he planned to do.

Chapter 30

March 27, 1911

Two days after the fire, Cormac handed his baby son to Mrs. Odermeyer. He couldn't stand to see the pity in her eyes, so he hurriedly donned his jacket and cap and left the apartment. He ran into Samuel Battle.

"What are you doing here?" Cormac said.

"I came to see you."

"Well, I'm on my way to work." Cormac walked past him and out the front door.

"Cormac, let me help you."

"Help me? How?"

Battle dropped his eyes.

"Can ye bring her back then?" Cormac raised a hand. "I'm sorry for that," Cormac said. "You din't deserve it." He started up the street.

Battle followed. "Did you talk to the Captain?"

"Aye."

"And?"

"And he said, "Officer Mead, are you mad? Have you taken leave of your senses? A hundred and forty six people were killed in that fire. Many by jumping out the window. I know your wife was one. And I'm sorry. But good grief, sir, a fall like that could cause any number of injuries. To think she was shot, well, it's outrageous. I won't have you following that line of questioning."

"But what did he say about the gunshot wound?"

"He said 'fuck-all' to the gunshot wound, to quote his precise words. "

Battle's mouth dropped open.

"He said she was no doubt pierced by debris as she landed nine stories on the pavement."

Battle blinked.

"So I asked him if he would allow me to bring her to the morgue for the coroner to view. Just to be certain."

"Yeah?"

"And he told me in absolute terms, no. He had City Hall, the Triangle families, and the unions down his throat and he wouldn't be dissuaded from his decision. To quit badgering him and to move on with my life."

Both men stopped walking and faced each other.

"I'm sorry," Battle said.

"You know, Samuel, it crossed my mind that Fiona's ties with Clara Lemlich and Frances Perkins had something to do with the captain's attitude. Perhaps he believes that I, too, am in league with the unions. And, by God, I'm tempted."

"What are you going to do now?"

"I'm going to work the case by myself and when I have the evidence I will attempt to present it to the captain once more. At that time he'll have no choice but to launch a full scale murder investigation. If not, I will climb higher up the chain of command if I need to. Job be damned."

"Are you sure you want to do this?"

"What would you do, if it was your wife murdered?"

A hint of a smile touched Battle's lips. "Same as you."

"Aye. That's it then."

"Cormac, have you considered talking to LaGuardia about this?"

"I did and Fiorello has been most kind in his sympathies. But right now he's embroiled in local politics and I don't wish to make trouble for him."

"Does he know you found a gunshot wound?"

"Nay, I never mentioned it."

"Well, I saw what I saw," Battle said. "I'm with you on this, Cormac."

Cormac nodded but a smile wouldn't come.

"What now?" Battle asked. "You do realize that conducting a personal investigation without sanction of the department could mean the end of your job?"

Cormac looked at him. "And yours. I'm ready for the consequences. But I don't want to hold you to them. You're free to do as you like, Samuel. I will understand, my friend."

Battle looked at the ground then up at Cormac. "What can I do to help?"

Cormac felt a surge of warmth for this man and tears welled in his eyes. He choked them down.

"I need proof and the only way to get that proof is to search for evidence, piece by piece, bit by bit."

"But where, how?"

"I'll start first with the remains of the fire."

"Surely there's nothing left there," Battle said.

"Probably not, but I intend to investigate every avenue open to me." He stared into space as if lost in memories.

"And after that?"

"After that, the body of the murder victim."

Fiona.

An hour later, Cormac stood on the sidewalk across the street from the Asch Building. Pedestrians walked slowly by, looking up to the top three floors and its broken windows, burned-out framing and blackened brick, reliving the tragedy.

Cormac shuddered when he thought of Fiona leaping out the window and falling to her death. Perhaps the bullet wound was a blessing. Perhaps she was dead before she hit the ground.

Jaw clenched, he crossed the street and stopped in front of the main doors to the building. His eye caught bloodstains on the pavement that the hoses couldn't remove. He walked up and down the street, picking up, studying pieces of debris, bits of clothing, even a shoe. One lonely shoe pressed against the cold cornerstone.

Next, he moved through the police barricades and guards into the main lobby. His uniform gained him entry without a word. The black and white tiled lobby floor was scuffed and scraped from the firefighting effort. Cormac could see trail marks of fire hoses being dragged through the corridors and up the wooden steps, now splintered and ruined. Everywhere he saw water damage, for the hoses had continued to spew water long after the fire was extinguished.

Indeed, the Asch Building would need major renovation and not only to the top three floors. The entire building was shut down.

The elevators were out of commission so Cormac started up the steps, careful to avoid the broken treads. When he reached the eighth floor he pushed through a door onto a production level, which should have been lined with machine tables and cutting tables. The lower of the three floors of the Triangle Shirtwaist Factory.

In his ten years' experience as a policeman, Cormac had dealt with burglaries, robberies, assaults, domestic violence, knife fights and murders. Murders by strangulation, poisons, beatings, knifings, and shootings. He had virtually no practical knowledge of fires. And what he saw now made him weak to the knees.

A shout came from below.

"Cormac, you up here?"

"Eighth floor, Samuel."

Battle walked gingerly over the debris to reach him. "Maybe this will help." He waved a sheath of papers.

"What is it?" Cormac asked.

"Statements from witnesses and survivors. Maybe someone remembers somethin'. Never know." Battle wrinkled his nose. "Man the stink in here is revolting."

"Read one of those statements aloud, let's see if there's anything worth bothering about."

Battle flipped through the pages. "From one James R. Tooson, blah, blah, here we go. *'There were cries of fire from all sides. The lines of hanging patterns began to burn. Some of the cutters jumped up and tried to tear the patterns from the line but the fire was ahead of them. The patterns were burning. They began to fall on the layers of thin goods underneath them. Every time another piece dropped, light scraps of burning fabric began to fly around the room. They came down on the other tables and they fell on the machines. Then the line broke and the whole string of burning patterns fell down.'*"

Cormac looked around him at the devastation. "There's the line that held the blouse patterns, or what's left of it."

"Jesus, it's tough to tell what kind of business had taken place here. I mean, there's not a table or chair that hasn't been melted, or broken, not a sewing machine that's even recognizable--just twisted chunks of metal."

"The walls and ceiling, scorched black," Cormac said and pointed. "You could still almost feel the heat radiating from them."

"Yeah."

"I'm going upstairs," Cormac said. "Why don't you keep reading? See if there's anything we need to follow up on. Maybe someone saw the gunman."

"Okay. You sure you want to go up there?" Battle said. "I mean that's where--"

"I know."

Cormac left Battle to his file and trudged up the stairs to the ninth floor. The death trap where many workers leaped to their deaths. Above the intersection of Greene Street and Washington Place, workers had been forced into the corner. They had no choice but to jump.

Cormac gazed at the ruins. Oddly, some of the tables whose sewing machines were connected to a common drive shaft were all that was still standing. He walked over wreckage to the windows. Several window sashes were gone, given way as the trapped workers pushed against them. His fingers came away blackened.

Questions plagued him. Why had Fiona been out on the floor? The offices were in a back corner office on ten, yet she went out the window right here. There was an exit there, closer to her work area. So why did she not escape? Did she run out to find a friend? To warn the workers? But the fire started on the eighth floor, how would she have known about it? Cormac licked his lips in exasperation. Had Fiona known this was about to happen? How?

"Cormac?"

"Here."

"Couldn't really find anything in the file that was useful. I'll go through it more thoroughly tonight."

"All right."

"Thought you might need a hand here, you know searching through the remains."

"I'm trying to figure out what path Fiona might have taken. From her office to the production floor to the window." Cormac's brain kept firing new possibilities.

"If she were shot in her office, she never would've made it this far. And the stippling around the wound demonstrates she was shot from no more than two feet away, so her killer was close. Maybe close enough to shoot and then push her out the window. There would have been so much noise, so much bedlam, the sound of a gunshot would've gone unnoticed."

"So we can assume that Fiona was shot somewhere between the office and the windows, probably closer to the windows," Battle said.

Cormac strode to the windows. He knelt down and carefully moved shards and fragments of the remains with his fingers. He sifted through rubble and trash lying in the path.

"What are you looking for?"

"The spent casing."

"Shit. You think it might be here?"

"Depends on what type of gun he used," Cormac said.

Battle dropped to his knees and helped Cormac pick through the rubble inch by inch.

What seemed like hours later the men were at opposite ends of the room, sifting through the detritus. They'd found nothing.

Slowly Cormac rose. "I think we're done here."

"I'm sorry, Cormac," Battle said.

"I'm sorry, Fiona." Cormac said to the empty cavernous space.

The men began the trek down to the first floor.

"There's still much to be done," Cormac said. "Thanks for your help, Samuel."

"Where to from here?"

"To the task I dread the most."

Chapter 31

March 27, 1911

Cormac strode through the darkened hallways, shouldering the satchel he carried. Samuel Battle followed close behind.

"I ain't never been in a morgue," Battle said.

"I thought all cops had been to a morgue."

"All cops who have been cops for more than a few months, mebbe."

"Good a time as any," was Cormac's reply. "You'll be ahead of your colleagues. I just wish I could find the bloody place."

"How come they don't have signs or something?"

"Might scare a lost visitor out of their wits, I guess," Cormac said. "What are you doing?

"I'm tiptoeing on this creaky wooden floor."

"Why?"

"Don't want to wake the dead," Battle said.

After a number of wrong turns, they found themselves in front of two large swinging doors.

"This'll be it, then."

"How do you know?"

"Instinct," Cormac said. "Most morgues are in the basement of a hospital and at the far end of the building. Out of sight, out of mind."

"Well, this is University Hospital and we're at a dead end," Battle said. "So how come there's no one around? No doctors, no nurses, no orderlies. Not even a janitor?"

"It's two in the morning."

"But this is a hospital," Battle said. "Never mind."

Cormac turned to his friend. "This is it, Samuel. There's no turning back now. I will understand if you just turned and left. Right now."

"No sir."

Cormac's mouth felt dry as a desert wind and his heart was about to implode in his chest. He was relieved that Battle was going to see it through.

"You all right?" Battle asked.

"I've examined many dead bodies over the years, but this is different somehow."

"Jesus, God, man, different somehow? This is your wife. Course you're all in knots." Battle shifted on his feet. "You know, the same is true for you as for me. You can quit this now."

Cormac squeezed his eyes shut and willed his body to ease up. "No."

He pushed open the doors. Blackness greeted him.

"What's that?" Battle said.

"What?"

"That smell. Phew. That what I think it is?"

"I forgot to warn you about, er, hospital smells."

"I know what alcohol and antiseptic smells like," Battle said. "That's a hospital. This ain't the same. Is it, uh, I mean--?"

"It's the smell of death. Breathe through your mouth."

It was eerily quiet.

"Where the devil is the light?" Cormac said. "I know electric lights were recently installed in the hospital. Check for a switch on the wall. Should be near the door."

He felt his way around the perimeter of the room, touching countertops of cold, unforgiving marble, bottles and jars, utensils for unimaginable probings.

"Here," Battle said. "A turn-switch on the wall."

"Crank it up."

A popping sound preceded the light and Cormac and Battle blinked in the brightness as banks of bulbs overhead flashed on.

"Wow," Battle said. "I like that. Light. The brighter the better."

Cormac set his bag down on the floor, caught his breath and listened. The only sound was the dripping of water nearby. His eyes scanned the autopsy room and came to rest on a table near the center. A table made out of metal, perforated with scores of holes to drain body fluids. The table was empty.

"Is that table what I think it is? And those holes what I think they are?"

"You should trust your instincts more, Samuel."

"So, um, what happens if the coroner shows up, or the police captain or--"

"Quit yer worrying. We'll deal with one thing at a time. Besides, we'll be out of here soon."

"It's probably too late to be asking this but without the coroner here to corroborate any evidence, who says the captain will believe you?"

"He may not. But you'll be there to verify it, won't you?"

"Yessir, I will. But I'm just a colored cop. Will they believe me?"

"They will. They'll have to. By the way, thanks for getting the body brought in without anyone knowing. I don't think I could've pulled that off."

"Yeah. Well, I still have a few friends. One of 'em happens to own a horse and wagon."

"How did they get her down to the morgue without anyone stopping them?"

"I don't know and I don't wanna know."

"All right. Now where is she?"

"Not in this room," Battle said. "There's no dead people in here."

"Through there." Cormac spotted another set of double swinging doors across the room and he made for them. Inside, he turned on a new bank of lights.

They stopped and stared at five stretchers, each with a body covered by a sheet.

"My stomach feels like a butterfly flew in, got trapped and is flappin' like a sum-bitch to get out."

"Just wait here a minute." Cormac lifted the sheets, one by one. No Fiona. He released the clench in his jaw.

"Over there." Battle pointed.

On the other side of the doors stood a lone gurney. On top was a corpse covered by a dingy white sheet.

Slowly, Cormac moved to the body and even more slowly, lifted the sheet. There lay Fiona. Cormac tried to swallow but his throat felt parched beyond dryness.

"Hey, I hear something. Footsteps?" Battle said. "Someone's coming. Shit."

The doors swung open and a little man in thick glasses wearing a stained blue jumpsuit walked in pushing a mop and pail.

"What are you doing here? Who are you?" the jumpsuit said.

Cormac stretched to his full height and walked over to the man, whose name said *Moe* on his name tag.

"Moe," Cormac said, tapping the name tag and edging the man back against the wall. "You the night janitor?"

"Uh, yeah."

"Ah, yes, Moe. Well then, as you can see from my uniform, my good man, I'm a police officer from NYPD. And this is another officer. We're here to investigate a crime and I will thank you to step outside and let us do our work."

Moe squinted his eyes at Cormac then at Battle and finally glanced at Fiona's body.

"Uh, what crime is that?"

"What crime would bring me to view a dead body, do you suppose?"

"Uh, murder?"

"Exactly. This may be a homicide case, so please get out of my way. I don't want the evidence contaminated."

"But, but, why, I mean, isn't the coroner supposed to--?"

"In case ye haven't noticed, Moe, there's been a major catastrophe at the Triangle Factory. There are one hundred and forty or more bodies that need attending to. The coroner is quite busy, you see. He's very probably at another hospital morgue as we speak."

"Oh, yes, of course, yes." Moe shook his head. "Terrible tragedy. Terrible."

"Don't you have work to do as well?" Cormac waited. "Can you start your cleaning in another room? We won't be long here."

"Yes, yes. I, yes." Moe scurried out of the room.

Cormac wondered if he had really convinced him or if he would be back with the authorities.

"We better move fast now," Cormac said and hurried back to Fiona. He pulled off the sheet without hesitation, took only a few seconds to study her face then rolled her onto her side.

Battle stepped closer.

"Oh man, oh man. Miz Fiona," Battle whispered.

"It's all right, Samuel."

"But she's, I mean--" Battle turned away.

"Of course she's naked. Look, look at this, Samuel. This injury was not from any fall."

Gently, Cormac rolled her onto her stomach and quickly pulled over his satchel. He reached in and pulled out a Box camera, an original Brownie Model from Eastman Kodak. He had already loaded the camera with film, so made quick work of the task.

"Take a look."

Battle leaned over to study a dark reddish hole.

"See? The wound is surrounded by gunshot particles embedded in the skin."

"Like a tattoo that can't be wiped away."

"And there's no soot around the bullet hole," Cormac said, "which proves the shooter had been only a foot or so away."

Did Fiona know he was behind her?

Cormac blinked the thought away.

"Let me get photographs." Cormac clicked the camera six times and obtained close-ups of the bullet wound and longer view shots so there would be no doubt that the bullet was, indeed, in his wife's body.

Then a thought struck him that was so wonderful and terrifying at once.

"What's that funny look on your face?" Battle said.

"Photographs of the wound are useful, but the bullet itself would be much more so."

"Whaa? You gonna take the bullet out of her? Oh man, oh man."

It would be like defiling her body, Cormac thought. His mind rocked back and forth.

"It's evidence," he said finally.

The two men looked at each other over Fiona's body.

Cormac turned, hurried to the counter where the surgical instruments gleamed in the artificial light. He snatched up a scalpel.

Breathing deeply several times, he leaned down and probed the wound. Within minutes, he'd dug out a bullet.

".32 caliber," he said.

"It's intact."

"Yes, It obviously didn't hit bone. Get the camera." Without hesitation, Cormac lay the bloodied bullet next to the wound and took several more photographs.

"Now what?" Battle asked.

"Tomorrow I'll have the body removed to the mortuary. With the Triangle travesty to contend with, the coroner will never even notice."

"I mean, the bullet," Battle said. "What'll you do with that?"

Cormac held up the bullet. "This damning piece of lead will be key to finding our killer." He dropped the bullet into an envelope he had in his pocket and sealed it. "Put the camera away," he told Battle.

He settled the sheet back on his wife and whispered, "Ah, Fiona, my love, I'll find out who did this to you and make him pay. Dearly."

By three thirty in the morning, the two men were back on the street.

"Samuel, you're a good man. I thank you for what you did tonight. Now go home and get some rest."

Samuel just gave a small nod. "Cormac?"

Cormac waited.

"What will you do now?"

"Now I will gather all my notes and diagrams, the photographs of the scene, of the bodies in caskets, the mourners and the roll of film I just shot in the morgue. And of course, the bullet. I will make detailed reports of everything I know and observed at the scene of the fire. I will document everything I can learn from others-- firemen, policemen, reporters, witnesses, even family members of the dead--"

"You realize you may wind up going head to head with the wealthy owners of the company--?"

"And, in turn, the political engine that runs our fine city." Cormac smiled. "Yes, I expect so."

"It's one thing to lose your job," Battle said. "It's another to lose your life. These are dangerous men to mess with."

Cormac said nothing.

Battle held out his hand and the men shook.

"I for one am going to go home to bed," Battle said, face somber. "Might get in two hours before my shift." He swiveled around and headed off down the street.

Cormac was locked in place, unable to move. Only his mind was active. His head bobbed up and down as thoughts ran into each other, his list of tasks taking shape. He suddenly felt lighter as if a great burden had been lifted from his back. He had a job to do and it was assured it would change the face of the investigation into the Triangle fire and Fiona's death.

His first task: to construct a murder book.

Chapter 32

March 24, 2011

6:00 a.m.

Frank woke early after barely four hours of sleep. He lay in bed staring at the ceiling. Amanda was in the next room and he didn't want to disturb her. She needed to get as much sleep as she could in the healing process.

She had a rough time sleeping, though. At four he heard her cry out and hastened into her room. When he woke her from her dreams, he'd tried to hold her, comfort her, but she shoved him away. Frank feared she'd be having nightmares for a long while. Everything that had happened to her in the last few days, all she'd been holding at bay, was finally setting in.

He would try to convince her to see a shrink, although he didn't have much confidence she would. A lot like him that way. Didn't need any help, could go it alone. Amanda wouldn't talk to him about her feelings. Talking to him about her private thoughts would ultimately lead to talk about 'Jeannie' and Amanda would avoid that at any price.

He wondered how much she knew about her mother. Frank felt a headache coming on. Had Jeannie been unfaithful? Did he know that for sure? Did Amanda suspect? Should he discuss with her? What good what it do?

No. If it was true, she didn't need to know the truth about the woman she worshipped. Amanda wasn't that strong right now.

Frank hoped that working on this case would take her mind off those painful memories that surfaced now that he was back in her life.

He heard the toilet flush and a soft squawk from Dexter. Dumb bird. He loved company and Amanda took to him right away. Dexter had ogled her from his perch. Then, tentatively he'd flapped to the couch and tilted his head so he could check her out more closely. Finally, he hopped onto her arm when she held it out. From then on it was mutual love.

Frank got out of bed and headed for the shower. He heard the water running in the other bathroom. His daughter was in the shower too. By seven he was dressed and in the kitchen making coffee.

Amanda walked out, dressed in sweatshirt and jeans. Dexter spoke first, " 'ello, 'ello. Awwwp."

Amanda smiled. "Hello to you too, Dex. How are you this morning?" She rubbed his chest with her finger as he preened. "You are a happy bird, aren't you?"

Dexter whistled.

"He's in love," Frank said. "Not surprising."

"You're sure he's a he?"

"That's what the vet said. Hopefully, she knows the difference." Frank poured coffee in two cups, handed one to Amanda.

"How did you sleep?"

She tossed a shoulder.

"I mean after your dream?" he said.

"Okay."

The puffy bags under her eyes said otherwise.

She sat at the dining room table and drank.

"Any breakfast?" he said.

"Not hungry."

He sat and faced her across the table.

"Are you mad at me? I mean, of course, you're mad at me."

"Why would I be?" she said.

"Oh, because I abandoned you for half of your life. Because I've been back in New York a less for almost three weeks and only saw you once." He paused. "Because I'm a lousy father. Let's see, what else?"

"You're a cop. Naturally you're a lousy father."

"Ah, Frick and Frack. I guess they go together."

"Don't you think so?"

"Is that a bad thing?" He tried a smile.

She didn't answer.

"Okay, then. What now?"

"You tell me," she said.

"I'd like to take another shot at it."

"At what?"

"You're not making this easy, are you?"

Amanda looked at him, then down at her mug.

"Look, Amanda, I can't pretend to be something I'm not. I don't really know what I want to do or how to do it. I know I missed a lot of your growing up. And, your teenage years. But, well, I'd rather not miss all the rest." He stopped, waited.

His daughter was silent.

"Can we try to be friends? Maybe not father-daughter stuff, yet, but just friends. Try to communicate better? Who knows, we might find we have a lot in common. Might even like being together. Like each other."

She looked at him.

"Okay." He got up, poured more coffee, looked out the window.

"I'll make a deal with you," she said.

He didn't turn.

"Let's work on the Triangle murder together and see how we, er, gel, you know? Then we can talk more about our relationship."

He faced her. "Deal." He couldn't ask for more.

"Now, where is the murder book?" she said.

8:30 a.m.

Frank left to pick up breakfast from the local Einstein's. When he returned, Amanda had spread out the contents of the murder book on the dining room table.

"Look at these," Amanda said. "When I untied the leather strings around the book, there were pages of notes, photos, sketches and this envelope."

Frank looked over her shoulder at the photos, stark black and white images, harsher and more gruesome than any color pictures could portray.

"This picture must be of the Triangle Factory floor right after the fire. God, there was nothing left. A pile of twisted metal and debris. Ugh." Amanda shuddered. She set it down.

"And this. . . this must be Fiona." She held up a photo depicting the body of a woman, unclothed and fragile. "She's still. . . I mean. . . you can tell who she is. She's recognizable. Poor Cormac."

Frank gawped at the photos, a strange sadness tugging at him.

"Isn't that amazing, considering she went out a ninth story window?" Amanda said.

He coughed, cleared his throat. "Let me put these bags down." He walked quickly into the kitchen and unpacked the bags. Then he brought food out.

Amanda sat in the same position, gazing at the photos.

With two large mocha containers, bagels and cream cheese, and a gold and blue Macaw whistling happily on his perch, Frank broke into Amanda's concentration.

"Let's begin at the beginning," he said. "With Cormac's description of the tragic day."

Frank picked up the loose pages of Cormac's notes and read out loud for several minutes.

"It reads like a thriller," Amanda said. "Right from his arrival at the Asch Building to the moment he discovered Fiona's body on the Charities Pier that night. . . and everything in between. The fight to reach the workers, the locked doors, the flimsy fire escape."

Frank added, "And the horror of watching over a hundred workers, mostly women and young girls jump to their death."

"Jeez, it was a hundred years ago. . . today," Amanda said.

They fell silent. Dexter did too.

"Dad?"

"Yeah?"

"Was Cormac in the same precinct as you?"

"No. In the early part of the century there was an 8th Precinct on Mercer Street. He was at the Mercer Street Station."

"Hmm. Not the 6th," Amanda said more to herself.

"Nope. They abolished the 8th, building and all, in the fifties or sixties."

"Abolished the whole precinct? Weird. No 8th even now? How come?"

"Good question. More for you to research."

"Never mind. Back to Cormac's writings. Go on."

Frank read the summary report out loud with the stunning revelation about Fiona's gunshot wound.

"It's still hard to accept. My great, great, great grandmother was murdered. But why? Why would someone kill her?" Amanda paused. "It had to be related to that letter, it had to be. Where is it, do you have it here?"

Frank scouted around on the table, pushing papers and news articles around until he found it.

"I agree with you, Amanda. The murder *is* tied to this letter, which, in turn, is tied to the Triangle fire."

"Arson," Amanda said.

"I've got Sergeant Jefferies looking into these names." He held up the letter. "See if there's a link to someone today."

"So Fiona found this letter somehow, probably at the Triangle factory itself, and maybe this guy Sweeney realized it, worried that she would take it to the authorities." Amanda waved a hand in the air. "Wow, talk about conspiracy theories. This is like a Hollywood script."

Frank rubbed his stubbled chin.

"What are you thinking?"

"If Fiona chanced upon this letter and realized it was dangerous, why didn't she tell Cormac?"

"How do you know she didn't?"

"Intuition," he said. "If she gave it to Cormac, why was it hidden in the back of a picture frame?"

Amanda blinked.

They sat thinking for a while.

"Do you think this may be the first murder book ever constructed?" Amanda said.

Frank held the battered book in his hand. "1911, NYPD. I can check, but I wouldn't be surprised. That's pretty astounding in itself."

"What's the real purpose of a murder book, anyway?"

"To document the crime. Notes from witness interviews, sketches of scene, diagrams of body and wounds, photos. Lists of all evidence found, weapons, trace, basically everything connected to the crime scene."

"Did you create one for Stephanie's murder?" she asked, a tiny catch in her voice.

"Sergeant Jefferies did. I'll be adding to it." He touched her shoulder.

"In Cormac's murder book," she said, "it looks like he made personal notes in the margins."

Frank flipped the pages gently. "Yes. That's not typical. Usually the investigator keeps to the facts, no outside comments."

"Apparently Cormac added his own thoughts in this one."

"Which makes an even stronger case for this being the first murder book ever created," Frank said. "Over time, they've evolved and today they're limited to the facts. No notes, no theories, no guesses."

Frank and Amanda looked at each other and then down at the murder book.

"Seems almost sacred," she said.

"Shall we begin?"

Chapter 33

March 24, 2011

9:00 a.m.

"Looks like Cormac set down the events in chronological order." Frank read:

"March 26, 1:15 a.m. Followed Fiona to morgue, but there was so much chaos, could not get the attention of anyone.

March 26, 4:30 a.m. Returned to Triangle site and attempted to talk to Captain. So many people clamoring around him, he paid me no heed. Will try again to see him tomorrow.

"What's that in the margin?" Amanda said.

Frank turned the book sideways. *"Must open formal homicide investigation."*

Amanda spoke. "I guess he never did. What about his son, Patrick Mead, your grandfather? I never got to meet him."

"No, he died in 1975."

"He also became a cop," Amanda said. "Do you think he knew what happened to Fiona?"

"Cormac would've had to tell him and share this book with him, or Patrick found it after Cormac's death. If he did, maybe he picked up the case that Cormac couldn't solve."

"And maybe, if Patrick had no better luck, maybe he passed it down to your dad, Grandpa Frank," she said.

"Could be how Lizzie is aware of it."

"Keep reading."

March 26, 7:30 a.m. Began a search of eighth and ninth floors of Triangle. Could not find any evidence of a gun or bullet casing."

He stopped reading. "Bullet casing? Why would he be looking for that?"

"What do you mean?" Amanda said. "Isn't there always a spent casing ejected when a gun goes off?"

"Only if an automatic or a semi-automatic is used. Not an old-fashioned pistol. I didn't realize they had automatics back then."

"How do we know what he used?"

Frank looked at her. "More research. Maybe you can find out what kind of gun he might have used in 1911. If Cormac was looking for a casing then there must have been automatics, but what kind?"

"Sure, yeah. I can check." She started jotting notes.

Frank returned to Cormac's report.

"March 26, 11:00 on until nightfall. Assisted with fire investigation, clean up, and notification of deaths to families."

"How awful," Amanda said. "146 deaths. Fiona."

Frank turned the book sideways again. "More notes. *Dear friend Battle accompanied me on this mission to morgue even though not part of official case. Thanks be to God, could not cope alone."*

"Battle?"

"Sounds like the name of his friend. Also a cop? Amanda, write that down too. Maybe his name is in the NYPD archives."

She did. "Go on."

"Brought camera. I planned to take photographs of her wound to prove that this was a case of murder whether the coroner agreed or not. After removing covers on some four or five bodies, I finally found her. Without a moment's hesitation, I turned her on her side and took several pictures, enclosed herein.

"I then attempted to remove the bullet itself from her back and photographed that as well."

"Holy shit," Frank said. "He had the bullet?"

Frank grabbed for the envelope, which had been tucked between the last page and the cover of the murder book, and now lay on the table. He fumbled the flap, finally opened it, then dropped it.

"Easy, Dad, here let me."

Amanda opened the envelope and a piece of hard metal bounced out, rolled off the table and dropped to the wood floor with a sharp rap.

Amanda reached down.

"No, wait," Frank said. He crouched on his knees.

Amanda did the same. "Oh my God, oh my God. It's the bullet."

"Don't touch it," he said.

"Is that red stuff, is that blood?"

Frank ran into the bathroom for tweezers. He lifted it by the tongs and held it up to the light.

"Unbelievable. This looks like a .32 caliber. That'll help in your research. Look for a semi-automatic with that caliber." He set the bullet gently back on the table and ran a hand through his hair. "And, yes, that's blood."

Frank burst out laughing.

"What?"

"Way to go Cormac. He knew how to preserve the evidence. Kept the blood-coated bullet dry within the paper envelope. We may actually be able to do DNA testing."

"Even though it's a hundred years old?"

"Depends on how degraded the blood truly is." He tucked the bullet back in its envelope. "There's even some blood in the envelope. Maybe there's hope."

"But why do DNA? Don't we know it's Fiona's blood?"

"Most likely. But to prove it we'd have to compare it to other blood."

She looked at him with a faint smile on her face.

"Other blood? You mean yours. . . or mine?"

"Let's take a closer look at the photographs," he said.

He spread them out on the table, brought over a magnifying glass. Both of them studied the prints for several minutes. One portrayed Fiona's back with a grisly hole clearly visible.

"Looks like a gunshot wound to me," Amanda said. She turned to Frank for confirmation.

"It is a gunshot wound. I'd say fired from ten to maybe fifteen inches away. No more than 24 inches."

"How do you know that?"

"See these black dots around the hole? That's tattooing, particles of soot embedded in the skin. If the range was closer, say three to five inches, there would be soot, which would have been wiped away."

"So in this case, the distance is a good thing. Like you can *see* the soot marks. Proving it's a gunshot wound."

"Exactly." Frank sat back. "Plus these pictures of the bullet next to the wound tell it all."

"Why shoot her, though? Let's say she had the proof that the fires were started for insurance money. Why not just push her out the window?"

"Picture the scene," Frank said. "Fiona was at work on March 25th. We know that because she died in the fire that day."

"She had the letter hidden at home," Amanda said. "We know that because I found it."

"Those are facts we know for sure. Exactly where was she when the fire started? On the eighth, ninth, or tenth floor? That we don't know." Frank paused. "When the fire started on eight, it wouldn't have taken but a few minutes for all floors to be alerted. What would she have done?"

"Try to help others get out?"

"According to all accounts, the fire took over the two floors so fast, there was no time for anything except to save yourself," Frank said. "So what did she do? Run for the stairs, the fire escape?"

"In a matter of minutes, Fiona would have realized it was too late. Like the others."

Amanda walked around the table and stared at the photographs. "At some point prior to the fire, though, she must've confronted the killer. Or how would he know she was a threat to him?"

"True. But think about it. The plan was to set the fire *after* the workers had gone for the day, like the earlier fires. What if he found out right then, at the end of the day, that Fiona knew about the arson plot. What if, instead of waiting for everyone to leave, he decided to start the fire earlier, using it as a cover up?"

"Holy cow, he planned to kill all those people just to eliminate one woman?" Amanda said.

"Maybe he thought there would still be time for most of them to get out," he said. "But the killer couldn't risk Fiona escaping."

"And a bullet would be a faster, surer way to shut her up," Amanda said. "While the others found an escape, Fiona would be left behind and her body burned."

"The evidence with it."

They both went quiet.

"What are you thinking?" she asked.

"How to open a century-old murder case."

His cell chirped. "Mead." He listened for several minutes then said, "You're shitting me?" He listened again.

"I think we need to meet--Katz's, an hour? Right." He clicked off.

Amanda looked at him. "I understand if you have to go. I'll continue the cold case investigation here."

Frank smiled. "That will make you-know-who happy."

Dexter flapped and squawked.

"There's still an officer outside the door, so you're safe here. Still, better lock the door."

She gave a tiny nod. "Hey, who needs to go anywhere? I've got the Net and I've passwords to *Lexis-Nexis* through the *Times*."

He smiled.

"Okay to feed Dex?"

"More than okay. Necessary."

Amanda ambled into the kitchen.

Frank sat immobile for a moment, mulling over what Jefferies had just told him. Things were heating up.

Chapter 34

Jefferies was gobbling up his usual corned beef on rye sandwich along with a Dr. Brown's when Frank slid into the booth bench across from him.

The sergeant swallowed his bite as Frank ordered a coffee.

"Don't you ever eat?" the sergeant said.

"When I have to. Don't you ever not?"

Jefferies grinned around the dripping mustard.

"Tell me what you found." Frank's coffee came and he just looked at it.

"Sweeney. Mike Sweeney. The so-called operative for *Soames and Slatten* did have descendants. Three sons, two daughters, six grandchildren and four great grandchildren."

"And one of those grandchildren is like I told you on the phone--"

"Sanford Russo's mother," Frank said.

"Sanford Trevor Russo. Our very own anti-corruption First Deputy Commissioner," Jefferies said. "His mother, ergo, he himself, is descended from a Master arsonist. Nice."

"What did you say? Sanford what?"

"Sanford Trevor Russo. Why?"

"Nothing. I guess I didn't realize his middle name was Trevor." Frank's mind did a somersault. The initials STR struck a chord.

He'd have to make a quick stop at Orchard Street to check on that later but he could swear he'd seen those exact letters.

"Lou, did you hear what I said? Russo's related to an arsonist."

"Yes. I heard." Frank leaned over. "Actually it's worse than that. It's not just arson, it's murder."

"You mean the workers killed in the fire?"

"I mean one in particular who was shot in the back to keep from talking."

"You kiddin' me?"

"I'm not."

"How the hell do you know this?"

"Because I'm descended from a long line of cops and my great grandfather, Cormac Mead, was at the Triangle fire and found the body. I'm sad to say the murder victim was his wife, Fiona, my great grandmother."

"Holy shit, I mean Holy fucking shit," Jefferies said.

"My sentiments exactly."

"How did you find out?"

"I've got the murder book, the one Cormac wrote, diagrams, photographs and--"

"And?"

"The bullet that killed her."

"Jesus. From a hundred years ago?"

"A hundred years ago *tomorrow*, in fact." Frank held out a plastic bag with the bullet.

Jefferies took it by the edge and examined it.

"Holy fucking shit."

"You said that already." Frank smiled.

"Want me to run it through ballistics?"

"Yeah, and the blood through DNA. I'll stop by and give a sample to the lab. Amanda is researching possible weapons that could have been used at the time."

Jefferies had stopped eating, which, to Frank's mind, signified the extent of his shock.

"What? Weapons?" Jefferies said.

"According to Cormac's notes, he believed there was a casing from the bullet at the crime scene. He looked but he never found it."

"Looked where? At the scene of the fire?"

"Apparently. With all the debris, it's not surprising he didn't find it."

"Interesting about the gun, though." Jefferies picked up where he left off on his sandwich. "An automatic in 1911?"

"Or a semi-automatic .32 caliber."

"Shit."

"The story that Stephanie Brandt was writing with my daughter's help," Frank said, "must've raised a few red flags to our chief. He wanted it killed before it hit the stands."

"So the First Commish has a little chat with the slimeball, Santiago, and sends him off to do his dirty work."

"Or he just plants the seed. Maybe all Russo wanted was for Santiago to talk to Stephanie, get her to quit the story. But Luis, dumbfuck yahoo, sees his chance to get ahead, please the boss."

I wonder how pleased the boss is now," Jefferies said.

"Here's what I think happened." Frank finished his coffee as the waitress came by. She stopped and looked at him, one hand on a hip.

"So how come ya nevah eat?" she said.

"How come everyone's concerned about my eating? I'm not hungry."

"Hmmph," was the reply.

"Besides, he eats enough for both of us." Frank pointed a finger at Jefferies.

"Hmmph," again. She refilled his cup. "Best food in the world and he don't eat." She sauntered off.

Jefferies grinned, head down in his plate. He looked up at Frank. "G'wan. You were going to tell me what you think happened."

"Yeah. Russo tells Santiago that the Triangle story needs to go away. Santiago has a chat with Stephanie. She says no way and, if she's anything like my daughter, is more determined than ever to write it. She, then, talks to Amanda who tells her she has a personal connection to the Triangle fire, not knowing the full extent of that connection.

"Santiago follows Stephanie to the Asch building that day to try to be more convincing. The class ends, she's alone, looking out the same window that so many women did a hundred years ago and the wheels begin to turn. Why not just push her out? Who would know? Who would tie the Triangle story, a harmless commemorative piece, to her murder? Reporter killed, end of story, literally."

Jefferies nodded. "Makes sense."

"But when Santiago nabs Stephanie's computer from the scene he finds out about Amanda. Now he's got a problem," Frank said. "Not only does he have to get rid of her, he has to get information from her. What does she know, who has she told about the story?"

"Don't you find it weird that he's already dated her a few times? Just a bizarre coincidence?" Jefferies said.

"Unless he knew about Stephanie's story and Amanda's connection to Stephanie weeks ago."

"Somehow I doubt that."

"Why?"

"Santiago doesn't seem like the patient type. He gets something in his twisted head, he acts."

"Okay," Frank said. "Maybe it is a coincidence he was dating her. I hate that."

Jefferies picked up the thread. "So now our boy has a problem. Amanda knows him. He's got to keep his pretty face out of the picture. He hires Espinosa to keep her locked up, beat her up a bit, scare her into giving up the information."

Jefferies paused. "But what information? I mean, what did Amanda really know?"

"Nothing at the time," Frank said. "But Santiago didn't know that. He was afraid she'd expose the Triangle fire and Mike Sweeney. She might even find the connection between Sweeney and Russo. And then Santiago would take the fall."

Frank leaned back in his seat. "No, Amanda was definitely a liability."

"Luckily for her, Santiago's not a rocket scientist and he hires Espinosa, who's dumb as a rock. Botched the whole bloody deal. Wound up dead for his trouble, too."

"And," Frank said, "With Amanda escaping, Santiago has no choice but to get rid of Espinosa."

"Himself?"

"I think by this time, the asshole doesn't trust anyone to do the job."

Both men sit thinking for several minutes.

"Anything on the gun that killed Espinosa?" Frank asked.

Jefferies shook his head. "Big zip on that."

"So now the question is how do we prove any of this?"

"What about Amanda? Is there anything she can link to him?"

"She doesn't even know he's involved," Frank said. "I haven't mentioned his name."

"Why not?"

"She's feeling a little vulnerable right now."

"I must say I don't care for her choice in men."

Frank smiled. "Yeah, well, it was only one movie and one dinner date, according to him. And, of course, she's not going to see him again. I'll make sure of that."

Jefferies said. "Actually, I was thinking just the opposite. What if Amanda, er, you know, gives Santiago a call, offers to cook him dinner--at his house, of course--and while she's there, happens to take a look around."

"Forget it. I'm not using her as bait."

"Hey, look, I understand how you feel, but she's the only one who--"

"No. It's way too dangerous."

"Not if we were right there," Jefferies said.

"Right where? In her pocket?" Frank sighed. "Forget it." He stared hard at Jefferies."

"Okay, okay."

"Did the crime team find any evidence of Santiago at Espinosa's place?" Frank asked.

"No. He probably was never there."

"What about phone records between the two?"

"Even Santiago's not that stupid." Jefferies paused. "Lieutenant?"

Frank looked up.

"You're going to have to tell Amanda about Santiago."

"Yeah, I know. Crap."

Jefferies blew out loudly through his nose. "Right now we don't have probable cause to look at Santiago at all. Nada."

"I know, I know."

"So what now?"

"I need some time to think," Frank said. "Something will come to me."

He didn't tell Jefferies what he wanted to think about. Maybe he was being a fool but he believed that Cormac Mead would help him resolve this case as well as the hundred-year-old cold case of Fiona's murder.

Chapter 35

March 24, 2011

3:00 p.m.

Frank had put it off long enough. He was back at home, watching Amanda poring over the Internet for information on automatics in 1911.

"Amanda, there's something we need to talk about."

"Yeah."

"Amanda?"

"What?" She stopped, looked at him.

"We need to talk about Luis Santiago."

"Luis . . . what? How did you know about him?"

"Long story."

"I've got time," she said, her voice sharp-edged.

He told her what he knew. She listened in silence.

"I don't believe it. You're all spying on me. Grandma, Aunt Irene, and now you."

"This is a murder investigation, Amanda. No one is sacred."

"But what makes you think he's involved?"

He told her about his meeting with Santiago, that he'd followed him on a hunch and caught him with Espinosa.

"God damn it. You actually talked to him about me? I don't believe this. What am I, chopped liver? You couldn't talk to me? How could you do that? I feel like a stupid child."

"I tried to talk to you. That's when I left you all those messages. When you were locked up in the basement of Espinosa's dump." He paused. "I'm sorry, honey, but I was afraid for you. I had to do whatever I could to find you."

She fell silent, collapsed on the sofa. Dexter flew over and sat near her but didn't make a peep.

"Is he really mixed up in this?" she asked.

"He's definitely connected to Espinosa, which leads me to believe he's at the heart of it all."

"Does that mean he murdered Steph? God."

"We don't know for sure."

"What do you think?"

"I think he murdered her."

"How could that happen? I mean, he's NYPD, he's--"

Amanda rubbed her eyes. "How could he get to the position he's in? Is he legit or what?"

"Good question. Jefferies is doing a thorough background check on him now."

"Wasn't there one done when he was hired?"

"Yes, but we have reason to suspect it wasn't done properly. That higher ups were pushing his app through."

"I can't believe I didn't clue into him."

"Why would you? You had no idea."

"I should have when he kept asking me all these questions about Stephanie's story, about the Triangle fire, about--" She shook her head.

"Remember, Amanda, these are still only theories. The only proof we have is that Santiago and Espinosa met at Santiago's house that one night."

"The night I escaped." She looked down at her hands. "What proof do you need?"

"Something physical would help like a gun, a written confession, something like that." He smiled, reached out and brushed her cheek with his hand. "Don't worry, if he's guilty, we'll get him."

"Does he think I'm a threat to him?" Amanda asked.

"You are a threat to him." He rubbed his chin. "I don't think he'll come after you. It's much too dangerous for him now. He knows we're watching. I'm watching."

Amanda played with her hands.

"Look, you go back to your investigation. Anything you can dig up that might help."

Amanda twirled strands of her hair. "Dad, um, I was hoping to visit Grandma. I'd really like to see her, you know?"

He nodded.

"Can you drop me off at the hospital? I'll stay a few hours then you can pick me up, if you're worried about leaving me."

"Sure. She'll be happy to see you. Maybe she'll quit nagging me."

They grabbed their jackets and headed out into a rainy, windy March day.

Amanda stuck her head back in the door.

"Later, Dex."

Awwp.

He dropped Amanda at the hospital and on the way back, Frank made a quick stop at his mother's apartment. He had to either confirm or deny his suspicions. Those letters had been niggling at him all morning.

In the spare bedroom, he made directly for the closet, reached up to the first shelf and brought down a small wooden jewelry box. Jeannie's.

He sifted through some of the more expensive pieces he had bought his wife over the years, knowing someday he would give them to Amanda. A pearl ring, an emerald pendant necklace, a charm bracelet and a silver rope chain with a diamond heart. At the bottom was a gold band. Her wedding ring. Something moved in his chest and Frank realized that no matter how many years passed, he still missed his wife. His hand shook as he brought it out, held it up with two fingers.

He dropped it as if it burned, then kept searching until he found what he was looking for. A gold filigree bracelet Frank had not given Jeannie. He may have been oblivious to her feelings, but he knew what jewelry he'd bought over the years.

He picked it up. Something inside of him withered. Engraved on the bracelet in delicate script:

To my love, J, from STR. Always.

Chapter 36

March 24, 2011

4:00 p.m.

Luis Santiago waited in the downpour outside Manhattan Memorial. He'd caught a glimpse of the red-haired bitch as she jumped out of her father's car. The bruises on her face were still visible and that gave him a modicum of satisfaction.

Took him back to his days in the Bronx, when he made it a career to bed all the white girls in the hood. Just for bragging rights. Women loved him. White women especially. He was exotic--dark, handsome, smart and sexy. Oh yeah.

Seems like a thousand years ago. What was it, ten? In ten years, he had developed a brand new persona. Street wise cop with the NYPD. Respected and on a fast track for promotion thanks to Russo. He laughed at that. Russo. He had him in the palm of his hand. And Santiago wasn't done with him yet. Russo owed him big time.

The rain came down hard. Santiago tucked himself tighter into a tobacco shop doorway and after three tries managed to light a cigarillo. He pulled his collar high and his hat low so no one would recognize him.

"Fuck this shit."

He sprinted across the street, climbed back into his sedan and settled in to wait. No sense getting wet. The car fogged up with smoke and he wiped the windshield so he could watch for the little slut. He considered snatching her when she came out of the hospital. Nixed that. Too many witnesses and she'd fight like a banshee.

Time was running out and he had to move fast but he had to be careful. That fuckin' Lieutenant would be watching his daughter closely now. No. Luis Santiago would play it smart and wait until the right moment presented itself. One thing he knew. He could not let her escape this time. She knew too much.

He didn't have long to wait. Amanda Mead burst out the hospital doors moving fast.

"What the--?" Santiago hissed.

She hailed a cab.

Santiago started his car and followed a car length behind. Pulled into midday traffic.

Within fifteen minutes they were approaching 42nd Street and the Queens Midtown Tunnel. Queens? Why the hell was she going to Queens? He gritted his teeth and followed.

Across the East River, Santiago continued to follow on the I-495. The same way he drove home to Forest Hills every day. Was it possible she was returning to the place Espinosa had kept her captive? Why would she go back to that dump?

He held his breath but the cabbie didn't turn off on I-278, the road he would have taken through the New Calvary Cemetery to get to Jackson Heights.

Where the fuck was she going?

Several miles further the taxi turned south on Queens Boulevard. Shit. He could close his eyes now and drive to his own house blindfolded from here. After a few miles they reached Yellowstone Boulevard and headed south again to Fleet Street. The cab stopped half a block from his house.

Santiago held his breath as if the bitch could hear him breathing. What the freakin' hell was she doing? Was she going to see him? In the middle of the day?   She knew he worked at NYPD.   No, something else.

He pulled closer to the cab as she got out and paid the cab driver. Then, glancing over her shoulder, she started walking, slowly, to his house.

4:30 p.m.

Frank arrived at the hospital and went straight to his mother's room.

"Frankie, what are you doing here?" Lizzie asked.

"Can't I come by to see you?"

"Sure you can." She smiled. "I'm going home tomorrow. Ain't that grand?"

"It is, Mom. Very grand." He gave her a kiss on the forehead. "Are you all set with a ride?"

"Irene's got it covered."

"Where's Amanda? I dropped her off a little while ago."

"You just missed her," Lizzie said.

"What?"

"Amanda. She said she had a few things to do and would be back."

"She left the hospital?"

"I don't know. I guess. Why? Problem?"

"No, Mom. No problem. Listen, I've got to get back to work."

"Talk about a short visit," Lizzie said.

"Sorry about that. Will you call when Amanda gets back? I'll pick her up."

"I'll call. I'll call. Frank?"

He turned.

"She's okay, isn't she?"

"Of course. She's fine." He winked. "We're both fine. I've got to get going. See you later."

Frank walked out of the room and dashed down the hall. He asked at the Nurse's station, hurried up and down hallways. Then he thought to try her cell phone. Connected with her voice mail. He left a message and knew he sounded angry. Angry and worried.

Where would she go? Didn't she know she was still in trouble? He speed-dialed Jefferies.

"Jefferies? Can you get over here to Memorial? Amanda's missing again." He hung up without explaining.

He paced the hallways, bumping into nurses and interns, paced again. Ten minutes and Jefferies was walking toward him. Frank pulled him into a small waiting room.

"Jeez, Frank, where'd she go?"

Frank knew what the sergeant really wanted to say was, "Can't you control your daughter?"

"I don't know. That's why you're here. To help me figure it out and fast."

"Okay, okay. What was the last thing you guys talked about? Something that prompted her to go somewhere, do something, know what I mean?"

"Yeah, yeah. I told her my suspicions about Luis Santiago."

"Was she surprised?"

"She was but she took it well. More like she couldn't believe she was duped by the scumbag."

"What else?"

"We talked about the fact that there was no physical evidence linking Santiago to any of the crimes. That we couldn't tie Espinosa to him directly. Or the Stephanie Brandt killing." He stopped, rubbed his forehead to help him remember. "That's when Amanda asked about Stephanie's computer. I told her it was missing."

Jefferies waited.

Frank looked at Jefferies. "Shit, she's going to Santiago's house to find the computer."

He leaped out of the chair and ran down the hallway, down the three flights of stairs and out to his car. Jefferies stayed on his heels. In the car, Frank turned north and headed to the Tunnel.

"God damn, would she really do that? Go to Santiago's house?" Frank said.

Jefferies got on his phone instead of answering.

"Marta, say is Luis around? This is Sergeant Jefferies." He listened. "What do you mean?" He listened again. "Thanks."

"Not there, is he?" Frank asked.

"He's been gone for hours. She has no idea where he is or when he's coming back. Acting strange, she said."

"How so, strange?"

"Missing appointments, canceling appointments, snapping at everyone in the office, more than usual even."

"She said that?" Frank asked.

"Exact words, scout's honor."

"Sounds like Santiago is a bit uptight."

"Ya' think?"

Frank turned the corner and ran into a traffic snarl.

"Amanda, what the hell are you doing?" he pounded the steering wheel.

"Look, Lieutenant. Your daughter assumes Santiago is at work. She has no reason to believe he's onto her or is anywhere near his house."

Frank snarled.

"Cut her some slack. She's just trying to get you the physical evidence. The proverbial smoking gun."

"Yeah."

"Too bad she doesn't realize it won't be any good if she breaks in to get it," Jefferies said.

Frank groaned. "Hell with the evidence now. I don't want her meeting up with him. Christ, what if he's been following her? That's why he's nowhere to be found. Maybe he's been watching her since I brought her home."

"Explains why he's been missing in action the last day or so. He'd have to be pretty frickin' crazy to go after her now, though. With all of us watching."

"He's a megalomaniac. He doesn't think we're watching. Arrogant prick," Frank said.

"I don't know about that. This is your daughter, a homicide detective's daughter, he's messing with. How can he not think you're keepin' an eye out? What the fuck is he thinking?"

"He's thinking that Amanda is the last obstacle in his path. With her out of the picture, he's home free."

"Man, can he be that stupid? Does he really believe we haven't connected the dots yet? Jesus. Maybe he is that stupid."

Horns honked around him and brakes squealed.

"Put the bubble on top," Frank said. "I'm sick of this freaking traffic."

5:30 p.m.

Santiago watched as Amanda made her way up the front door to ring the bell. When she got no response she moved around to the side of the house. Looking for a way in, he thought. Then she was out of sight around back. Fuck. The kitchen door might be open. Damn cleaning woman always forgot to lock it.

When Amanda didn't come back within a minute, he knew. She had gained entrance to his house.

He exited his car and, eyes alert, walked to his front door. He unlocked it and entered silently, ears tuned for sounds. Treading lightly, he made his way to his office, his sanctuary. He'd decked it out with antiques, or so the salesman at *Corner Galleries* claimed.

Queen Anne, Victoria, or Queen somebody. All he knew was the pieces were dark and massive, the better to impress with.

The bitch had found it first and was searching through his desk, opening drawers, riffling through the file cabinet. Then she opened a narrow closet and went through the shelves, pulling out folders. Finally she lifted a small box down from the top shelf. She set it on the desk and opened it. Her eyes bulged as she picked up a white Mac laptop decorated with pink flower decals.

"Stephanie," she whispered.

"So. I see you found it."

Amanda jumped a foot yet managed to hold onto the laptop.

"Clever girl to come here. But you know it's against the law to break and enter."

"I didn't break in," she said, breathless. "The door was open."

"But you're here illegally and going through *my* things in *my* office in *my* house," Santiago said with deadly calm. "How do you thing the law will view that?"

"Like they should. You're a freaking murderer. And this will prove it." She held it up.

He smiled and took a step toward her.

"That doesn't prove a thing. There's nothing in it."

"Even if you wiped it clean, the question remains, why do you have it at all?"

"I am on the police force. Perhaps I'm planning to turn it in as evidence."

"A little hard to do when it's hidden in your closet," she said.

"I think you've been watching too many CSI's."

"If you're so sure this can't be used as evidence, why don't you let me take it and leave? Take your chances." Amanda threw her chin out and started walking toward the door.

Santiago laughed. "I don't think so. I've come this far. You don't think a little white bitch like you can stop me?"

"What are you going to do, kill me too?" She sucked in a deep breath and started past him. "You can't stop me."

He pulled his .38 from his pocket and pointed it at her chest. His face wore no expression but the hint of satisfaction. "This can."

Chapter 37

March 24, 2011

6:00 p.m.

Frank had Jefferies turn off the siren about a mile from Santiago's house. Then he pulled up Fleet Street.

"That's his car," Jefferies said.

"No way to know if Amanda is inside." Frank got out of the car and rushed up to the front door. He turned to Jefferies who was right behind him. "Frontal assault. Keep your weapon at the ready."

He rang the doorbell, then, impatient after two seconds, pounded the door. Finally, he shouted, "Santiago, it's Lieutenant Mead. Open up." He pounded some more.

"I'm going round the back." Frank took off, Jefferies following.

They found the kitchen door unlocked. Frank opened it and stepped in.

"Santiago, it's Mead. Where are you? I know you're here."

Frank burst through the door between kitchen and living room, shouting, "Santiago, come out now."

He spied a room off of the living room and moved, gun leading the way. Jefferies was behind him.

With his left arm, Frank pushed open the door. Santiago's office.

Jefferies nudged him, pointed to the desk.

Frank spotted the laptop with pink decals. He turned to Jefferies. "Stephanie's?"

Jefferies said nothing.

A noise upstairs like something heavy dropping to the floor. Frank prayed it wasn't Amanda.

Jefferies did a quick search downstairs then nodded. Frank took the stairs two at a time. The upstairs hallway was empty, four doors, two on the left, two on the right, all closed.

He burst through the first door on the right, gun drawn. Nothing.

Jefferies kicked through the second door and shook his head.

A scuffling noise from the last room on the left.

"Santiago, come on out. It's over," Frank shouted. He stepped closer to the last door, while Jefferies kicked open the third. Nothing.

"Amanda? Are you here?" Frank called. No answer.

He reached for the doorknob, twisted it. Locked.

"Santiago, one more chance. Don't make this harder on yourself. You still have a chance to explain your story."

Silence.

Suddenly Santiago exploded out of that room, shooting wildly. The men ducked and dove into the other rooms.

Santiago made a break for the stairs. Frank leaped out and tackled him in the hallway. The two men crashed to the floor and rolled. A shot blasted a hole in the wall. A second exploded.

Jefferies crept out of the bedroom, gun drawn. He pulled out his cell and called for backup and an ambulance. He followed the two wrestling men as they fought near the top of the stairs. Just as they were about to go over, Jefferies grabbed Frank's arms and the two cops watched Santiago pitch and roll down the flight of wooden steps, roaring in pain and rage.

Frank started down but Santiago had already rebounded and split for the front door.

"Fuck." Frank took after him. He staggered out the front door and could hear a car start up. Tires screeched as it barreled down the road.

Jefferies called in the vehicle information and turned to Frank. "Shit, Lieutenant, you went and got yourself shot."

Frank looked at him, then at his left arm. The shirt was drenched with blood.

"Siddown, lemme take a look at that," Jefferies said. "Medics on the way."

"Amanda." Frank groaned. He pushed Jefferies aside and launched himself up the stairs. Jefferies followed right behind him.

At the fourth bedroom he pushed open the door. Amanda was lying half-unconscious with a new bruise to her head.

"Baby, you okay?"

She rolled over, touched her head and said, "Call me Sweet Pea."

Frank smiled.

"What happened. . . you're bleeding," Amanda said, forgetting her own injuries. "Oh God, Dad, were you shot?"

"I'm okay. Just a scratch."

He slumped over on the bed.

11:00 p.m.

That night, while Amanda slept in the second bedroom, Frank went back to Cormac's murder book, flipped through the journal entries. A bottle of pain pills sat on the coffee table. His injury had only been a flesh wound but it bled like a son-of-a-bitch and he still felt woozy.

Amanda came out, rubbing her eyes.

"Why aren't you sleeping?"

"Can't." She joined him at the dining room table.

"Feeling any better?"

"Yeah, just a headache. Which I deserve." She sighed, sat down. "How do you feel? Take any of those?"

"I'm fine. No pills. They blur my detective abilities." "I'm sorry, Dad. That was really stupid of me."

"He could have killed you, you know. He would have killed you."

"I know. But at least now, there's hard evidence. Right?"

"Yeah. Hard evidence and a dead daughter. Great trade off."

She reddened and reached over to touch the pink-flowered laptop. "Poor Steph. All over a hundred year old murder." She looked at her father. "Did you find anything new in Cormac's murder book?"

"Nothing really," Frank said. "Apparently Cormac was unable to get the murder case opened, despite the sympathy from some of his colleagues."

"You mean there never was a case file about Fiona?"

"No."

"What about Patrick?"

"He didn't open the case either."

"Or Grandpa?"

"Apparently not."

"Why?"

"Lots of reasons," Frank said. "Maybe Patrick knew about the murder book, kept it hidden and forgotten, and his son, my dad, never actually saw it. Remember too, no one saw that letter until you found it by accident. Probably even Cormac knew nothing about it."

"You mean Fiona hid it and never showed Cormac? Why? Why didn't she go to him with it? He was a cop."

"Maybe she planned to but got killed before she could. My guess is she deliberately chose not to show it to him."

"Why?"

"Several reasons. One, she was afraid he would get into trouble on the force by pursuing any hint of arson at the Triangle. Remember the owners were very powerful people."

He drank from his Coke can.

"The other reason, the one I'm leaning toward, is that Fiona was afraid he wouldn't believe her, even with the letter."

"What?"

"He was a cop with the NYPD when the City of New York was run by the politicos of Tammany Hall. I hate to suggest it, but maybe Cormac was part of that machine. He wanted to succeed, get ahead, and the only way was by playing with big boys. Preserving the status quo. Exposing crimes at the Triangle would have been career suicide."

"Jeez," Amanda said. "Things weren't very different back then, were they?"

Frank shook his head. "But when Cormac realized Fiona didn't just die in the fire, she was murdered, he couldn't just let it lie. That was too much. So he investigated as best he could. Forensics was in its infancy then so he didn't have many resources. He attempted to open the case officially, met resistance with the higher ups and continued on alone."

"And Patrick?" she asked. "I can't believe he wouldn't have wanted to find his mother's killer."

"Let's ask Lizzie what she knows about the second and third generations of Mead and this murder investigation. Right now, I've got a modern murder to solve."

"Of course. Steph." She ran her finger over Dexter's head and he preened.

"Still, do you think it's too late to open a cold case now?"

He half-smiled. "We'd need a lot more than these old photographs as evidence. Even the bullet may not be enough.

"Why?"

"There's no way of proving that bullet came from Fiona. Only Cormac's word."

"What about the photo of the bullet near the body?"

"That only proves there was a body and a bullet. Not that the bullet came from that body or that the body was Fiona."

"But with those photos, his notebook and the letter that clearly implies someone--not just someone, Mike Sweeney was going to set the fire--that still isn't enough?"

Frank realized his daughter didn't know what Jefferies had found out about Sweeney and his relationship to Russo. He decided not to get into that yet.

"I'll talk to a friend of mine in the DA's office," he said. See what she thinks about all this. Whether there's enough to launch a cold case investigation."

"Why would they?" Amanda asked. "The killer's long dead."

"It resolves a mystery, vindicates my great grandfather, gives NYPD a good name. Who knows?"

"What about DNA from the blood on the bullet?" she said. "Did you give a sample for a match?"

"I'll be doing that in the morning. If there's a match and the body is Fiona's, then there's a good chance they'll believe the rest of Cormac's story about murder."

"God. I hope so. I believe Cormac, don't you?"

"I do. And I believe Fiona was shot like he said. Let's see if the evidence is convincing enough to warrant an official case file."

Frank picked up the murder book, looked at it wistfully. "The last date of his entries is January 17, 1915, so he pursued Fiona's murder for almost four years. Then the trail went cold."

"Which brings us back to Patrick again. I hope Grandma knows more about this." Amanda leaned back. "Dad, do you know how Cormac got to own Orchard Street? I don't imagine he made enough money as a cop to buy a whole building even at prices back then."

"No. According to Lizzie, after Fiona's death, a friend he met at Ellis Island was responsible. Do you know the name LaGuardia, Fiorello LaGuardia?"

"Wasn't he mayor of New York a long time ago?"

"He was that and more. He'd befriended Cormac and Fiona when they landed in New York and from what Lizzie tells me, he and Cormac had a falling out about politics."

"Yeah?"

"LaGuardia was no Tammany fan. But after Fiona's death, they evidently reunited."

"Hmm."

"LaGuardia took up a collection from some of his rich friends to purchase the building. It was a present to Cormac and his baby son, Patrick."

"Wow, no kidding."

"That's one of the reasons your grandmother doesn't want to sell the tenement. She'd rather keep it in the family."

Amanda smiled. "Yeah, it's a great old place."

"It may be yours someday."

They fell silent.

"I'll be doing some more research today," Amanda said.

"I'll be trying to hunt down Santiago."

"Yeah, that creep is still out there, free as a bird."

"Awwwwk, freeee." Dexter's contribution.

March 25, 9:00 a.m.

The next morning, Frank took Stephanie Brandt's laptop to his office at the police station. He wanted to look more closely at her notes without Amanda peering over his shoulder. Jefferies was already there. He came into his office without knocking.

"Any bright ideas?" Jefferies said.

"Just one," Frank said. "I'm going to talk to the big man himself."

Jefferies raised his eyebrows. "What are you going to tell him? I mean besides the fact that one of his troops is a murderer and kidnapper and is currently on the run? Which, he no doubt knows already. And that his grandfather was Mike Sweeney, who, at this moment, we don't have any evidence against."

"I want to know what role he played in this scenario." *And maybe confront him with having an affair with my wife.*

"And you think he'll confide in you? You nuts?"

"Let's just say I want to set his cage to rattling."

"Lieutenant, some animals are really dangerous when caged. Like ferrets and weasels, for instance. You might get seriously bitten."

In answer, Frank picked up the phone and dialed an extension. "Molly, this is Lieutenant Mead. Can I get a few minutes with the Commissioner?" He listened. "That'd be fine." He hung up.

"What?" Jefferies said.

"He's out until this afternoon." Frank rose. "In the meantime, I've got a few more details to work out. I'm heading over to the crime lab. Want to come along?"

Chapter 38

March 25, 2011

10:00 a.m.

The New York City crime lab at OCME had been updated a year ago and now housed one of the more technologically advanced units in the country. At the entry to the unit was a large blue wall boasting raised letters:

The City of New York

Police Department

Detective Bureau

Forensic Investigations Division

A few years earlier, the Crime Lab achieved top scores from the Accreditation Board. They had had their share of controversy before that.

Frank and Jefferies walked down the maze of corridors, looking for ballistics.

"Christ, they changed everything," Frank said. "Looks nothing like CSI New York now."

Jefferies made a gurgling sound.

They passed dozens of people, many wearing lab coats. A few were in civilian clothes like themselves and looked like cops or even fibbies. A few higher class wardrobes suggested attorneys. Occasionally a member of the legal profession wanted to get a thorough understanding of one of the lab processes and would request a quick tutorial from a tech.

"Kate," Jefferies called out to a young woman darting into a glassed-in room, like all the rooms in the lab.

She stuck her head back out and pushed a pair of large black-rimmed glasses up on her nose. "Oh hi, Will. Come on in."

They followed her in.

"Katie, this is Lieutenant Frank Mead, Kate Smothers," Jefferies said.

"Hey. The new boss, eh?" she said with a crooked smile.

"That's what they tell me," Frank said.

"So you're here about that 100-year old bullet, right? I can tell you, the lab is abuzz about that. Not often we get to recreate history."

She moved across the room to a light table, switched the light on. Just so you don't freak, we did remove some blood samples from the bullet before we did our tests. They're still waiting for your sample in DNA, so you'll have to check with them."

Frank and Jefferies leaned over the light table.

"Here's your slug," Kate said. "In good shape, surprisingly, for its age. Lands and grooves, twist of the spiraling, very distinct."

"Which means?" Jefferies asked.

"Which means that the rifling inside the barrel was not too worn, which means the gun was relatively new or not fired much."

"That's good news," Frank said. "If it was severely damaged, we'd have more trouble identifying the weapon."

"Right," Kate said.

"What else?" Frank asked.

"We know that it's a .32 caliber. That's easy. Also that it's not composed of soft lead or it would have been distorted a good deal more. Unless, mind you, unless it only passed through soft tissue, no bone." Kate moved in a circle, getting into her presentation. "Now, I assume no casing was found?"

"Correct," Frank said.

"If the jacket was copper or steel, it would distort less but if it hit bone, it might shatter. So it's safe to say it didn't hit anything hard."

Frank nodded, rubbed his chin.

"Tell me, Lieutenant, how did you come by this amazing find?" Kate asked.

Frank explained.

"You're kidding? This slug may have killed your great grandmother? Wow."

"Any way of knowing what kind of weapon fired this bullet?" Frank asked.

"That would take some research," she said. "But if you can give me a time frame, I might be able to work on it, on my own time. I'm afraid I can't do it on company time since it's not an open case."

"I understand and I appreciate that. It was 1911, by the way, but I've got my daughter working on the research so don't spend any time on it. When I find out more, I'll let you know." He shook her hand. "Thanks very much for all your work."

"No problem. DNA has been moved upstairs along with all other Bio. Good luck." She waved and turned away.

"Upstairs it is. Sammie Chu still work in DNA?" Frank asked.

"He's in charge."

Frank smiled.

In the upstairs maze, they located DNA and tracked down Sammie.

"Frank Mead, hey, how ya' doin'?"

They shook.

"I'm doing great, Sammie. Congratulations on your promotion."

"Hey, you too. How does it feel to be back in the big city?"

"Not bad, actually, not bad."

"So I bet you're here to give me some of your DNA, right?" Sammie said.

"You got it."

"Siddown on that stool and I'll get a swab."

After he took the sample, Sammie asked, "So this is pretty cool stuff. Century old, huh?"

"Think you could work with it?"

"You bet. I could work with a hair that's been buried under the Rocky Mountains for five hundred years and suck out some DNA."

"A hair, maybe. For that you could use mitochondrial DNA. Problem is that only traces the maternal lineage. I need paternal."

"Aha," Sammie said. "Well, let's see how degraded the sample is. Blood can last forever if it's well-preserved. I'll perform Y-STRs; all the males in the paternal line would have the same Y-Type."

"PCR technology?" Frank asked.

"Yup."

"How long for the results?"

Sammie winked. "I'm making this my personal priority, mainly because it's a challenge."

"You know this is not an open investigation," Frank said.

"Not yet, it's not."

Frank slid off the stool. "Thanks, Sammie. Here's my number. Let me know what you find." He handed him a card.

"You bet, Frank."

"Later," Jefferies said as they exited the lab.

Noon

Back in his office, Frank started to sift through myriad piles of phone messages and paperwork. His cell rang and saved him.

"It's Amanda," she said.

"Hi." Both still tentative.

"I've been doing that research on guns."

"Yeah, right. Did you find something?"

"Maybe. If Cormac was searching for a bullet casing, then he certainly knew there were automatics at that time. So, I checked. The best fit is something called a Colt Model 1903 Pocket Hammerless."

"Describe it."

"Semi-automatic, self-loading, designed by John Browning for the Colt Firearms Company, Hartford, Connecticut. It was produced from 1903 to 1945. It was a .32 caliber. A .38 was added in 1908, the 1908 Pocket Hammerless. Anyhow, they called it a single-action Blowback, whatever that means." She stopped.

"Keep going. Anything about the gun itself?"

"Let's see. Special features include a serrated slide to prevent slippage during manual cycling and two safety mechanisms . . . a grip safety and a manual safety. Despite the name, Hammerless, the Model 1903 does have a hammer but it was hidden from view by the slide. Metal finish was blued or nickel and some special order finishes were available such as engraved, silver or gold-plated."

"What was the barrel length?"

"Uh, let's see. 205 milimeter, the weight unloaded was 640 grams and the barrel length 127 millimeters."

"Capacity?"

"The .32 was eight rounds, the .38 only seven."

"Amanda, this is great. Sounds like a good possibility. I'm going to give this info to our ballistics guru and see what she thinks."

"Sweet."

Silence

"Will you let me know? It'll be cool if I actually found the murder gun."

"I'll let you know." He paused. "How you doing?"

"Going stir crazy now that I'm 'sleeped-out'."

"Will you promise me something?"

"What?"

"Don't go anywhere alone?"

"What about grandma? I'd love to help her move back home."

"Not a bad idea. Why don't you call Irene and see if she can pick you up? I'm sure she'd love the help with Lizzie."

"Really?"

"Really."

"I'm on it. Talk to you later." She clicked off.

He hoped he was doing the right thing, letting her out on the loose again.

He searched for Kate's card on his desk and called.

"Kate, it's Frank Mead. Right. I've got some information on a possible weapon for that bullet. Ready?"

Frank gave her the stats he'd written down from Amanda's description. Colt Model 1903 Pocket Hammerless. He wondered if Michael J. Sweeney owned such a weapon. And if his grandson, the First Deputy Commissioner of the NYPD, Sanford T. Russo, was now the owner.

Chapter 39

March 25, 2011

2:00 p.m.

That afternoon, Frank found himself outside Russo's office twenty minutes early. When the First Deputy Commissioner turned the corner and spotted him, Frank could swear his face drained of blood.

"Lieutenant, Frank, good to see you. Are we meeting or something? I've been away from my office all morning."

"Carol said you had a few minutes now. Is it a problem?"

"Nah, come in, come in. If Carol says it's so, it's so."

The big man hustled in to his office, set his briefcase down and settled into his leather high back.

Frank noticed he was breathing hard.

Russo picked up the phone. "Carol, Can you bring in two coffees? Thanks."

"Sit, sit."

"Didn't mean to throw you off."

That's exactly what Frank meant to do.

A blond haired woman knocked, entered with two coffee mugs.

"Thanks, Carol," Russo said. To Frank, "Milk, sugar?"

"Black's good."

Carol left closing the door behind her.

"I expect you're here about Santiago and the reporter's murder?"

"How much do you know?" Frank asked.

"Not a whole hell of a lot. I was hoping you'd be talking Jane into calling a briefing soon, since the press will be all over me. That s-o-b Santiago would be the one to handle it all. Now. . . shit, what a cluster fuck. I guess the department cleanup should've started in my office." He sipped his coffee.

It should have started with you, Frank mused.

"Talk to me," Russo said.

"Here's what it looks like. Santiago killed Stephanie Brandt, call it stupidity, call it a crime of opportunity. Wanted to kill the story, instead killed the story teller. He snatched her computer, found out that my daughter was a friend and involved in the story as well. A new problem to deal with."

"Your daughter? Jesus," Russo said.

Frank knew this was an act. Russo knew all about his daughter. He watched him fidget in his seat.

"Santiago had to find out what Amanda knew," Frank continued. "He hired Salvatore Espinosa to keep her holed up in his basement until he got the information. Amanda escaped. Santiago freaked. He killed Espinosa. Now he's not sure whether Amanda can tie him to murders or not. So he follows her to his house where she's looking for Stephanie's computer. She finds it, he finds her, threatens to kill her." Frank slowed, drank his coffee.

Russo shook his head but said nothing.

"Jefferies and I arrive. Santiago starts shooting, takes off."

"And is still at large," Russo said. "Goddamn it. Everything I've tried to do for the department to clean it up and my own fucking staff is dirty. Think anyone inside or outside the Department will believe *I didn't* know about this?"

Russo stood abruptly and walked to the window, coffee mug in hand. "How much hard proof do you have that Santiago killed the girl and had your daughter kidnapped?"

Frank didn't answer.

Russo turned from the window to face him. "With what you're telling me now, all we have is Santiago finding Amanda in his house, breaking and entering and, for all we know, planting Stephanie's computer."

"What?"

"I'm looking at every possible angle on this, Frank. Right now it's Amanda's word against Santiago's."

"You fucking with me?" Frank leaned forward.

"The D.A. will. They'll fuck with you until you find hard evidence."

"Santiago started shooting."

"Yeah, he's a fucked-up whacko. Freaked out. Maybe he's on dope, who knows? Still doesn't prove he killed the reporter. We may be able to get him on assaulting Amanda but that's iffy. After all, she just broke into his house. Look, even if she found the computer there--"

"If? She did find the computer there," Frank said.

"All right, she did. But she found it illegally. It can't be used in court." Russo rubbed his chin. "Until you get more evidence on the two killings, I just don't know."

Russo sat back down as if he felt satisfied that his problem was resolved. "Have you talked to the D.A.?"

"Not yet. Got a few more pieces of the puzzle to put together."

"Oh, like what?"

"I think this case is tied to a murder a hundred years ago. The common denominator is the Triangle Shirtwaist Factory fire. Stephanie and Amanda were working on historic research for the article and were going to break open a cold murder case."

"You're joking, right?"

"Nope."

Russo blinked, caught himself looking aghast and straightened his features. "What murder are you talking about?"

"One of the factory workers found out that the Triangle owners were going to torch the place for insurance money. They hired a detective to take care of it. That person killed the worker."

"What does it have to do with today's case?"

"That killer has descendants today. Descendants who will not be happy to have this crime publicly revealed."

Russo frowned. "How can you possibly know all this from a century ago?"

Frank looked at his watch, stood. "Sorry, I've got to get going now, Commissioner. I'll touch base with you later today when I have more details."

He headed to the door.

"Frank, you didn't answer my question," Russo called out. "How do you know all this history-mystery stuff is true?"

"Let's just say I have a personal connection to the case."

He exited leaving Russo staring after him.

3:30 p.m.

When Frank returned to his office, Jefferies was waiting.

"How'd that go?"

"As expected. I set a few things in motion. Gave him food for thought, you know?"

"Right. I'll bet. Commish didn't go ballistic?"

"Nah. Not his style," Frank said.

"Speaking of ballistics, Kate called. She has some news."

"Let's go."

Twenty minutes later they were in Kate's lab.

"Wow, you guys got here fast," she said but smiled.

"And I appreciate your working this so fast," Frank said. "Whatcha' got?"

"Well, with the information you gave me yesterday on the Colt Hammerless? First, I checked around to see if I could get hold of one, you know, so I could physically test it? A good friend of mine is a collector and, would you believe, knew someone who had one. There are not many left of the Model 1903." She moved across the room. "It's going to cost me a dinner, you know, but I talked him into bringing it in for me."

"Hey, dinner's on me," Frank said.

Kate lit up as she held up the revolver. "Check this out." She held up a Colt Model 1903 Pocket Hammerless. Frank took it from her hand. The barrel was about four inches in length, it weighed only about 30 ounces. The grip was brown checked hard rubber, the metal finish blued or nickel.

"This is it?" Frank said. "Light, sleek."

"Awesome," Jefferies said.

"Yep, just like Amanda described," Frank said.

"So what about the bullet?" Jefferies asked.

"Definitely could have come from this gun," Kat said. "Well, not this, this gun, but one exactly like it."

"Kate, you are amazing," Frank said.

"I know. I am, really, aren't I?"

Frank grinned. "One piece of the puzzle solved. Now, how do we find out who might have owned it in 1911?"

"Well, I can check gun registrations today. But I don't know if the registry dates back that far."

"Also that's just for guns actually registered," Frank said. "That's a problem. If the person who owned it in 1911 passed it down through the generations, the gun might not have been re-registered."

"No, but if we assume Mike Sweeney owned it originally," Jefferies said. "Then chances are his descendant has it now."

"Ah, yes. The very man I just had coffee with," Frank said.

What about the DNA?" Jefferies asked.

At that moment Frank's cell chirped. He looked at the caller and smiled. "Ask and ye shall receive."

"Yeah, Sammie, that was fast," Frank said. "What do you have?" He waited, listening, bobbling his head. "Thanks, guy, I owe you one. You're a freaking whiz."

Frank looked at his sergeant. "The blood on the hundred year old bullet matches mine. The victim was my great grandmother, Fiona Kathleen O'Hara Mead."

Jefferies' cell rang. He answered, listened, face showing no expression. He nodded at Frank.

"You going to tell me or do I have to subject you to torture?" Frank said.

"What? You gonna take away my corned beef sandwiches?" Jefferies said with a smirk. "Good news. They caught Santiago at a motel in the Catskills, small college town called New Paltz. Just waiting for things to cool down, I guess. Asshole. Went kicking and screaming."

"I guess the D.A. will want to see us. Can you set something up?" Frank said.

"Right."

"In the meantime, I'm going to check in with the Captain, fill him in and see if I have better luck with him than Cormac had with his captain."

"Oh yeah? Luck at what?"

"Opening an official murder investigation." Frank grinned. "A hundred year old cold case."

Chapter 40

March 25, 2011

4:30 p.m.

Frank was pleased with the progress he'd had made on several fronts. First, he easily convinced his Captain to allow him to open a murder investigation into Fiona's death. After showing him Cormac's murder book and giving him details of the current crimes, he was given permission to formally open the case. He grabbed all the paperwork needed to get started that night.

Then he headed to the D.A.'s office to brief her on the Stephanie Brandt murder and Amanda's kidnapping. The difficulty, she explained, was that the murder charges were built largely on circumstantial evidence, as Russo had pointed out. Even the dead girl's laptop found in his home could be interpreted in more than one way. In any event, the computer would prove problematic because of how it had been retrieved.

Frank knew Amanda would be devastated with this news. She'd blame herself. But in all actuality, the contents of the laptop had no direct evidence against Santiago. It was merely the fact that he had the computer of a dead girl stored in his house that would be beneficial in the case. So the computer as evidence was out.

Hard proof was what he needed. Frank believed he knew where he could get that hard proof. Sanford T. Russo. The Commissioner knew much more than he was telling. Frank had ended their last meeting abruptly to give Russo a chance to come to terms with the fact that Frank was onto him. This time Frank was prepared to do battle.

He reached in his pocket and touched Jeannie's gold bracelet. As a last resort, he would confront the big man. A glance at his watch told him it was time. He didn't call ahead for an appointment, just drove downtown to his office. Even though it was late in the day, Frank knew he'd find him there.

Sanford Russo was waiting for him. Frank predicted the Commissioner would assume a fighting stance, his last stand. From his slumped posture and soft voice, it was clear the Commissioner anticipated defeat.

"Sit down, Frank. I've been expecting you."

Frank remained standing.

"Sit down."

Frank sat.

"We both know why you're here," Russo said. "Why don't you tell me anyway?"

"All right. I'll begin with a story. An interesting tale, one of historical significance, but also a modern day crime drama. There are a few chapters missing and I'm hoping you can help me with those."

"Go on."

"I believe that your grandfather murdered my great grandmother one hundred years ago."

Russo's lip quivered but his face remained neutral. He leaned back in his chair and the shift made it squeak.

"You don't seem surprised."

Russo half-smiled. "You come from a long line of NYPD cops, don't you, Frank, going all the way back to your great grandfather?"

"That's right."

"I wish I could say the same. I come from a long line of cop wannabes, men who couldn't get onto the force or were kicked off the force so they formed private security companies. Kind of like the Pinkertons."

"Was Mike Sweeney a Pinkerton?" Frank said and watched the commissioner's face blanch.

"So you know about Sweeney?"

"My great grandparents left evidence behind," Frank said.

Russo slumped.

"Fiona worked at the Triangle factory," Frank began. "Somehow she chanced upon a letter from a 'private security' firm, as you call it, and an operative by the name of Mike Sweeney. The letter implied that the Triangle owners were planning to torch the factory." He paused. "For the fifth time, I might add. Evidently Sweeney found out that Fiona knew and had to add murder to arson. He shot her in the back and then pushed her out the window with the other workers who were jumping. A bit of overkill, wouldn't you say, since she had nowhere to go but down."

Frank crossed his legs, let his words sink in. "The window, by the way, was the exact same one that Stephanie Brandt was pushed out of. Isn't that a strange coincidence?"

"How did you know that your great grandmother was shot?"

"Cormac Mead, my great grandfather, a member of New York City's finest, found a bullet wound in her back. He photographed it and included it in his murder book. Along with the blood-covered slug."

"Murder book? He constructed a murder book? My God, that would probably be the first of its kind." Russo's eyes focused on nothing. "And the bullet itself? You tested it?"

"The blood matches mine. It belonged to Fiona Mead."

"The murder book. You have it?"

Frank nodded. "Oddly enough, Cormac was not able to convince his captain to pursue an investigation. A murder case file was never opened. I was able to convince my captain, however, and with the evidence I have, I'll be opening one."

Russo leaned his head back heavily and blew out a deep breath. His face looked gray and sweat beaded on his upper lip.

"Shall I go on?" Frank asked.

The phone rang on Russo's desk. He grabbed it, spoke. "Cancel that. I'll be in conference awhile." He hung up.

To Frank, "Go on."

"I think you knew about Sweeney and his role in the Triangle fire and Fiona's murder," Frank said. "When Stephanie Brandt came to you for an interview, she'd already done her homework, with the help of my daughter who had the incriminating letter."

"How did you know of her interview with me?"

"Stephanie's computer."

"Of course," Russo said.

"You wanted the story to go away so you went to your lap dog, Santiago, gave him the information and sent him on his way. But it got out of hand, didn't it?"

Russo blinked, said nothing.

"Santiago tried to kill the story, but instead he wound up killing the reporter. He snatched her laptop, found out about Amanda and knew he had to do something about her too. Then, of course, that left his hired thug to be dealt with. He did that personally. So Sal Espinosa winds up with a bullet to the brain. All tidied up."

Frank directed his eyes to Russo's, who met his gaze. "How'm I doing?" he said.

"Real good. Except for one major flaw--"

"Let me tell you what that flaw is," Frank interrupted. "I think you asked Santiago to make the story go away. Nothing more. It was Santiago who decided the reporter needed to die. It was Santiago who figured Amanda knew something and Santiago who hired Espinosa to abduct her for the information. And it was Santiago who later killed his own guy."

Russo sat up, rested his arms on his desk. "If I told you that you were exactly right, would you believe me?"

Frank tilted his head to one side. "It doesn't matter what I believe. The fact is you knew that Santiago was out of control. Committing one crime after another and you kept silent. That's aiding and abetting."

Russo nodded. "I'm going to make it right."

"Not for Stephanie Brandt you're not."

Russo dropped his eyes.

"Commissioner, I'll be honest with you. I don't give a rat's ass what happens to you and your career. It's Santiago I want. Right now that son-of-a-bitch is in lockup but who knows for how long? He might make bail despite the fact that he's a flight risk. He's heavily lawyered up and the evidence is pretty much circumstantial." Frank stopped, took a breath. "There's actually a chance that fucker could walk."

Russo stared at Frank a long moment. Then he opened the middle drawer in his desk and pulled out an envelope. "I think I can help you with that."

He handed the envelope to Frank. "You see, I want Santiago too."

Russo swiveled his chair and turned his gaze out the window to the grimy buildings in his view.

"I wrote this to my mother but you should read it. It essentially verifies everything you just said." He picked up a pitcher and a glass, poured some water and drank until the glass was empty. "I wanted her to know the truth about her father from me, not the newspapers. I also wanted my family to be prepared for my, er, career change?"

Frank opened his mouth, but Russo waved him not to speak.

"I mostly wanted to keep the department from sinking into another scandal, especially since I've been so determined to fight this very thing. You know, Frank, I really do care about NYPD, despite this debacle. I trusted the wrong man and now two young women have paid the price for it."

"Don't forget Sal Espinosa," Frank said.

"Right. Now it's time for a few ideas of my own. You may not have physical evidence to use against Santiago but you have this." He reached in his drawer again and pulled out a small tape recorder. "Santiago was proud of the way he handled things. He really didn't understand me at all. And because he's got the I.Q. of a gerbil, he actually confessed the murder to me. As if I would be pleased." Russo shook his head. "It's all in there."

Frank picked up the recorder, hit play and heard two voices. He listened a minute then clicked it off.

They fell silent and both men stood at the same time.

"Now," Russo said. "I'm going to hold a press conference. I'm going to announce that we've caught the killer of Stephanie Brandt, etc., etc., and own up to my role in it. Whatever happens, happens."

Russo walked out from behind his desk to shake hands with Frank.

Frank looked at the hand, then balled up his fist and sent it hard into Russo's jaw. The big man fell backward onto his desk, mouth agape.

"What the hell. . . what the hell was that for?"

"That's for this, Commissioner." Frank set the bracelet on the desk and left.

Chapter 41

March 25, 2011

9:00 p.m.

Four Meads sat in front of the fireplace at the Orchard Street tenement on the anniversary of the Triangle factory fire--a cold, blustery day unlike its counterpart a hundred years ago. The Matriarch, Lizzie, her daughter, Irene, her son, Frank and her granddaughter, Amanda. The only Mead missing was Thomas. Thomas was usually missing, but rarely did anyone notice.

Frank filled them in on the status of the case. "Santiago is now in jail until his trial. Russo's taped recordings made the prosecutors very comfortable with a first degree conviction. Unfortunately, it's a black mark on the NYPD, again." He turned to Amanda. "You know you'll be asked to testify?"

"Of course I will," Amanda said.

Lizzie reached for her hand.

"What about Russo?" Lizzie asked Frank. "What will happen to him?"

"Don't know yet. He might be charged with aiding and abetting since he knew about Santiago's crimes. But, at the very least, he's resigning from the force."

All were quiet.

"What do you think about Russo, Frank? Was he an okay guy who let things get out of control?" Lizzie asked. "Maybe to protect his mother?"

Frank thought about Jeannie and had a hard time answering. Finally he said, "I think he honestly did want to clean up the department. As far as his mother goes, I don't know. Would I be protecting you by hiding the past, no matter how bad it was?"

"I'd want to know the truth. But maybe that's just me," Lizzie said.

"Well," Amanda said. "*He* may be a good guy at heart, but his grandfather certainly wasn't. Mike Sweeney was responsible for the deaths of 146 workers at the Triangle Shirt Waist Factory. And one directly, Fiona. What I don't understand is why he felt he had to shoot her. Why not just leave her to the fire?"

"He couldn't take that chance. What if she managed to escape? There were survivors," Frank said. "Besides, even if they found her, found the bullet, forensics was in its infancy then. He had no reason to believe they'd link him to a murder."

"I have the feeling that Fiona wasn't a shy wallflower either," Amanda said. "I think she may have confronted him, gave him no choice but to get rid of her."

"Not a shy wallflower, hmm?" Lizzie said. "Now where did you ever get that idea?"

Frank smiled. "Look at Fiona's female descendants. That's a clear indication of her moxie for you."

"Makes me proud, actually," Lizzie said. "Like having a celebrity for a relative."

Amanda smiled. "I might just write a story about her, maybe even finish Steph's story."

Irene said, "What's so amazing is that Cormac kept that bullet. God. This would make a helluva thriller."

"Thanks to Amanda for a lot of the evidence," Frank said. "She was the one who found the letter and--"

"That was pure accident," Amanda said.

"And for finding Cormac's murder book," Frank said. "She also figured out what kind of gun Mike Sweeney used and brought everything around to the Russo clan."

"Amanda paid a high price for it, too." Lizzie said.

"Let's not go there, Grandma, okay? Still gives me the creeps to think about it."

Lizzie waved a hand.

"Mom, maybe you can clear a few things up," Irene said. "Why didn't Patrick or even Dad follow up on Fiona's murder?"

"According to Frank, they both did. In fact they worked on it together in their spare time. They simply couldn't get anywhere."

"But they had the murder book," Amanda said.

"Yes, and that convinced them that Fiona was shot to death. But the key piece of evidence that we have today was missing then."

"The letter," Irene said. "So until Amanda found that, they might have known what happened but not who did it."

"The science of forensics was still new in both Patrick's and Dad's time, so it would have been hard to convince a jury, even if the letter had surfaced."

"Yeah," Amanda said. "In 1911, or in Patrick's time, through the 50's--even in Grandpa's time through the 80's, the blood on the bullet could not prove a match to Fiona. DNA typing didn't really take off until the 90's and wasn't used in court until 1996."

"You really did your research, didn't you?" Frank asked.

"It was an interesting case where DNA evidence actually landed in court. Guy was convicted of the rape and murder of a four-year-old girl after mitochondrial DNA profiling matched him to a hair found on her body."

Frank added, "*IBIS* was developed about the same time, so comparing a bullet to the gun was a lot tougher before the 90's."

They sat in silence.

"Hmm, not a very satisfactory ending to Fiona's murder," Irene said. "You are going to open the case, Frank, aren't you?"

"You are?" Lizzie said.

"I am. A century-old cold case has wide appeal for our detectives."

"And for the press. When you get further along, I'm going to propose the story for the *Times*. They'll love it," Amanda said.

"What's wrong, Mom?" Franks said, taking Lizzie's hand.

"Nothing, nothing." She wiped her eyes with her hand. "It's just, well, I'm happy that Fiona will be able to rest in peace now. Finally."

"And Cormac too," Amanda said.

"Maybe all of the Meads." Lizzie sniffled.

Amanda looked at Frank. "Dad, remember you mentioned Fiorello LaGuardia took up a collection and bought the tenement for Patrick?"

"Fiorello LaGuardia?" Irene said. "*The* Fiorello LaGuardia?"

"Yeah, it's true," Lizzie said, stretched out on her favorite sofa. "You should've asked me. Over the years I'd wondered how the building was purchased. Your father, even, didn't seem sure. He thought maybe life insurance or something."

"Life insurance in 1911?" Amanda said.

"But when I checked the papers in the attic couple of months ago" Lizzie went on, "I learned about Fiorello LaGuardia. He and Cormac were friends. Isn't that amazing?"

"My guess is they met him at Ellis Island," Frank said. "Did you know that LaGuardia was an interpreter there before he went into politics?"

"What? You're kidding? Imagine," Irene said.

"I also think Cormac had quite a few high level friends." Frank said. "I found a party invitation for him and Fiona to go to a fundraiser for Al Smith."

"Al Smith? Who was he?" Amanda asked.

"Only the governor of New York, elected four times," Frank said. "He was also the democratic presidential candidate in 1920--something. Can't remember."

"Wasn't LaGuardia fairly liberal in his politics?" Irene asked.

Frank nodded. "I bet he and Cormac bumped heads a few times. After all, Cormac had to tow the Tammany line."

"Conservative, huh?" Amanda said.

"Yes and no. They cared about social programs to a degree but they were really about power for a few at the top."

"So what's different?" Lizzie said.

"You really think Cormac was a Tammany man?" Irene said.

"Probably," Frank said. "At least until Fiona was killed.   That changed things."

"Imagine," Irene repeated. "Fiorello LaGuardia."

Amanda sighed and everyone turned to her. "If it wasn't for Stephanie's article. . . and her murder, we wouldn't know any of this today," Amanda said.

"It's sad to think that someone had to die to find out the truth about another murder," Irene said.

"Cormac's murder book buried up in the attic, the letter hidden in a picture frame," Frank said, shaking his head. "Waiting for a curious young lady to find a hundred years later."

About the Author

With a Masters' Degree in Science and more than 28 years as a science museum director, Lynne Kennedy has had the opportunity to study history and forensic science, both of which play significant roles in her novels. She has written four historical mysteries, each solved by modern technology.

Time Exposure: Civil War photography meets digital photography to solve a series of murders in two centuries.

The Triangle Murders was the winner of the Rocky Mountain Fiction Writers Mystery Category, 2011, and was awarded the B.R.A.G. Medallion Honoree Award for independent books of high standards.

Deadly Provenance has also been awarded a B.R.A.G. Medallion and was a finalist for the San Diego Book Awards. With the release of *Deadly Provenance*, Lynne has launched a "hunt for a missing Van Gogh," the painting which features prominently in the book. "Still Life: Vase with Oleanders" has, in actuality, been missing since WWII.

Pure Lies, won the 2014 "Best Published Mystery" award by the San Diego Book Awards, and was a finalist in Amazon's Breakthrough Novel Award.

Lynne blogs regularly and has many loyal readers and fans. Visit her website at www.lynnekennedymysteries.com

Made in the USA
Middletown, DE
21 September 2017